$ACRED $ILVER

By Susan Reiss

Ink & Imagination Press

Cover Design by Damon Freeman
Interior Design by Gemma S. Boyer
Author Photo by Bob Bader

Website: www.SilverMystery.com
Facebook: SterlingSilverMystery
Susan Reiss
Twitter: @SusanReiss
Goodreads.com: Susan Reiss

To the real
Adeline

More then family, true sisters

CHAPTER ONE

It is the Butler's responsibility to see that the table is set correctly for a formal dinner. Always select and position the silverware in the order it shall be used. Place it from the outside inward toward the plate in the center. Thus, the organization is guaranteed and a peaceful atmosphere is assured. If a guest is unsure about which piece to use, the hostess will provide the lead.

—"The Butler's Guide to Fine Silver" Mr. Hollister, 1898

"Simon, are you ready?" It was the question I asked my black Labrador puppy every morning since our move to this little cottage on the Eastern Shore estate called Fair Winds, owned by Lorraine, my employer and friend. We burst out the front door into the crisp December morning air. A pale mist hung over the waters of the Miles River and a lone goose floated among the autumn leaves. Like him, I'd landed in a good place after I lost my dream job at a software company, inherited a mountain of sterling silver pieces and been used for target practice in the past few months.

Now I was in a safe place, though it was going to take some getting used to the river views, rolling lawns and big white main house with high columns. Like the goose, I felt good floating along in this beautiful place without having to worry about anybody else. Too often in the past, caring about other people ended in hurt and grief. Sometimes it was just life; other times, the injury and betrayal inflicted on me was intentional. My heart was bruised and my mind was tired. I needed to heal. Right now, the best medicine for me was some alone time, just me, Simon, Lorraine and the peace and calm of this place.

Suddenly, the goose shattered the early-morning quiet with a plaintive call for his flock. In response, my loveable bundle of black fur charged across the grass down to the water's edge. Though still a puppy, Simon was growing into a big Labrador retriever. His wild barking caused the goose to thrash the water into white foam and take off as his flock responded in the distance. Simon stood on the shoreline wagging his tail. I didn't know what he'd do if he ever caught one and I didn't want to find out.

"Simon, come on."

He retrieved his bright orange ball from under a bush, dropped it at my feet and sat primly with his tail wagging so hard, his whole body rippled with anticipation. I threw the ball as far as I could and walked slowly toward the main house. I was looking forward to some quiet time over the holidays in this beautiful place. I hoped to tackle the stack of mysteries piling up on my nightstand, take afternoon naps or sit by the fire and *not think* for a change. That leisure time would only happen if I caught up on my work cataloguing and organizing Lorraine's sterling silver collections. I also had to deal with the extensive inventory I'd inherited from my Aunt Agnes, a part-time antique silver dealer. But first, we had to get through the activities of the Christmas in St. Michaels Festival.

The morning chill and the aroma of something fresh-out-of-the-oven nudged me along the path to the main kitchen. "Come on, Simon! I've got a lot to do and there are goodies inside."

When I opened the door, the sounds of a busy kitchen overpowered the morning's tranquility. A whirring mixer, a beeping oven timer and a chorus of voices signaled that Mrs. Clark, a woman approaching sixty with an ample tummy wrapped in a brilliant white apron, was orchestrating the organized chaos of making pastries, cookies and cakes for tomorrow night's Kick-Off party for the volunteers.

Simon ran on ahead in search of Lorraine's three large Chesapeake retrievers while I moved down the hall on the sly. Maybe I could grab some coffee, a delicious goodie and sneak into my office without anyone noticing.

No such luck.

"Here at last!" Lorraine announced right behind me as she slipped on her coat. Medium height, trim and full of energy for a woman in her late fifties. Her shoulder-length brown hair was expertly trimmed and the highlights accented her movements. "I thought you and Simon were going to sleep all morning."

"No, we just stopped to enjoy the view."

Lorraine smiled. "I know. Though I've lived here a long time, I never get tired of it." She ducked back into the breakfast room. "But we've no time for that.

The police chief called requesting... insisting that our presence is required at First Presbyterian Church of Saint Michaels right away."

"Not me," I pleaded. "I have so much work to do and—"

"Oh, he asked for you specifically."

"What have I done wrong?" I asked, assuming I'd offended a villager unintentionally.

"Nothing that I know of. He said they need our help with some silver. It'll be good to get away from all the cooking and decorating for a little while."

"Did someone say *decorating*?" asked a singsong voice from the hall. A short-like-a-pixie middle-aged woman with long dark hair pulled back on one side with a feather barrette appeared in the doorway. "Kat Designs, at your service." She sniffed. "Do I smell fresh coffee?"

"That you do. Since you're here, pour yourself a mug," said the cook as she raised her eyes to heaven. "But try to stay out of our way, please."

Kat, the interior decorator, was a little trying. Perky, eager and a little nosey described her perfectly. Sometimes, she could be exhausting. Overwhelmed by the thought of getting the house ready for the holidays, Lorraine brought her in to deal with the tree, holly, garlands, tinsel, glass balls... everything. We got a detailed running commentary from Kat every day. I had to admit that she was turning the rooms into magical places.

"Oh, sugar cookies!" Kat squealed as she snagged one. "My grandmother, a real Western Pennsylvania mountain woman, made the best." Cook stiffened as she was closing an oven door, her round face flushed by the heat, but Kat recovered nicely. "Yours are the finest I've had around here, Mrs. Clark. Besides, I should be partial to my Granny's cooking, right?" Kat took a bite and moaned in delight. Slowly, a smile spread over Cook's face, making her cheeks round like small apples, and everyone relaxed.

I followed Lorraine into the breakfast room as she gathered her keys, purse and gloves. "I *really* need to stay here and work," I declared.

She stopped and gave me that Lorraine Look: she lowered her chin and tightened the area around her brown eyes that threatened to shoot daggers at my heart. "You *really* have to come with me." Confident she had made her point, her face resumed its natural, lovely expression. "Do you want coffee to take with you? This might take a while."

"I have it right here for you, Miss Abigail." Dawkins, the new house manager, silently appeared behind me, almost scaring me to death. An American, he'd probably have done well in an important English house about a hundred years ago. He towered over both of us and his posture was almost painfully erect, commanding attention in a very quiet way. His dark hair was tamed into place and didn't dare move. Everything about Dawkins was all business, except his blue-gray eyes. They were soft and suggested a good soul... if you could get past his prim and proper attitude and the way he moved around silently.

I turned to him slowly. "I wish you wouldn't sneak

up on me like that and I've told you to call me Abby."

With a hint of a smile on his angular face, he handed me a travel mug and left.

"The way he pops up really creeps me out."

Lorraine put on a red felt hat and cocked it at a stylish angle. "It's the job of a good butler or house manager to anticipate. Dawkins does it very well." She bustled past me and held open the door to the garage. "Come on, let's go. The sooner we get there, the sooner we'll find out what's going on."

The drive through the center of St. Michaels was slow thanks to the traffic and tourists dashing between the cars. Christmas shopping was in full swing. Fortunately, the church was on the other side of town just beyond the basketball park and had its own parking lot. Done in the old Gothic style with stone and stained glass windows, Lorraine said it had been part of the community for more than a hundred years. We hurried up the brick walk and entered the peace of the sanctuary. Bright red and soft white poinsettias were everywhere. A stately Christmas tree waiting to be trimmed rose toward the massive beams high above. We rushed forward to the altar where the Chief and two men wearing white collars stood.

A sharp voice cut the silence to ribbons. "At last!" The old man standing at the altar was as thin as a reed with wispy gray hair. His intense attitude along with his black suit, shirt and brilliant white collar suggested he was the man in charge.

"And good morning to you, Pastor," said Lorraine as she bypassed the clergyman and shook hands with police chief "Lucky" Lucan. "Chief, we came as fast as we could. What's happened?"

"What's happened?" whispered the Pastor. "What's happened? We've been robbed!" His voice seemed to echo in the silent church. Then, he raised his hand to his chest and breathed, "The Gordon Communion Chalice is gone!"

CHAPTER TWO

Placement of forks to the left of the plate is limited to three. As a rule, they are: the fish fork with a notched wide left tine to separate the fish from the bones ; the large dinner fork with long tapered tines for the main course; and the salad fork that has a wide left tine to provide strength when cutting lettuce or vegetables.

—"The Butler's Guide to Fine Silver" Mr. Hollister, 1898

Pastor Francis McFarland's eyes drifted back and forth between us looking for a reaction of shock and horror, but Lorraine's face was wreathed in confusion, and mine, which wasn't familiar to him at all, must have looked blank. I really didn't know what to make of the situation. Disappointed by our lukewarm reactions, his shoulders sagged. Hunched over, he was still taller than everybody else. His black suit hung limply on his skinny frame, but the little bit of white at his neck dazzled like a sword of justice in the dark.

"Oh, for heaven's sake." His voice cracked with strain. "The Chalice has been stolen! Pilfered! Spirited away!" With a flourish, he waved a large piece of paper in our faces. "And this is what the thief left in its place."

The sheet was covered with words and pictures.

"That looks more like a children's puzzle than a ransom note," Lorraine said.

I turned to the Pastor. "Somebody's playing a game with you. A treasure hunt, maybe?"

"A game?" The Pastor's pale face was turning the color of blood. "This is no game, young lady." He turned to the Chief. "Who is she and what's she doing here?"

The Chief, as big as a football player and as dark as chocolate, moved in front of me. "Sir, just calm down. Could we get some water?" The other clergyman rushed out.

The Chief guided the pastor to a pew and helped him sit down. "There, that's better. Now, Pastor, when you first showed me this paper, you said that the first symbol looked like the hallmark on the bottom of the missing silver chalice. Abby here works on Miss Lorraine's silver collection and might be able to help decipher the letter."

The younger man returned and placed a glass of water in the Pastor's shaking hand, then helped guide it to his lips. After a few sips, he turned to us, his face tightened into a maze of worry lines and wrinkles.

"I'm sorry. This is dreadful. Why would someone take our precious chalice... and just before the Christmas season of holiday services? We only use it once a year and now it's gone." He shook his head sadly. "I don't know what we're going to do." He bit his lip and looked at Lorraine and then me. "I pray you can help."

Lorraine stammered, "Well, I don't know what we can do, but," she looked to me. "We'll do our best to help." I nodded in agreement.

The young cleric brought his hands together as if in prayer and tapped them lightly on his lips. "Thank you." I wasn't sure if he was thinking of us or a higher power. In his mid-thirties, he had short blond hair and was a little taller than my 5'8". "Let me introduce myself. I'm Pastor Paul Thomas, assistant pastor here at First Presbyterian." He extended his hand and mine was almost lost in his fleshy grip. I suspected the excess pounds masked by his black suit came from too many church suppers and bake sales.

"Paul, please explain why we need the help of those who know antique silver," the Pastor asked.

"Of course." He turned toward us. "As you know, silversmiths in the 1700's signed the pieces they made with a hallmark. It could be the name of the craftsman, his initials or a symbol that was particular to him." He pointed to the message. "The first symbol in this message is the same hallmark used by the silversmith who made the communion chalice. It was a one-of-a-kind item commissioned hundreds of years ago by the Gordon family in England. The chalice came to Maryland when the family moved here to escape religious persecution." He whispered the next part. "They were Catholic."

The Pastor's face softened as he picked up the story which seemed to bring him comfort. "They could worship freely here because this was known as a Catholic state. Down through the generations, the family used the chalice as their communion cup whenever a priest visited to conduct services. It was passed down along with the land to the eldest son."

Paul spoke up as if to protect the Pastor from dwelling on more bad news. "Then, tragedy struck. While the son was in Baltimore on business, a band of outlaws raided the family estate. They'd heard rumors about *the cup of silver covered with jewels.* They killed everyone in the family and the boy's fiancée but they never found the cup. When the son returned and found out what happened, he gave it to this church for safekeeping and to protect his house from future assaults. In the eyes of the church, it's ostentatious, but considering the person asking was the head and only surviving member of a leading family here, the pastor agreed."

Pastor Francis added, "How could he say no? With the chalice came the offer to build a new church building to house it." The man shrugged. "In the eyes of worshippers, this church would be on an equal footing with the Episcopalian church up the road that was given a silver chalice by Queen Anne in 1710."

Paul continued. "There was a caveat to the gift: the chalice must be used at the Christmas service."

"What happens if it isn't?" I asked.

"The family can take back the chalice and we could do nothing to stop them," Pastor Francis said with a hitch in his voice from barely controlled fear. "That's why it's so important to find and return the chalice to its rightful place."

"I'm sorry," I interrupted. "Could you describe exactly what was stolen?"

"The silver communion chalice," Paul said.

"The chalice," I repeated, not fully really understanding.

Pastor Francis snapped. "For heaven's sake, you see it at every communion service. You know, the part about the body and blood of our Savior?" He looked away. "The young people today…"

I was going to keep quiet but something in his manner made me say, "No, I'm afraid I don't know, because I don't take communion. I'm Jewish."

The chiming bells high overhead marking the quarter hour filled the silence. Lorraine looked a little surprised because the common Semitic stereotype of coal black hair, Middle Eastern look and substantial nose didn't match up with my curly auburn hair, light complexion and bright green eyes. My observant Jewish grandmother was a natural blonde.

Paul tried to cover the awkward moment. "Oh, oh, I see. Well…"

Lorraine jumped in. "Abby, the chalice is used to bless the wine for the communion service. It's about fourteen inches high, wouldn't you say Pastor Francis?" He nodded.

"All silver?" I asked, willing to move on with the treasure hunt.

"Oh, yes," he stared off into empty space seeing something we did not. "The silver is unlike what you see today. Its sheen has a hint of blue to it."

Lorraine cleared her throat and clarified his romantic description so the information was helpful. "It's called the patina. Don't confuse it with the black tarnish you see on silver that's been exposed to pollutants in the air. The patina takes many years to develop. It's really a web of tiny scratches from normal use and handling

12

that creates the warm, rich color. Some people buff their antique silver and lose the patina. I think it's a crime."

"Any ornamentation?" I asked, trying to get a clearer picture of the piece.

"Only a king's ransom in jewels," said the Pastor. "They're not modern but they're large and valuable."

"Great, so the thief doesn't have to sell the chalice to make his crime pay. He can dig out the stones."

As my words sunk in, the Pastor swooned, his face going white and his body caving in on itself as he slumped to the side. The Chief gave him support while Pastor Paul ran to get more water.

After a few minutes, the Pastor recovered and the Chief directed the conversation. "The first thing we need to do is to hear exactly what happened this morning when you found the chalice missing, if you feel up to telling us the story, Pastor."

"Yes, I suppose I must." With a deep sigh, he clasped his hands together and dropped them in his lap. "I arrived at the church about 7:30 this morning as usual to spend a few minutes here alone." He looked down at his hands and his voice turned soft. "That time at the altar is precious to me. When I came into the sanctuary, I saw the vestry door was destroyed."

Pastor Paul stood up. "Let me show you." He led us to an opening in the paneled wall to the left side of the main altar area. The wooden door was splintered. The sharp points stuck out in all directions ready to injure anyone who got too close, a defense that was too late. We took turns leaning in to see the small room on the other side.

"This is where we store and put on our vestments before a service," Pastor Paul explained. There was a large cupboard for clerical robes, a long mirror and a simple wooden chair. Built into one wall was a small storage area, its door almost torn away. It was empty.

We listened as Pastor Francis continued. "I was shocked and stepped over the splintered wood to investigate the damage. Whoever did this had no regard for the sanctity of this place or the antique value and design of the wood. That's when I saw the secret alcove, open and empty except for that awful note." He sniffed in distaste. "Destroying church property is reprehensible to say nothing of the breaking of the Eighth Commandment."

"Thou shalt not steal," quoted the Chief. "The thief knew right where to go, found the cabinet and tore right into it."

"An inside job," I murmured.

Pastor Francis shook his head, not in contradiction, but in disbelief. "It can't be one of our parishioners. To cause such destruction and to take this particular silver piece." He raised his chin and stuck out his chest, proudly. "It is very valuable, as you can imagine." Then his shoulders slumped. "But it means more to us than just its monetary value."

Pastor Paul pointed to the silversmith's mark at the beginning of the puzzle. "If that symbol is meant to represent the chalice, some sick person is indeed sending us on a treasure hunt with very serious ramifications and tight time constraints."

I pointed to other symbols. "If the Pastor is correct,

these other symbols could be silver hallmarks as well." I shook my head and looked at Lorraine. "This will take a lot of research and —"

"We have an extensive collection of research books." Lorraine said quickly. "Plus Abby is a whiz on the internet." I closed my eyes wishing she hadn't said that. I wanted the church to have its chalice, but I had enough work to finish before the holidays and was hoping to take break for a little while before the new year. "And we know museum and auction experts—"

"No! You must not tell anyone about this... this theft. It must be a secret or news of this sin might destroy the spirit of the season. This is a time of love and hope, not breaking commandments. Please, please tell no one of this, this..." The Pastor worked his lips as he struggled for the right word. "...this situation."

"I happen to agree with the Pastor," the Chief said. "The fewer people who know about this, the better. It will deny the thief the attention he... or she wants." The Pastor smiled in satisfaction until the Chief continued. "Let's organize a search of the building. If this person is playing games, the chalice might be right under our noses." The Pastor's head swiveled around, searching as if it was in plain sight. "While we're doing that, you ladies work on solving that puzzle."

"If you're right that those other symbols are hallmarks, we have to take the puzzle back to Fair Winds where we have our research books," Lorraine pointed out. "I don't know enough about them to identify the different ones listed off the top of my head. Plus I don't know a lot about solving puzzles. It looks simple, but it might be more difficult that it seems."

"No problem. Do the best you can," said the Chief.

"You'll let me know as soon as you have the solution," instructed Pastor Francis.

I responded. "With all due respect, I think you might be expecting miracles here, which is more your line of work than ours. Deciphering this puzzle probably requires more than an understanding of silver. We could make our reference books available to you or a real puzzle expert—"

"No, no, no. I'm sure you can do this. I certainly don't have time since the Christmas in St. Michaels Festival is this weekend and the Choir Concert Saturday evening is here." I looked at Pastor Paul. "I couldn't spare him, no, no, no." He was shaking his head.

The Chief volunteered, "Don't look at me. Playing with words isn't my thing."

"Abby is logical and loves a challenge," said Lorraine as she took out her car keys and jangled them, anxious to leave. "Give her the paper, Chief." She started moving toward the door. "Let's get to work."

The Pastor cleared his throat. "Wait, perhaps you're right. You may need help so I'll have our own Edward Chandler contact you."

Out of the corner of my eye, I saw Pastor Paul's eyebrows shoot up in surprise then he rubbed his nose trying to cover his reaction.

"He is one of the pillars of our church and a model of discretion. After all, we'll do anything we can to find it and fast."

"Find it? Oh, no." A man's voice behind us caught

us all off-guard. We all turned toward the back of the sanctuary, but no one was there. A creepy feeling moved over my skin and made me shudder, a sign of how unnerving this situation was. It felt like a long time, but it was probably only moments before a man emerged from the shadows. He was a short man wearing a green corduroy jacket pulled around his round body. He pushed his thick round glasses up on the bridge of his broad nose. Even in the weak light, it was easy to see his face scrunched up with worry. "Dear heaven, is it really gone?"

"Yes, the chalice has been stolen," said the assistant pastor.

Pastor Francis shot up. "Paul!" Only the pews kept him from launching himself at the younger man. "Please! He doesn't need to know." The pastor whirled around, drew himself erect and said in a barely-controlled voice to the little round man, "Stewart, this is a private meeting. Why are you interrupting?"

"He's here because I called him," declared the young pastor, raising his chin a little.

"I came as soon as I got your message," the man explained, as he seemed to stagger into the sanctuary wearing rubber galoshes. He pulled off his knitted gloves and stuffed them into his coat pockets, ready to do something with his hands, but not knowing what, he fidgeted with his coat buttons. Finally, he gave up and stuffed them into his pockets with the gloves. "What are we going to do?"

The Pastor dropped onto a pew, rubbed his forehead and groaned.

"Stewart Greer is chairman of the Finance Committee," Paul said by way of an introduction. "I thought he should know in case we have to call the insurance company about the loss."

The little man trailed his right hand through the thin, graying hairs on his head. "What are we going to do?" He appealed to Paul. "We need it for collateral on the loan to repair the roof. We can't take another loss."

The Pastor winced. "I told you we'll get the roof fixed without using our sacred things."

"But I thought —" Stewart's head swung back and forth between the two pastors, trying to understand.

"Look, we're going to find it," said the Chief with false bravado so, I suspected, he could get on with his investigation. "The Lord has provided for this parish in the past. He will do so again."

"Besides," said the Pastor. "If these ladies can do their job, there will be nothing to report."

"But..." Paul said.

"There are no buts," countered the Pastor. "They will solve the puzzle and everything will be as it should for my last Christmas celebration as Pastor of this fine church." He looked at the broken wood around the doorway. "Our challenge is to get that repaired before the concert on Saturday." He put his palm flat against his cheek and shook his head solemnly.

"And to find the chalice," Paul added. "Perhaps if we spoke with our trusted church leaders, maybe we could—"

"I am your most trusted church leader," the Pastor said while jamming his own index finger onto his chest.

"Do you think that alerting the elders or the entire congregation is going to help?" He turned and started to pace. "No, our flock needs the steady hand of a father." He sat down with a flourish and draped his arm over the back of the pew. "But if you want to ruin everything, why don't you call Harriet Snow and it will be all over the Shore in minutes."

I gasped. I remembered a few encounters with Harriet Snow, the town gossip, and the memory made me cringe.

The Pastor continued. "Or you could tell Miss Cunningham."

"Did someone call me?" The voice came from another doorway as a frumpy older woman dressed in a plaid skirt and sweater appeared. Her huge eyes darted from one person to the next and back again.

Lorraine whispered to me. "The church secretary. She knows everything that goes on here or is hell-bent on finding out." She chuckled at her little joke.

The Pastor covered his face with both hands as the woman rushed toward us.

"What can I do to help? I'm always ready to help in any way I can, you know."

I barely heard the Pastor's response: "You can go away."

"Excuse me, sir? I didn't catch that." Miss Cunningham cocked her head to one side. Her dishwater blonde hair, which looked like it was cut with a bowl on her head, hung lifeless around her face.

The pastor sighed. "Why are you here?"

"Oh!" It was more of a squeak than a word. She

straightened up to give her report, but first, her eyes scanned to make sure she had everyone's attention. "Sonny Jennings hasn't shown up for work."

Miss Cunningham looked startled as questions and comments erupted, then she took a step back to watch the commotion she'd caused. A small smile tickled the corners of her mouth.

"He's the thief!"

"I told you we shouldn't hire him!" The Pastor's voice was heard over the noise.

The Chief countered, "Don't jump to conclusions."

I didn't have to whisper to ask Lorraine, "Who is this person?"

The Chief answered my question. "He works here as the janitor/handyman and as a part-time pizza delivery guy. He got into a little trouble, but this? It doesn't fit."

The Pastor got our attention as he used a voice well suited to deliver sermons. "Miss Cunningham, you've made your report. Why are you still here?"

"Well, sir. I thought—"

"We pay you to type and file and organize." The unspoken words *not think* sounded in my mind. "Have you finished preparing my report?" Her silence answered his question. "Return to the office and limit yourself to things that concern you."

She turned her head toward the door, her shoulders and body swiveled around to follow. Her pointy nose popped up in a harrumph. As she marched out the door, everyone else started sharing opinions again.

Lorraine tugged my arm and led me away toward

the back of the sanctuary. "What a mess... and right before the Festival! Go into town. It's not far. See Mr. Cavanaugh at his jewelry shop near the Cove. He carries antique silver along with estate jewelry. He'll have some reference books and a slim volume of all the English and American hallmarks. I'll pick you up in a few minutes."

Gratefully, I slipped out of the church and saw Miss Cunningham moving slowly through the breezeway connecting the church to the parish hall. I double-timed my step to catch up.

"You might have solved this situation and in record time. Do you really think Sonny..."

She burst out, "Is he a suspect? Could it mean...?" She rolled up on her toes in anticipation as her questions came in rapid-fire.

"I think you gave the Chief important information he can use to check out Sonny."

"I knew he was a bad seed from the first moment I laid eyes on him. It's his eyes – they're pale blue, too pale."

"I think it's called ice blue."

She raised her shoulders and quickly shook her head. "They're ice all right. No warmth." Without warning, Miss Cunningham's hard exterior fell away and her face filled with concern. "And Pastor Paul tried to help him get back on the right track. Even Mr. Chandler, our former president mentored him on some things." Her voice quieted as if she'd forgotten I was there and she was speaking to herself. "I should have known. I should have seen it before this terrible thing happened."

I didn't know what information this woman—who seemed to be a nosey old maid—could offer but it was worth a try. "And why would you?"

Her head jerked in surprise to find me there. "I... well, I should have seen it coming." She raised her chin and looked down her long nose at me.

"How?" I asked.

She shrugged and looked down at her shoes. "I notice things." Her nose shot back up in the air, the façade firmly in place again. "Now, if you'll excuse me. I have to get back to work." She strutted back to her office, leaving me in the middle of an empty hallway to figure out a collection of random clues and antique silver hallmarks pasted on a piece of paper to retrieve a valuable, bejeweled communion chalice... as fast as possible.

I wrapped by scarf around my neck. *Sure, how hard can it be?*

CHAPTER THREE

The correct single spoon for the soup course is placed to the right of the plate. The soup spoon is as a large tapered oval to allow the eating of soup made with bits of food such as meat, vegetables or grains. Though not appropriate for a formal dinner, the cream soup spoon has a wide round bowl and the pureed soup is sipped from the side.

—"The Butler's Guide to Fine Silver" Mr. Hollister, 1898

It felt so good to drive through the entrance to Fair Winds. The big house with its air of calm and serenity balanced the confusing mystery and puzzle we found outside the front gates and that feeling lasted until we walked into the big house. Kat, the decorator, had Dawkins at the top of a ladder, hanging garland. When he saw Lorraine, he scrambled down, leaving the greenery uncoiling into a puddle on the floor.

"Ah, Madame, you're home. Thank goodness," he breathed.

Kat dashed over. "Lorraine, you must tell Dawkins not to drop everything like that."

I escaped down the hall with the books I'd borrowed from Mr. Cavanaugh at the jewelry store. While putting them on the desk, a whimper grabbed my attention. Simon stood by the door, decked out in bows and bells. He dragged himself toward me, trailing red and green ribbons. I rushed over, sat down and forty pounds of gangly puppy curled up and overflowed on my lap. Then, he let out a long, pathetic sigh.

I started untangling the strands wound around his neck, tied to his collar and stuck on his tail. "Who did this to you?"

Kat ran into the room and skidded to a stop. "There you are, you naughty boy. Abby, what are you doing? I was decorating him for the holidays."

"First, we don't *decorate* Simon. He's not a doll, he's a dog." With a clatter, I pulled off a bunch of tiny metal bells. "And you don't put bells on a dog – a cat, maybe – but not a dog." I scooped up all the decorations and handed them to her. "Let's just leave him alone, okay? He's handsome just as he is." I scratched his favorite spot behind his ear and he licked my nose.

Kat held out an impressive red velvet bow. "How about just one?" She decoded my silent stare. "I guess you're right." She wandered over to the desk and looked at my reference books. "I still have some decorating to do in here before the party. I could do it while you're working. I can be very quiet."

"Sorry, I need to work alone. It shouldn't take too long, once I can get to work."

She got the hint and started toward the door, but turned around with a long face and a pouting lower lip. "Too bad they suspect Sonny."

I almost squealed, "What? How do you know...?"

Too late, I added, "Who's Sonny?"

She smiled a slow Cheshire-cat smile. "He's the janitor/handyman at the church. Miss Cunningham called me a little while ago, asking if I knew where he was."

"Why did she call you?"

"He works for me sometimes on installations or when I get a big shipment. I didn't think anything of it until the Chief called, too." She strolled back to the desk and picked up a book. "I see you're researching really old silver. Did you know that old, landed families liked to give ecclesiastic silver to their churches? They must have thought it would reserve a place in heaven for them. The fancier, the better. Pieces like the chalice at First Pres." She shrugged. "It adds up: you and Lorraine dashed off to the church this morning, Miss Cunningham called me, then the Chief called looking for Sonny and now you're doing research on old silver. He probably took off with the silver, right?"

It was my turn to shrug. I didn't dare open my mouth. If the pastor found out that Kat knew about the missing chalice, he'd probably blame me and I didn't want to be the object of his anger, which I suspected could be unpleasant.

"Well, I'll let you get to work. See ya." She left me alone on the floor with Simon.

A little dazed by how quickly news traveled in a small town, I went to the desk and laid out the copy of the puzzle in the center of the desk. I was glad it wasn't out yet. Who knows what Kat would have done with that tidbit of information?

I sat down and looked at all the pictographs, words and symbols that leaped off the page. I took out a pad of paper for notes and... no more stalling. It was the moment of truth. Were the other symbols silver hallmarks? I opened a slim volume with columns and columns of marks listed. Originally, the family that donated the chalice came here from England. It made sense that the other marks would be English. It was a place to start.

"Abby?" I almost jumped out of my skin. A man – a stranger – was standing in the doorway to the hall. Simon didn't pause. He rushed at the man, barking. I leaped after him and had to wrestle him away from the man's pant leg.

"I'm sorry. He's still a friendly puppy, probably lick you to death," I said.

The man knelt down and scratched Simon behind the ear. I couldn't help but notice that his fingernails were well manicured, not feminine, but neat and clean. His attention to detail extended to his closely trimmed beard and a thick head of hair, both gleaming silver. All in all, a distinguished-looking gentleman, about my height, dressed casually with a striped tie tucked into a blue sweater that matched his eyes. I thought *a companion for Lorraine?*

"I'm afraid I scared you," he said with a hint of a southern accent.

"Startled is more like it."

He gestured over his shoulder. "The lady decorating the entry said I could find you here in the library."

Just like Kat to let a stranger wander around the house

26

by himself.

"I'm Edward Chandler." He lowered his voice. "Pastor Francis sent me. He thinks I can help you or..." He pressed his lips tight. "Or he wants me out of his way. But, no matter, I'm here and at your service. I have a little experience with puzzles and I'm willing to help."

Edward seemed so kind, so sincere, but there was work to do that required some background in sterling silver. This was not the time to train someone about the intricacies of sterling silver. Besides, I could probably tear through the work much faster on my own.

"I appreciate your coming, but I think I can handle it. I've already made a breakthrough. I'll probably have the solution by early afternoon." My smile felt strained.

"Really? That's wonderful." He paused and almost shyly asked, "Since I'm here, do you mind if I take a look at the puzzle... since I'm here?" He cocked his head a little to the side and gave me a look that reminded me of Simon when he really wanted a treat.

What could it hurt? I motioned him over to the desk so he could look at the large sheet. He adjusted his bifocal glasses and leaned over with his hands held behind his back.

"Hmmm. Interesting," he said almost under his breath. "It appears to be a rebus where pictures represent sounds. For example..." He made three quick drawings on a blank piece of paper and turned it toward me. "Tell me what that says."

I laughed. "I loved solving these puzzles as a kid. Okay, let's see. Eye - heart - ewe or I Love You! I guess we create rebus messages today when we text." I wrote down BRB and CU. "Be Right Back and See You."

"Don't forget one of the most famous." He scribbled o's and x's. "Hugs and Kisses."

I tapped my lips, thinking. "So, you know about puzzles?" I knew many people enjoy puzzles in newspapers and such but I had to follow up. What could it hurt? There weren't a whole lot of clues in this curious affair. Wouldn't it be funny if the pastor sent the thief to help solve the puzzle?

"A friend of mine studied puzzles at Indiana University and he used to bore me with stories over many beers. He's the expert, not me. The university has a curator of puzzles, someone fluent in French, German plus graduate work in..." He scratched his head. "Oh, what did he say? Graduate work in math, engineering, history, philosophy of science. I can't even finish a Sunday crossword puzzle. I like trivia. It comes from being a retired college history professor."

"I wanted to major in history but I didn't know how I'd pay the proverbial light bill so I went into software development. It seemed smart at the time, but not as much fun."

"I know what you mean. I landed a tenured position and, with Laura's help, we raised our boy and carved out a good life for ourselves." His voice cracked a little on her name.

I was impressed to meet an older man who respected his wife for putting her marriage and family first and didn't take it for granted. Though their relationship might be called traditional or old-fashioned, I would want my husband, whoever he might be, to have that same look of love and admiration on his face while talking about our life together. His loss broke a little corner off my heart.

"Now, I'm alone and rattle around in a nice house, do volunteer work, sail, even served the church for many years. It's been a good life." He raised and dropped his shoulders. "About the puzzle..."

I pointed to the first symbol in the puzzle. "That's the mark on the chalice." Pointing to other symbols, I said, "I think these are other silver hallmarks but I haven't researched them yet. Since the thief only took one piece of silver—"

"That we know of," he interrupted.

I stared at him with sudden concern. "That we know of," I repeated. "Nobody thought of that. I hope there aren't more pieces missing. I think the Pastor would just pass out... or burn down the town."

"Well, we can't let that happen. I'll talk to Paul and he can check on the other pieces. See, I'm being helpful already." His smile was infectious.

I was about to hand him the book with columns of hallmarks when his cell phone rang.

He looked at the caller ID. "It's the Pastor's office. I need to take this." Excitement crackled around him as he rushed out to the hallway. "Maybe they found it."

I looked at what the thief had left in place of the chalice.

THE IS . H- THE BELL OF

TRUTH. ALL IS IN OUR .

FOR THE OF HAPPINESS

WHERE NOW THERE IS ONLY

THANKS TO ,WE R LIKE THE

AT . THIS -LONGS TO

. NO ONE SHOULD IN F- .

IF OUR LEADER WILL  UP A , WILL. MAY THE

US BUILD S AND THE WALLS

---TWEEN US. WITHIN OUR

CONGREGATION .

THE IN THE PLACE OF THINGS

AND THE IN THE AND THE OF THE .

When Edward came back, he reported it was just Miss Cunningham.

"The lady I met this morning at church?"

"Yes, she's a little meddlesome but a nice lady. I hope you didn't start without me."

I gave him the hallmark book and together we started to work our way through the symbols to decipher the thief's message. It took a lot of page flipping through the reference books but my confidence grew as we identified all the hallmarks. But the list didn't mean a thing:

The Chalice

BELL	LEADER
WRIGHT	COOKE
PYNE	ANGELL
PAYNE	BRIDGE
LADYMAN	WALL
HATFIELD	MAKEPEACE
CASTLE	GODBEHERE
CROUCH	EAST

Edward and I peered at the list in silence, hoping for inspiration. Nothing.

I was disappointed. "I thought identifying the hallmarks would solve the puzzle."

He smiled. "Whenever my wife Laura faced a big problem or a crisis, she'd ask me if everything would work out, if it would be all right. I trusted that we could handle just about anything as long as we faced it together. By telling her it would be all right, she relaxed and didn't worry as much. Often, she was the one who came up with the best solution."

What a sweet man. "That was a nice thing to do. She must have felt relieved."

"When our son was sent to detention in middle school, she was worried he'd grow up a troublemaker or worse. She came and asked, Edward, will it be all right? And I said yes."

I looked away, not sure I should ask, but I wanted to know. "And was it?"

"He got through middle school and all the other schools and is now a fine attorney in Boston." He turned his head and stared out the window but I didn't think he was seeing the beautiful view. "Whenever she asked if it would be all right, I told her it would be. I didn't want her to worry. She was the love of my life. I would do anything for her, for us. We always tried to live a good life so we could spend eternity together. Even after the cancer diagnosis, I was so sure the treatment would work and it did…" His voice caught. "For a while. On the night she died, she said…" His breath caught and his voice was rough with tears. "She said, Edward, it will be all right." He gave his head a sharp shake and focused hard on the window.

With perfect timing, Dawkins appeared with a tray of coffee, jam and Cook's biscuits warm from the oven. *I don't know how he does it but at this moment, he is just what we need.*

"Will you have a biscuit before it gets cold, Miss Abigail?" He handed me a small plate and, without a whisper, left the room.

Fortified, we went back to the mysterious document. Edward seemed to bundle his emotions into a quiet place again and move into the present moment. He sat down in the chair by the desk, eyes bright and eager to deal with the puzzle. He laid the list of hallmarks next to the rebus and I picked up a pencil to record our guesses. We cobbled together a solution and I read it aloud.

The chalice is safe. Hear the BELL of truth.
All is not WRIGHT in our church. I PYNE for the smiles of happiness where now there is only PAYNE.
Thanks to LADYMAN, we are like the HATFIELDs at war. This CASTLE belongs to us all. No one should CROUCH in fear.
If our LEADER will not COOKE up a solution, I will.
May the ANGELLs help us build BRIDGEs and tear down the WALLs between us.
Let's MAKEPEACE within our congregation for GODBEHERE.
Look for THE CHALICE in the place of old things and the light in the EAST and the spirit of the season.

"Before we go any further, I have to say one thing. Stealing the chalice was a bad thing. Destroying that beautiful woodwork wasn't good either, but whoever put together this puzzle was very clever. Just saying..." I held up my hands. "Creativity deserves a little recognition."

"Maybe so, but we need to figure this out and find the missing chalice."

"You're right. Back to work." I ran my finger along each line slowly. "It seems to be pretty straightforward until we get to here. What... or who is a LADYMAN?" I sat back in the chair. "Do you think the thief is a homophobe? I thought we were getting beyond all that."

"I haven't seen anything like that in our church," he said.

A thought hit me. "Is there a woman who comes across like a man? Not all macho and masculine but, I don't know..."

"You're too nice to say it. Is there some woman who the older, more conservative parishioners think is aggressive and unladylike?" He smiled, making the question less offensive.

"Um, well, yes. I guess that's what I was trying to say."

"I, for one, think there are a lot of young women in this world today who have forgotten... or never learned how to be a lady. They want the same professional opportunities and the same pay. That's fine. If my wife Laura had ever caught me being a male chauvinist, she would have skinned me alive."

He laughed and the little lines around his eyes crinkled to show he'd often enjoyed funny moments in his life. I couldn't help myself. I laughed, too. Relaxed again, I listened to more Wisdom by Laura, a woman I wish I'd known.

"I don't think they have to act like jocks to get what they want. Laura said that women are clear thinkers and often interpret situations and come up with solutions better than men could. Do you agree?"

"Yes, but the tough part is getting the chance to compete, to play the game… without being betrayed." Memories of my hopes for the software startup I'd help launch and its sudden failure began to flood my brain. *Stop it! This is not the time to wallow in thoughts of what-might-have-been.* "Okay, if I'm such a clear thinker, why am I stymied by this line, *Ladyman is a fox in the garden?*"

"You don't know the people at the church. I'll think of some names that might fit."

"This line might help. *Thanks to Ladyman, we are like the Hatfields at war. This castle belongs to us all. No one should crouch in fear.* If a woman is throwing her weight around, she might be upsetting a lot of people. Any idea who it might be?"

He rubbed the palm of his hand over his face. "We have a number of women in important positions in our church. We even have a female head of our governing council. It could be any one of them, I suppose."

"Think about it, Edward. It might be important." My finger moved along the words again. *If our leader will not cook up a solution, I will.* "It looks like the writer is taking control of the situation – whatever it is – and is going to force a resolution."

"That all seems like church business. We're here to find the chalice. Skip to the bottom."

Look for the chalice in the place of old things and look for the light in the EAST and the spirit of the season.

"A place for old things… an old house, a museum, maybe?" I raised my arms and let them flop against my sides in frustration. "There must be hundreds of museums in this region."

"A little local knowledge might help here." I looked up, waiting for him to fill me in. "We have two museums right here in town: the Chesapeake Bay Maritime Museum and the museum at St. Mary's Square."

I shook my head. "The Maritime Museum doesn't work. It's big and professionally run. Somebody would notice any tampering or changes. Tell me about the other one."

"There are three old houses cobbled together to make the museum. Furniture, clothes, cooking utensils and maps are on display. It's been a while since I've been there."

I read that part again. "I guess it could work." I felt like the light at the end of the tunnel might not be an oncoming train, finally. "It's all we've got. Guess our next stop is the museum. Better call the Chief so he can arrange it," I said.

"And the Pastor."

I put up my hands. "Not me. That's your job, my friend."

"Miss Abigail?" Dawkins had appeared by magic, yet again. "Mrs. Andrews wanted you to know that a meeting of the Christmas in St. Michaels committee, St. Michaels Business Association and the Choir Concert committee is about to commence in the main living room. She asked if you planned to attend."

"Are they here about the missing silver?" I asked in horror.

"No, Miss. That would not be prudent considering

the expressed need for discretion."

I groaned. "I hate office politics and small-town intrigues have got to be worse. Why would she want me there?"

Dawkins suggested, "Perhaps to, as they say, keep you in the loop."

"Dawkins! You used jargon."

"Yes, Miss Abigail. It seemed appropriate this one time."

Edward rose. "I should be on my way."

"No! You should stay. Go with us to the museum," I urged.

He smiled and, when he did, his face lit up and the little laugh lines around his eyes reappeared. "Why don't you call me if you need me? I wrote my number on the pad." He started toward the door.

"Wait," I scrambled past Dawkins. "I'll walk you out."

Hoping Lorraine wouldn't see me, I tiptoed across the blue and white marble tiles in the foyer, around the walnut table with a cut-crystal vase brimming with chrysanthemums and pussy willows and past the living room. Outside, I glanced through a tall window and saw a small group of people – men and women, robust and graying – huddled together in serious conversation.

"I wonder what they're talking about." I whispered though they couldn't hear me.

"They're ironing out last-minute details that threaten to *ruin everything*. Maybe the fresh flowers didn't arrive in time for the committee to do their work or a major parade float sponsor is threatening to back out."

He raised his hands in mock horror then lowered them with a smile. "There are so many details to manage with such a major event and everyone is so passionate about its success that they fret about everything. Claudia, the festival chair, will be calm. Grant from the St. Michaels Business Association will have one more deal to offer. Both parade organizers will have bitten their fingernails down to the nub. The lineup changes right up to the last moment."

"And will somebody be here about the concert?"

"Yes, the choir concert is a spiritual event to help balance the commercial side of the festival and it's very important for the participating churches, too. The choirs rehearse for hours and invest their emotions and creativity in the performance. Some say it's the one thing that kicks off the Christmas celebration for them. Last year, that representative would have been me. The new head of the council, Josephine Quinn is here." His voice sounded a little strained as he said the woman's name. "I am an elder and served on the council for many years. Until this new term, that is. I lost my position to Josephine." He walked toward his car and called back over his shoulder. "Call if you need me."

I waved. *How wrong I was to think the helper sent by the Pastor would be a problem. Edward was a nice man and helped shoulder the stress of solving the puzzle to find the chalice.*

CHAPTER FOUR

There is one exception to the rule that all forks are laid to the left of the plate. The seafood fork is set to the extreme right of the knives and oval soup spoon in a place setting. Its short tines may rest in the bowl of the spoon with its long handle angled to the side for the ease of use by the diner.

—"The Butler's Guide to Fine Silver" Mr. Hollister, 1898

I stood at the library windows overlooking the river, waiting for Lorraine so we could meet the Chief at the museum and finish this treasure hunt. I wrapped my arms around myself. The little whitecaps on the water whipped up by the wind and the last crinkled leaves blowing across the browning grass sent a chill over my skin. Winter was coming.

Kat's voice pierced my thoughts. "Have you found the missing silver yet?" She was arranging greenery on the mantel. "Don't look at me like that. The world doesn't stop because a piece of silver is missing. I still have a lot to do to get this house ready for the party."

She was right. My life didn't revolve around just Simon and me anymore. "Sorry, I didn't hear you come in."

"That's okay." But it didn't sound like it.

Simon trotted in, saw Kat and retraced his steps. I had to suppress a laugh. "Kat, you're doing a great job."

"Thanks. It's nice to talk with you for more than two seconds before you run off to something *very important*. You're always working at your computer or in the silver closet." She stopped fussing with the holly and looked at me with a frown. "Now that I think about it, if I didn't know better, I'd think that it was *you* who took that chalice."

My mouth fell open in surprise. "What? That's ridiculous."

Her hand touched her chest in an all-innocent pose. "Not really. Of course, I would never think that... because I know you... but other people might wonder. They know you're an expert in sterling silver. If anybody would know where to sell it off, it would be you, wouldn't it?"

"That's the most ridiculous—"

She went back to arranging. "It *is* ridiculous. You have more important things to think about – like getting yourself ready for your date with Ryan tomorrow night."

I would never admit to her how much I was looking forward to seeing Ryan again. Ever since we'd met several months ago at the Tilghman Island Day Festival, his handsome face, his muscular body, his easy, playful manner had interrupted my thoughts more than once. "It's not really a date." I felt my face getting hot.

"I thought you might get a manicure, maybe get your hair done," she tossed off.

"My hair?" I spun around, my hand touching the

curly hair I'd inherited from my mother. In pictures, hers always looked perfect. She died before she could teach me how to tame mine. "What's wrong with my hair?"

Kat paused and considered. "I don't know, maybe a trim, maybe a conditioning treatment. Something special for your not-a-date with a gorgeous man." She stepped closer and lowered her voice. "You have to consider every man, every opportunity that comes your way very carefully, Abby. I know. What feels right – physical attraction and all, might not be right for you deep down in a marriage."

"Marriage?!" My voice went high in surprise. "Don't you think you're rushing things?"

"Take me, for example. Larry and I fell in love in college and got married after graduation." Her perky attitude was gone. Her perpetual smile had vanished. Her shoulders slumped a little.

"I went to Pitt so I could stay close to my mountains. Larry loved the Eastern Shore. When he got a chance to work in a local insurance agency here, he jumped at it. I figured he'd learn the business and we'd save up to open an agency close to my hometown." She clutched the decorations to her chest. "But it didn't happen. First, a little group of women adopted me, which was great at first, me being a newbie and a newlywed. Then I started losing track of the real me. They gave me a new nickname because they already had a Kathleen, my real name, and a Kathy. They called me Kat, and it stuck." Her voice went flat. "I hated it."

I could understand. My own name, Abigail Adeline, was a mouthful. Though I preferred to be called Abby, being saddled with such an old-fashioned name wasn't a bad thing. In our family, we had to have names starting with the letter A in order to receive an old trust fund, now only three years away. Mom and Gran went a little overboard, I think. I didn't want to get caught up in memories so I humored Kat by asking, "What happened?"

She smiled, but it didn't reach her eyes. "Larry loved selling insurance. The money rolled in and he spent more time hunting and fishing. Then, I got pregnant. The doctor said the last thing I needed was to pack up and move." She made a fist and bounced it lightly against her lips, trying to control an urge to cry. "I'll never forget the afternoon he announced he'd bought the agency! I had no idea he was even thinking about doing such a thing. He probably didn't tell me because he knew I'd explode. That wasn't our plan. It just wasn't."

I cringed. "What did you do?"

"I taught myself interior design, made lots of contacts, spent my time with beautiful things while my son was in school and my husband was off shooting, fishing and meeting with clients. Then, he dropped dead fourteen months ago. Massive heart attack. Was this my chance to go home? No, the agency was in debt and our son Evan's college fund was less than I thought." She swallowed hard fighting a wave of emotions that showed on her face: a jaw clenched in anger and eyes tearing up. "Ever the optimist, Larry just ran out of time." She bit her lip and marched to a table and started decorating again. "I've paid off the debts and funeral bills, but I don't have enough to move back home. But I swear I'm not going to spend the rest of my life here on this flat spit of land."

She whirled around on me, raised her arms and dropped them to her sides in frustration. "That's why you need options, Abby, and you need to make smart decisions. Ryan is a nice guy who isn't hurting for money. But be sure he's your best option." She picked up the decorations. "I need to finish decorating. Think about it." She scurried away.

What just happened here? Now I have two puzzles: Kat and the letter on the desk.

Lorraine walked into the library and plopped down in a chair by the fireplace. "I thought they'd never stop talking. I'm exhausted."

"Don't get too comfortable, we've got a lead on the silver chalice." I thought that might perk her up and it did. She sat up straight and her eyes gleamed with renewed interest. I filled her in on the details. "It's time to go to the museum."

We turned into St. Mary's Square to find the Chief's car already parked at the curb. In the car, Lorraine had mumbled something about being too old for all this hysteria. I wanted to tease her out of her funk. "Maybe you should downsize to a house like this."

Her love of history always sparked her interest and today, it brought on a flood of information. "The waterman's cottage dates back to the Civil War. They raised six children in there. Three brothers built the other house around 1850 and then bought their father and sister out of slavery. In the back is a building that was once a bank, a mortuary, a barber shop, the jail and who knows what else. All were moved here for the museum."

The Chief's voice boomed across the yard. "I'm glad you ladies were finally able to make this little party." As I passed him, he whispered, "You pulled me away from some real police work on this case." Before I could say anything, we faced a very irritated museum docent.

"Are any more going to push in," she asked through pinched lips.

The Chief pasted a friendly smile on his face and stepped up. Glancing down at the older lady's nametag pinned to her green and white gingham blouse, he said, "Mrs. Stangler, I really appreciate your cooperation. We're involved in an investigation of a delicate matter and—"

She was having none of it. "I'm sure it's important, but I want you to know I have four dozen cookies to bake and decorate for the festival this weekend. Four! I don't have time…"

As she rambled on, Lorraine moved in to placate the woman, freeing us to look around.

"Okay, Smart Cookie," the Chief said to me. "What are we looking for?"

I pulled a slip of paper out of my pocket and read the note I'd made. "It said, 'Come find the chalice in the place of old things and look for the angel of the season' or something like that."

"Okay, let's fan out and find anything having to do with an angel or a star or a light…"

"Or a candle flame. The puzzle used a picture of a

flame," I added.

"Excuse me, candle flame." He winked. His smooth skin, the color of mahogany, contrasted with the starched white shirt that was part of his uniform as chief of police. He turned to begin his search.

I called after him. "You might include something with a cross." He turned around and gave me a quizzical look. "It's a Christian silver piece." I shrugged. "Maybe? I don't know."

When Lorraine joined the search, she leaned close to my ear. "We need to do this quick! That woman is like a pressure cooker, about to blow her top."

Inside the museum, artifacts of every size and description were displayed everywhere. I didn't hold much hope that we'd find this needle-in-a-haystack clue. Maybe the chalice itself was hidden somewhere. I narrowed my eyes and refocused my attention.

"No, you can't do that! You must leave. I insist!" Mrs. Stangler's voice was shrill as she rushed to the Pastor who was pawing through a display of vintage period clothing.

The exasperated Pastor responded in kind. "My hands are clean. Don't you know who I am?" The Pastor with his sarcastic tone that seemed to surface when under stress was about to make a serious enemy.

Lorraine zoomed in and tried to settle things. I took what I feared were our last moments in the museum to do one more sweep. That's when I saw it: a rough, hand-carved cradle with a baby quilt draped inside. Its alternating light green crosses and butter yellow stars were like a beacon in the jumbled collection of old things.

"I found it!" Everyone crowded around the antique wood cradle. "At least I think it's what we're looking for."

"Take it out and open it up." The Pastor's words came out like orders.

"Don't you dare," declared the docent. The ice in her words stopped me cold. "I just refolded that quilt. I swear, no one has any respect anymore. They put their trash anywhere."

Lorraine and I approached Mrs. Spangler. "What do you mean?" Lorraine asked kindly.

"I was dusting earlier as I always do on Thursdays and I found some trash someone had tucked into the cradle by the quilt." She rubbed her cheek with the palm of her hand then shrugged. "It looked like an advertising announcement, that's all."

"And what did you do with it?" I asked in my most polite, most respectful voice.

She scrunched up her nose. "I threw it in the trash basket, of course."

"This one's empty." The Chief's voice bellowed from the entrance area.

"Of course it is. I empty every trash basket into the bin out back before I leave. It wouldn't do for us to have…"

The rest of her words were lost as we rushed around to the back of the museum. The Chief grabbed the big bin and shook the contents on the ground. The Pastor approached the pile, but the Chief used his *I'm-in-charge* voice and ordered us to stay back. He took a pair of latex gloves out of his pocket and gently started poking through the mess.

"There!" I pointed to a paper with printed words written in black ink. The bottom was torn. We searched in vain for the rest of the note, but at least we had something.

"What does it say? Let me see it!" The Pastor's hand shook as he reached for the paper.

"This is a piece of evidence and I'm taking it to my office."

"But…" pleaded the Pastor.

"My office and into an evidence bag. We're going to do this right, just in case."

At the police station behind the Acme grocery store, we packed into the Chief's office to look at the paper safely encased in plastic, trying to figure out what it meant.

Come one and all to hear the good news!
Seek the true path to salvation and
you'll find the gift you want.

"It's obvious," said the Pastor. "The paper was in a cradle so it must refer to the Christ child in the manger. Christmas, when the Child was born."

Lorraine gasped. "You think the chalice is going to appear during the Christmas in St. Michaels Festival? I can't imagine…"

"The thief will probably hide it somewhere in plain sight." He looked out to the hallway to see if anyone was listening; then he came back to the group and leaned close, ready to share a secret. In a low voice, he confided, "I'm on to his scheme now. It's a publicity stunt and those money-crazy shopkeepers are behind it all. They stole the chalice and will hide it in a place where everybody can see it, then announce it's been found!" He stood up straight and threw his arms up in the air. "Announcing the newest event of the festival weekend: the St. Michaels Treasure Hunt!" He dropped his arms. "The media will love it and the congregation will skin me alive. When I get my hands on those business association people, I'll—"

"Pastor!" The Chief saved us a tirade.

Lorraine and I moved into the hallway. "What do you think?" I asked.

"I think he's wrong. A hoax like this would take too much planning and carries a very real penalty. Neither the police nor the church members will see this as an elaborate joke. Somebody is going to be charged."

"Would the store owners go to such extremes to increase sales?"

Lorraine shook her head. "Who knows? I don't think we can take any chances."

"What do you mean?" I wasn't sure I wanted to hear the answer.

"I think we should fan out during the festival just to make sure the chalice isn't the drinking cup for Santa at the big breakfast on Saturday or on a mantel at one of the homes on the House Tour." She rolled her eyes. "There's so much to cover and the Pastor will never let us enlist the help we need to do it right, but I think we have to try."

Hoping I had the strength, I agreed.

CHAPTER FIVE

Place the dinner knife to the immediate right of the plate. Its dull blade is used to cut and push food onto the dinner fork. The fish knife is placed to its right as the fish course is served before the entrée. Additional knives for fruit or salad may be required. Always position the sharp knife edge toward the center of the plate. Facing out, it may convey a hostile message as well as be considered bad form.

—"The Butler's Guide to Fine Silver" Mr. Hollister, 1898

After dinner, I settled down on the library sofa and arranged a soft afghan over my knees when Kat walked right up to me, looked over her shoulder to make sure we were alone, and said, "Have you found *it* yet?" I sighed and she had her answer. "I did some poking around on the internet and talked to an antique dealer/friend of mine up in New York. He said he might be low-balling the value because he didn't know the size or quality of the stone, but he thought it would be worth between $15,000 and $20,000. If the purchaser was a private collector, *it* would bring a lot more." She turned and stared into the fire. "What I wouldn't do to make a killing like that."

"Look who's talking." I shook my head in amazement. "After what you said to me this afternoon, that people would think I took the chalice."

"Well, would you? If it meant you could finally do what you've always wanted?"

"Like what?"

"For me, move back to the mountains where I belong."

Lorraine seemed to stagger into the room. She looked fine with her hair in place and her soft rose cashmere skirt brushing her legs, but her face looked pale and drawn from all the activity. "Oh, hello Kat," she sighed. She made her way to the fire and dropped into a comfy chair. "I didn't know you were still here."

"I'm on my way home. Just saying good night." As she left, she sent a pointed look across the room as if to say to me, *Remember what I said.*

Lorraine and I sat together listening to the fire crackle until I felt like I was going to explode. "Do you think Assistant Pastor Paul took it?"

Lorraine gasped, then her eyes narrowed. "The chalice? Paul?"

"His boss belittles him in front of others. Maybe he hid it to get back at him."

I could see from the look on her face that the idea made her sick. "I hope he didn't do something like that."

We both looked back at the fire and watched the flames.

Lorraine said, "Today was a day for surprises."

"Yes, it was. This thief or treasure hunt person turned the Pastor's day upside down."

"That wasn't the only person who gave the Pastor quite a shock." I looked at her for clarification. "You did, young lady."

"Oh," I said quietly.

"When you said you didn't know about the chalice because you'd never taken communion, I thought the man would faint. I hope he doesn't start a campaign to convert you."

I chuckled. "He wouldn't be the first."

Lorraine licked her lips. Not wanting to pry, she asked gently, "Your grandmother raised you in the faith?"

"Yes, everyone in the family was Jewish except my father. I don't think Gran was thrilled when Mom brought him home, but he worked his charm on her. After Mom died, Gran raised me while he continued his naval career. It was natural for me to attend Hebrew school and, at thirteen, to have a bat mitzvah. Since I lost Gran and Aunt Agnes, I really don't celebrate holidays anymore."

"There's a very nice rabbi in Easton," she offered.

"I heard there is a temple there, but I'm okay." Simon crawled up on the sofa and curled up next to me. "Searching for the chalice today reminded me of a silver piece that's been in my family for a very long time. It's a menorah – a nine-candle candelabra – used to celebrate Hanukkah. Our family menorah was smuggled into this country under the skirt of a relative from Russia years and years ago."

"She took a huge risk," Lorraine said.

"She was young and pretty so she dirtied her face, stained her teeth with tobacco juice and ate raw garlic. No immigration officer would go near her let alone search her clothing."

"What a clever lady," Lorraine said with a smile of admiration.

I nodded slowly. "Because of her, I have a valuable piece of our history. Gran kept it on a shelf year-round, but at Hanukkah, it came alive when we lit the candles and sang the songs and prayers. She always made it special."

"Where is it now? You should bring it out for the holiday."

"No, it's packed away in storage with so many other things from the old house. I haven't lit my own menorah since I settled Gran's estate and sold the house." I snuggled into the afghan.

Raindrops beat a gentle counterpoint on the window panes. Little did we know it was the calm before the storm. Someone started pounding on the front door as if to knock it down. Simon rocketed off the sofa and raced out of the room barking. All the commotion sent a spark of fear through us as Lorraine and I sat frozen and looked at each other.

"Dawkins will handle it," Lorraine whispered.

The pounding stopped, then wet footsteps squeaked across the marble floor as a man yelled at Dawkins. The words became clearer as he came down the hallway toward us.

"No, it can't wait! Are they in the library? I must see them now!" All angry words filled with fire and brimstone. The Pastor had arrived.

I threw off the afghan and stood as Lorraine rose from her chair.

"Good evening, Pastor." Her calm voice contrasted with the breathy gasps coming from his open mouth.

Raindrops caught in his hair, crowned his face red with rage. "It is not a good evening, Madam." He planted his wet shoes on the Oriental carpet, made his hands into fists and planted them on his hips, then stared at Lorraine.

She did not cower but merely offered him a brandy while Dawkins took his wet coat. Lorraine handed him the glass. Still angry, he shook a rolled-up piece of paper in her face.

"I found this tacked to my office door when I came back from the pageant rehearsal." He unrolled it for us to read. The challenging words leapt off the paper:

You think you know what's right for everybody. You don't! You got the puzzle wrong! I believe in Christian love and forgiveness so figure this out to save your silver!

If a house is sheltering a divided heart, it fights against itself. That our house cannot stand.
Any more derision is clear. Remember, he who is not loving thinks not with his heart. For me, it is possible to stand against all that threatens you and me. We must come together at this time, not stand in the dark of midnight.

Lorraine and I exchanged a look. It didn't make any sense. The words made coherent sentences and certainly described what seemed to be going on at the church, but, what did they mean and what was the connection with the silver chalice?

"Nothing to say?" And just like air escaping out of a balloon, he collapsed in a chair and dropped his face into the palm of his hand. "What am I going to do?" Agony was in every word. He looked up. "I have to tell the Council now. The Lord only knows what they're going to do to me... and only months away from retirement."

"It's not your fault," Lorraine said gently.

"Not my fault?" His voice went higher as he jumped out of the chair. "Not my fault? This thing was tacked to *my* office door. What am I supposed to do with it?"

As he ranted, I watched as he waved the paper in front of the fire. That's when I saw it.

"Excuse me, Pastor." I didn't wait for permission as I slipped it from his grasp. When I held it steady in front of the firelight, pinholes of light appeared above certain words.

○ ○ ○   ○
If a house is sheltering a divided heart, it fights against

 ○   ○   ○   ○   ○
itself. That our house cannot stand. Any more derision

          ○ ○   ○
is clear. Remember, he who is not loving thinks not with

        ○   ○   ○
his heart. For me, it is possible to stand against all that

        ○   ○
threatens you and me. We must come together at this

        ○
time, not stand in the dark of midnight.

"Lorraine, write this down." I read out the words under the points of light.

If a house is itself that house cannot stand. Who is with me is against me at midnight.

"What does it mean?" Lorraine shook her head.

The Pastor pushed in, confident that it would be clear to him. It wasn't. "It's gibberish!"

I drew in a deep breath and blew it out in a rush, hoping to release my frustration with this whole exercise. "I have no idea."

Ever the steady hand in a difficult situation, Lorraine said, "Let's look at this again. Part of the message seems to make sense." She pointed to the words as she spoke. "If a house is against itself... that could mean there's strife or discord within the church."

The Pastor was quick to respond. "We have our little disagreements but there is no strife."

"I'm not saying there is," she said carefully. "It could be the thief's perception, that's all."

"It's the next part that's beyond me," I said as I started to pace.

"Look at the end," Lorraine showed me the paper again. "It says 'is against me at midnight.' Maybe there's going to be a fight at midnight and the winner gets the chalice?"

"Please don't trivialize this situation." The Pastor stood with his feet together and his hands clasped at his waist. "A contest like a duel with the silver as a prize? Really."

"How are you at twenty paces, sir?" I couldn't help it. It was too good an opening and I was getting a little tired of his attitude. One glance at Lorraine's disapproving expression and I apologized. "I'm sorry. That was just a little joke."

My apology either didn't come fast enough or wasn't sincere enough for the man. He walked over to the fire in a huff. Lorraine's expression delivered a silent reprimand.

I repeated, "I'm sorry. I know you're under a lot of pressure and my—"

He raised his hand and thrust his index finger toward my face. With every word, he jabbed that finger of accusation at me, closer and closer. "Your little joke was uncalled for."

Lorraine tried to salvage the situation. "Here, Abby. Take this." She held out the sheet where she'd written the message I'd dictated. "Maybe you can see what I'm missing."

I took the paper from her hand without much enthusiasm, but seeing the words made a difference. "You're right, there's something missing." I held it so Lorraine could see it.

The Pastor couldn't stay away. "I see it. It says 'Who is is against me. What could be missing?"

"There is a word missing." I went back to the fireplace and held up the original message. No more holes appeared over words.

"Look on the back," Lorraine suggested.

I took the paper over to a lamp with a strong light and examined the other side of it. There were little bumps where it should have been smooth. I picked at a spot with my fingernail and the bump came away. Quickly, I turned the paper over and held it up to the light.

"We have hanging chads. Remember in the 2000 presidential election, some of the Florida ballots were challenged because the holes to indict the voter's selection were not made clear through?" I held up the paper. "That's what we have. I uncovered another word after the first *is*: *divided.*"

"Got it," said Lorraine. "Any more?"

I went to work on the back of the sheet, gently scraping away the bumps. Once it was smooth, I held it up to the light and read it out. Then I looked at what Lorraine had written down. She added a comma and a period so it read:

If a house is divided against itself, that house cannot stand. He who is not with me is against me. Come at midnight.

Lorraine broke the silence with a question. "What does that mean?"

"Isn't that from Lincoln's House Divided speech against slavery? Except I think he shortened it to 'A house divided cannot stand.' I don't know about the second part."

The Pastor croaked and cleared his throat. "It's from the Bible. The house divided verse is Mark 3:25. The other is Luke 11:23: Jesus said, he who is not with me is against me."

We stood in silence.

After a flurry of phone calls, the Chief and Paul stood with us in the library. I remembered what Lorraine said; that there was no way Paul could be responsible for the theft, but something about him made me uneasy. Without being obvious about what I was doing, I kept an eye on the assistant Pastor.

Quick to get to the heart of the action, the Chief said, "What does it mean?"

The Pastor and I started talking at the same time. I paused and the Pastor was off quoting Biblical passages. He concluded with, "It's about the Protestant Reformation and the split from the Catholic Church. It must mean we have to go to the big Catholic Church in Easton." Pastor Paul nodded in agreement.

"Why not another Protestant church?" asked Lorraine.

The Pastor explained. "The only church we're 'divided from' is the Catholic Church. It has to be it."

"What? Where?" The words tumbled out of my mouth. "No, the first part relates to Lincoln's speech about the nation and slavery." The Pastor shook his head sadly but I continued. "Is there a Civil War monument around here somewhere?"

The Chief thought aloud. "Yes, there's a statue outside the courthouse in Easton, but it's a monument to the Confederate soldiers."

"Not surprising. This area is south of the Mason-Dixon Line and was a tobacco-growing area with slaves." I tried to persuade the churchmen that we had to go to the statue but they wouldn't budge. They wouldn't even consider sending people to both locations.

The grandfather clock bonged the time: 11:30.

"We're out of time," declared the Chief. "Pastor, it's your chalice. Your decision."

"The church."

The Chief raised his shoulders in a silent apology to me and led the group off on what I considered a wild goose chase. Lorraine went with them at the Chief's request to keep the Pastor calm.

Simon and I sat alone as the fire died. A chill crept over my skin. "They're wrong, Simon. I just know they're wrong."

I jumped a little when I heard a door closing down the hall. Someone else was up late, too. Probably Dawkins. Simon brought me a toy and I tossed it a few times. He sensed my heart wasn't in it so he curled up on the rug. It wasn't long before Simon was dreaming. He shifted over to his side and those long front legs started moving. He was running in his sleep.

"Oh Simon, I envy you. If all I had to worry about was catching a squirrel… " I let out a long sigh. I wanted to help but I supposed it would take them a long time to accept me since I was an outsider. *I hope everything will be all right.* I thought about that phrase, Edward's phrase, and smiled.

There was a soft knock and Dawkins stood in the doorway.

"Thank you for knocking. I think if someone said *boo* to me, I might faint dead away."

"Yes, Miss Abigail, that is probably a valid assumption. You seemed to be lost in your thoughts.

Normally, I would respect your right to be alone, but I have a question."

"I'm not surprised. People in Easton could have heard us." I rubbed my forehead. The confrontation with the Pastor had given me a headache. "I'm sorry, Dawkins. I didn't mean to take out my frustration on you."

"That's quite all right, Miss Abigail."

He was being nice so I dropped my normal request to call me Abby. "What do you want to know?"

Dawkins squared his shoulders. "Miss Abigail, I normally don't get involved, but in my humble opinion, you were correct and, with all due respect, the Pastor was wrong."

I moved my head up and down in tired agreement. "Thank you, Dawkins, but as you can see, my argument and logic didn't make a difference. They ran off to the Catholic church."

"A wild goose chase."

"Yes, but here I sit in front of the fire." I looked at the glowing embers in the grate.

"If you believe you are correct, why *are* you sitting here?"

"Because I once ran off somewhere on a hunch and almost got myself killed, that's why."

"I know the story." I looked at him in surprise. "Lorraine felt I should have a full understanding of Fair Winds so I could perform my job. The story is safe with me, I assure you."

I looked at the man – pleasantly handsome, courteous, knowledgeable – and an enigma. I wondered what secrets lay behind those deep brown eyes that were starting to drill into me.

"I appreciate that, Dawkins and—"

"Forgive me, Miss Abigail but I don't think this is the time for polite chitchat. I believe you are right and should take action based on your deductions." I started to explain it was futile but Dawkins continued. "Perhaps an additional piece of information might be beneficial."

I nestled into the afghan and sofa pillows, ready to listen. "Okay, hit me."

"Do you know the history of the Presbyterian Church?" I shook my head. "Around 1860, a faction of the U. S. Presbyterian church split off over the issue of slavery. The Church of the Confederacy created a house divided." Quietly, he left the room

I sat stunned. The Presbyterian Church itself was once a house divided. The thief was waiting at the statue in the courthouse square, not at the Catholic Church.

The grandfather clock chimed the quarter hour before midnight. *Fifteen minutes. The thief wants to see the pastor, but if I can identify the thief...* I threw off the blanket and jammed my feet back in my shoes. Simon sprang to his feet. He swayed as he tried to wake up.

"Simon, you can stay here." He whined a little. "Really, I'll be okay."

I rushed to the back door with him on my heels. There wasn't time to take him down to our cottage. I grabbed a handful of cookies from a jar kept by the door and piled them under his nose. He looked up at me pleading with his head cocked to the side. "Nothing bad will happen. Eat your cookies." As I sprinted to my car, a fleeting notion urged me to bring him but I shook it off. I was going to the courthouse square to look around. That's all. What could happen?

CHAPTER SIX

Do not react if you notice someone picking up the wrong fork. The hostess sets the tone. If the guest of honor has committed the mistake, she may wish to salvage the situation by also using the wrong fork. The other guests must always follow the hostess regardless.

—"The Butler's Guide to Fine Silver" Mr. Hollister, 1898

I only made one wrong turn on my way to the courthouse square. I parked in a space on the side and out of the way. When I got out of the car, the cold wind kicked up and slapped my face with some fat raindrops. The bare branches above my head creaked. A high wrought iron fence surrounded the impressive old brick building bright in electric spotlights. On the side closest to me, there was a bronze statue of a man carrying a musket set on a stone pedestal. The old soldier and I were alone. I waited by the fence. Shadows of tree limbs danced around me. Usually, the dark didn't bother me, but I was starting to shiver though I had on a warm coat.

What was that? I looked over my shoulder. *Something rustled. Was someone there?* Nobody.

In the square, landscaped beds of frozen ornamental cabbages—

There it is again, that sound. I whipped my head around, but there was nothing there. *No, the sound isn't coming from behind me. It's close to the statue. The soldier has a midnight date.*

I crept up to the fence and looked between the iron rails. I wasn't imagining it. Someone was in the murky light near the base of the statue.

I couldn't get any closer without walking around to the front of the square where the fence stopped at a broad walk leading up to and around the courthouse, right up to the statue. If I made any noise, I was sure I would scare the person away. I slipped my hand into my coat pocket only to find it empty. My phone was on the console in my car.

I couldn't leave or call for help. Then, I smiled. I had a plan. *I'll watch... and when the person realizes that the pastor isn't coming, I'll follow whoever it is. Get an address, at least a license plate number... and deliver it to the Chief on a silver platter. Lorraine had enough of them.* I stifled a giggle. *They thought I was wrong. Won't they be surprised?*

Something was happening at the base of the statue. Movement. A small flame of light was struck in the dark. Then another. Two candles burned near the base of the statue. There was another rustling sound. Someone stepped in front of a spotlight and a huge shadow of a person with a head and arms burst on to the side of the building. It moved like a monster with its arms crooked and its head distorted. Suddenly, the shadow jerked upright, alert; then the person moved and the shadow shrank to nothing. I had an eerie feeling it was moving, coming for me.

It was a relief to see a real person enter the courthouse square. At least I wasn't alone. The person walked quickly up the main sidewalk, then turned toward the candlelight.

The breeze died and faintly, I heard a woman say, "Oh, it's you."

The rain had stopped, but the wind picked up again, blotting out the specific words, but it was clear that two angry voices were doing battle. Their feelings were clear as their words faded away. I leaned against the iron rails hoping to catch a sound or glimpse of what was happening. Suddenly, two distorted shadows moved across the brick wall as the bodies did a macabre dance by the light of the candles and the spotlight. They moved around then came together. One jerked away. The other moved close so the shadows became one. With a cry, they split apart and one fell away, leaving a single shadow on the wall. A wail in a deep voice, a man crying out over the wind. And his shadow fled.

Without thinking, I ran around to the sidewalk and followed the woman's path to the base of the soldier's statue. Her body was sprawled on the pavement, the face sheathed in darkness. A lighted candle fell from its perch and rolled along the walkway, a dark puddle oozing out to meet it. The light flared, then was extinguished by the blood. In that moment, I saw the face of the woman.

It was Kat.

CHAPTER SEVEN

The family places its solemn trust in the Butler who offers service, care and protection in all things. While sterling silver is a valuable commodity, its true worth is the way it reflects the family's character and position.
— "The Butler's Guide to Fine Silver" Mr. Hollister, 1898

After hours and hours of talking with the police about the little I saw and heard of Kat's death, the Chief brought me back to Fair Winds. Lorraine had waited up, Dawkins too. She gave me a soft flannel nightie and tucked me into the big bed in a guest room with Simon at my side.

"Sorry, buddy. I know you wanted to go with me. Did you know that something really bad happened?"

Suddenly, I felt a cold shiver. If I'd taken Simon, something bad could have happened to him. I put my arms around him and he let me hug him for the longest time.

"Okay, you two. Abby, drink up." Simon nestled down next to me and Lorraine sat while I sipped the hot drink Dawkins had prepared. In moments, I was in a dreamless sleep.

The next morning, I awoke to a soft tap on the door. Confused by my surroundings, I watched Lorraine come and sit on the edge of the bed, her face filled with concern and sadness. In that moment, it all came back to me, the vision of two shadows moving on a brick wall. With an anguished cry, I remembered. Kat had died in front of my eyes.

Lorraine rocked me while I sobbed and wiped away my tears. She didn't say anything. She didn't have to. Her silence alone was comforting. When I'd pulled myself together, I threw off the covers and stumbled into the shower. While I showered, Lorraine brought up a breakfast tray and we shared cups of hot coffee and Mrs. Clark's piping hot biscuits. When I couldn't eat another bite, I burrowed into the pillows and Lorraine moved away the tray table.

"It wasn't your fault," she spoke in a gentle tone.

My response was a rattling sigh. I didn't want to cry again. I didn't want to think. I didn't want to remember. Someone killed Kat right in front of me and I couldn't grasp how helpless I was to prevent it. Pain and sadness were stalking me. First, there was my mother when I was too young to understand. Then, there was Gran and I could do nothing to stop the cancer. Aunt Agnes gently fell asleep. Now, the shadows dancing on the wall last night would join my nightmares. Every time I got close to someone, I got hurt, hurt down to my core.

In an instant, my stomach muscles tightened and my eyes clamped on Lorraine's face. As if reading my mind, she reached out and patted my arm.

"I'm not going anywhere."

Simon laid his head on my leg and I closed my eyes.

They were still there when I woke from my little nap. I started to get up, but Lorraine gently pushed me back on the pillows.

"I want you to listen for a moment." Gently, she placed her soft hands on mine. She lowered her chin and wiped any expression from her face. Her eyes bored into me, but they were filled with caring. "Last night was not your fault. You argued your point with the churchmen but, frankly, it wasn't your call. It was their decision to make and they made the wrong one." I bowed my head and she rushed on. "Abby, listen to me. You can't stop people from doing what they want to do... and I'm not talking about the Pastor now. I'm talking about Kat."

"One," She started ticking off points on her fingers. "You told me yourself, she wanted more than anything to get off the Eastern Shore and go back to her beloved mountains. Two, with her son in college at Pittsburgh, she was free to leave, but moving costs money. Three, she needed a stake, cash to make the move; cash to set herself up in a new place and cash to still support her son though he's on scholarships. Four..." She tapped her index finger. "And this is probably the most important point, Kat loved to eavesdrop and poke around where she didn't belong. I'm not going into details, but I caught her more than once. Actions like that can only lead to trouble."

I covered my face with my hands.

"No, listen. You couldn't prevent this from happening. You certainly couldn't stop it."

"But who would kill Kat?" My voice was rough. "I

know she talked a lot and was a little nosy but—"

"It's not your problem. The Chief will work it out." Abruptly, she stood up. "Right now, it's time for you to get up and get back to it."

"Get back to what? I—" I sounded pathetic.

"Get back to life. We have things to do, places to go, people to see, if you'll excuse the trite phrase but it's very appropriate in this case. Come on, your jeans are on the chair along with one of my big, comfy sweaters and a pair of warm socks. Get dressed, thank Mrs. Clark for your breakfast, Dawkins wants to see you about... well, he didn't tell me." She bustled around the room opening curtains and window shades in rhythm with her words. "Then you can go back to the cottage and dress to go into town. I hope you'll have time to return Mr. Cavanaugh's reference books before your hair appointment."

"Hair appointment?" I touched my mess of curls and remembered. "Kat told me I should get it trimmed and conditioned before seeing Ryan... but I can't."

"Oh yes, you can. I got you on their schedule, just barely." She planted her feet and stood at the bottom of the bed with her hands on her hips. "Don't even think about curling up like an old slug. I need you. I made a decision. I've thought about it and I've decided that we are going ahead with the festival kick-off party for the volunteers. It's the right thing to do."

"You're having the party?"

"Yes, Kat worked so hard decorating this house. I wouldn't want it to go to waste." We both remembered Kat rushing around with garland and micro-managing Dawkins as he worked at the top of the ladder. "She wanted the people coming to the party to enjoy the atmosphere she created and get into the spirit of the season. So many of them started working on Christmas in St. Michaels last January. That's eleven months. They deserve the recognition and appreciation shown by an invitation to Fair Winds, delicious food and beautiful..." Her voice caught. "They deserve their special evening, as do you. A little cruise in the boat parade with a hunk of a man will help take your mind off things." She threw open the bedroom door, grabbed the breakfast tray and marched down the hall with Simon at her heels hoping for another scrap of bacon. "We'll see you downstairs."

Reluctantly, I dragged myself into the kitchen unsure how people like Mrs. Clark and her staff would look at me. What would they think? Right away, I found out.

"Ah, there's my girl," announced Mrs. Clark as she wiped her hands on her apron, her mouth pulled up in a big smile, her eyes sparkling. "I'm glad you ate my biscuits. They're always good for what ails you and I see they're working for you." I barely got a thank-you out of my mouth when she continued. "Your little buddy here is a big help to me and my staff." She pointed at Simon, tummy flat on the floor, ready to spring on any random crumb that appeared. "He's keeping my floor mighty clean though if he gets any bigger, we're gonna need a bigger kitchen."

I couldn't help but smile. Somehow, Simon and his antics always set my world straight.

"Any Christmas cookies for a hungry police officer?" Chief stuck his head around the corner and flashed one of his famous smiles.

When he looked my way, I could see he was worried. This tall man, well over six feet, looked like his toned body could handle dozens of cookies with no problem. Though his manner was light and playful, his wrinkled brow was my first clue that he was concerned about me and what had happened. It wasn't his fault that I was at the courthouse square last night and saw what I saw. He had told me to stay at Fair Winds. It was my brilliant idea to jump in the car and go to Easton. The best thing I could do for my friend was to show him I was okay, even if I had to fake it. "Just the man I wanted to see. I have something for you. Wait right there."

I was back in a flash. "Earlier, I did a little research on the clip art and narrowed down the possible sources to these websites." I handed the list to the Chief. "Of course, there are hundreds, if not thousands of sites, but I think you should start with these URLs. But if the thief used books of clip art, all bets are off." The Chief gave me a blank look. "What?"

"Clip art?" He said almost meekly. The authoritative tone that was always in his voice was gone. "Now, a URL, I know what that is but what am I supposed to do with them?"

I'm an idiot. The man knows all about guns and criminal behavior, but clip art?

I almost laughed, but at myself. Instead, I laid it out for him. "A website of clip art is a good place to find those little pictures the thief used in the puzzle. I did a quick search on some of the bigger ones and found several of the pictures he used. They weren't free…"

He completed my thought. "So, if I can get a warrant, we might find out who bought these pictures."

"It's a long shot, but it might work."

"Thanks, Abby. You gave us good information last night, but, as you know, it wasn't very specific. Every little thing helps." He folded the list and put it in his pocket, his lips pressed together in determination. His forehead smoothed out and the furrows disappeared. The Chief was back on track.

Dawkins appeared in the doorway as silent as a stealth airplane. "Miss Abigail, shall I put out the silver pieces for the party?"

I'd forgotten. Kat had offered, but Lorraine wanted me to do it. *I guess she wasn't saying those things upstairs about Kat just to make me feel good. I remembered she didn't want Kat to have direct access to the collection before I finished the inventory. Lorraine must have been aware of Kat's behavior of lurking around corners and snooping where she didn't belong. It must have made her uncomfortable, even suspicious. But she didn't steal the chalice because the thief was the man I saw at the statue last night who pushed her. Could he have been her accomplice? If so, she put her trust in the wrong person.*

Lorraine trusted Dawkins. So did I, but working with the silver might help me get back to normal. "I'll do it," I said, walking toward the silver closet. "Would you help me?" I was ready to step away from the treasure hunt for the chalice and deal with the treasure right here at Fair Winds.

Though we called it a closet, the storage area for the silver was more like a room. Glass-enclosed shelves running floor to ceiling lined the walls. Rich wood chests with silver flatware – basic knife, fork, and spoon table settings – nestled inside. Other shelves covered with anti-tarnish cloth held every type of silver tableware or hollowware imaginable: Serving trays, candlesticks with all kinds of candelabra configurations, bowls in various sizes and shapes, teapots, sugar bowls and more. After Dawkins and I ferried many pieces to the table, including slotted serving spoons, olive forks and three different kinds of asparagus servers, I headed to a far corner of the silver closet for a very special piece that dated back to before the Civil War. I slid open a glass panel and reached for the piece. Tonight, the center of the table would feature the epergne.

"We'll use this as the centerpiece, but first I have to take it apart." The tall decorative structure was designed to offer fruit, candies or flowers from the intricately designed piece. I gently unhooked small hanging bowls, fluted flower vases and the bases of eight candleholders. Dawkins watched my every move and, though he tried to hide it, his eyes were glowing with excitement. The epergne was a magnificent piece that wasn't used very often anymore, unfortunately. The piece took a lot of time to set up. Even after it was put together, one had to have special things to put in each little basket. Too complicated for most people in this fast-paced world. It took several trips to the main dining room to move all its pieces to the long dining table stretched out with additional leaves and covered with an elegant lace tablecloth. The dark walnut chairs with needlepoint seat cushions stood along the walls of the large room ready for guests who might prefer to sit with the buffet close at hand. I suspected the staff had spent hours cleaning the many prisms, pendants and faceted glass chains of the three-tiered crystal chandelier above, and the effect was dazzling.

While I reassembled the epergne, I said to Dawkins, "You probably know that the word *epergne* comes from the French word for *saving*?"

"Really?" He waited for me to continue.

"It was designed to save guests the trouble of passing around sweets at the end of a meal. With an epergne in the middle of the table, everyone could reach what they wanted when they wanted it." He raised his eyebrows and cocked his head to the side a little. "Okay, you knew that."

"I don't mind when you tell me things, Miss Abigail. I might learn something I don't know. After all, you are the resident expert on silver."

I lifted the crowning silver piece – a large basket – to the center high above the radiating branches below. "I guess it will be your job to decorate it now."

He dropped his head a little. "I hope to do something with the materials she set aside, something worthy of the piece and..." He didn't have to say her name. I knew. Dawkins didn't display his feelings, but I knew that last night's events had touched him.

"Well, I'll leave you to it. Lorraine has set up a full schedule for me today."

I backed out of the dining room to stand in the foyer so I could get the full effect... and I crashed into Edward. We fumbled around making sure we were both all right.

He said, "I came by to see..." His words trailed off. "What's wrong?"

His question tore me away from all the distractions of Simon, the biscuits, silver pieces and Dawkins. Reality slapped me in the face.

Before I could find any words, Lorraine swept in. "Edward, please join me in the library. Abby run along, you have appointments to keep."

Grateful to be dismissed, I called Simon. As we walked toward the door on our way back to my cottage, I heard a low moan from down the hall. Lorraine had delivered the news.

The next words stopped me in my tracks. "That's just wrong!" Edward bellowed. "The chalice is not about death. It's the symbol of life, life everlasting. Not death. Not *her* death."

CHAPTER EIGHT

The Butler must ensure that each item on the evening menu is presented with the appropriate silver serving piece. He must understand the design and function of each piece so he can make the proper selections.
—"The Butler's Guide to Fine Silver" Mr. Hollister, 1898

Torn between going into the library and leaving Lorraine alone to deal with Edward, I stood in the hallway where Simon found me and pawed my leg. He had his big neon orange ball in his mouth.

"I didn't listen to you last night and look what happened. Let's go outside and play."

After what felt a hundred throws, one tired puppy was willing to go inside the cottage.

Though he was ready for his morning nap, Simon knew the drill and plopped down at my feet in front of the refrigerator. It was time to do my *Plan for the Day*, a little game played with refrigerator magnets that my grandmother made up when I was a very little girl. After the car accident that killed my mother, I refused to talk. Doctors said there was nothing physically wrong and I would speak again when I was ready though it could take months, maybe even a year. Gran wasn't willing to wait that long to communicate with me. She started this game using magnets with pictures or small items so I had a way to respond to her questions, and later, together we could focus and plan my activities. It became a habit to use them to leave messages for one another and to let her know what I had planned for that day. Even though I'd been to college and lived on my own for a long time, I still worked with the magnets every morning. Through this simple action, I reconnected with the woman, now lost to cancer, who I'd loved so much and relied on when things got tough.

I needed that connection today because, after what happened, it was going to take some doing not to go back to bed and hide under the covers. *Might as well get started.* I pulled a fluffy white cloud magnet to the center to represent the serenity here at Fair Winds. I added the one I'd made from a small silver spoon to represent my new work that gave me a sense of satisfaction I'd never had before. My pleasure faded as I picked out a magnet I rarely used... a kitten. Sadly and with a little wave of guilt, I had to admit that Kat wasn't my kind of person. Yes, she was often annoying and nosey, but she didn't deserve to—

Lorraine's voice echoed in my mind. *It was not your fault. Kat loved to poke around where she didn't belong and that could only lead to trouble.*

I contemplated the kitten and wondered what the woman had seen or heard that motivated to go to the courthouse. Then, I remembered. After everyone left for the Catholic Church and the house was quiet, I'd heard a door closing. Kat had eavesdropped once too often and believed I was right that the message pointed to the Confederate soldier's statue at the courthouse. Lorraine said it was up to the Chief now. With a heavy heart, I picked up the kitten magnet and moved it back to the collection. Lorraine was right. It was time for the professionals do their job and for me to move on.

I reached for the sailboat and smiled. Ryan – the tall, tan, handsome man I first met at Tilghman Day – had finally forgiven me for my insulting behavior with an innocent young man he was mentoring. Let's start over, he'd said and invited me aboard his sailboat for the Christmas parade on the water to open the Christmas in St. Michaels Festival. Yes, it was a good day to start over.

Dressed and finally ready to face the day, I went into town and walked along the main street where shopkeepers were sweeping away leaves, putting out tempting children's toys and unfurling a variety of flags. I drew my scarf tighter around my neck against the wind and hustled along to the Little Jewelry Shop only to find a sign that read, Back in 30 minutes. I retraced my steps and headed to the drugstore and the Cove for a hot cup of coffee.

Bells tied with holiday ribbons clattered as I walked in the main door of the local drugstore. The Cove was the coffee shop/soda fountain tucked in the back corner. "Good afternoon, Maureen." The middle-aged queen of the front cash register flicked her eyes up at me then down again to the rolls of coins in her cash drawer, which gave me the full effect of her brilliant green eyeshadow. Somebody had said she loved everything Irish so she even dyed her hair red so she'd have something in common with the gorgeous actress Maureen O'Hara.

"Good morning, Maureen. Do you have an extra "New York Times" today?"

She scowled. "Haven't I told you, Missy, all I get are spoken for?"

"Is there somewhere else I can get the paper here in St. Michaels?"

"Nope, all the copies come to me and to get one, you have to be on my list."

"Would you put me on the list?"

"No room. You have to wait your turn. You're from Washington. Read one of the Wasington papers. That's good enough for you."

"But the *"New York Times"* is special."

"I know. That's why there's a list."

The door bells jangled, she looked and her nose went up in the air. "If you'll excuse me, I have a customer." She flashed a big smile at an older man in a black cashmere coat. "Good morning, Dr. Lancaster. You're in early for the weekend."

The man nodded. "They're calling for snow up north and we didn't want to miss the festival this weekend." With deference, he asked, "You don't happen to have an extra…"

Maureen leaned down behind the counter. "For you, always." With a flourish, she presented him with the current edition of the newspaper I wanted. "I'll put it on your bill."

"Thank you! Santa should be very good to you this year!"

After he left, the smile on Maureen's face melted away. She looked at me and raised her eyebrows as if asking if I understood that this was her domain. .

Not knowing what else to do, I wished her a good day and went in search of some hot coffee in the Cove. I was happy to see that Lulu Mae was working the counter instead of the uppity waitress Patti-with-an-i.

When she saw me, her ever-present smile broke into a wide grin. "Well, look what the winter wind blew in. Sit yourself down and I'll get you some coffee."

"It's not winter yet, Lulu Mae," said the man sitting on the other side of the counter, hunched over a half-eaten plate of toast and a coffee mug. "Not until the 20th or something."

"I know that and you know that, Jeff," she shot back over her shoulder. "But who's gonna tell Mother Nature?" She put down a mug of steaming coffee in front of me. "How are you this morning?"

I ignored her question. It wasn't the sort of thing to talk about in front of strangers. Instead, I whispered, "You have an interesting group here this morning."

She nodded and I followed her gaze from the bleary-eyed man on the far side of the counter, past Stewart, the finance chair from the church who was sitting at a table by himself, staring into space while stirring his coffee round and round to a thin young woman sitting alone at the large round table in the corner. She looked meek. She'd blend into the wallpaper at a party. She was huddled over her mug, crying silently. A crumpled tissue balled up in her hand suggested that she had been at it for a while and had given up trying to stem the tears that now fell in her mug and on the table.

"Poor Millie. She's been like that for a half hour."

"What's wrong?" I asked, keeping my voice low.

Lulu Mae shook her head. "Not sure, but I suspect it's man trouble."

"A breakup? A divorce?"

"No, she'd be lucky to get that far along in a relationship. She's always the one left on the dock. Nobody notices her. She pours herself into that little gift shop down the way. Her daddy set her up after high school thinking a nice little business might attract some guy, but she's still alone after ten years. She has a real knack for picking out things the tourists love. I see them carrying her little bright yellow bags in here all the time. She says she likes to spread a little sunshine. Wish someone would bring some sunshine into her life."

We both looked back at the girl and sighed.

"What can I get you?" she asked.

"Nothing, just..." All of a sudden my stomach overruled my brain and demanded sustenance in the form of comfort food. "Can I get a couple of eggs and some of your fried potatoes really quick?"

"Ready in a jiffy." She scribbled on her pad and hustled off to the kitchen pass-through.

"You shouldn't rush a meal like that, you know. It could upset your whole system," said the winter expert who was about thirty-five years old. His sandy hair was finger-combed, his seen-better-days denim jacket pulled over an Oxford-cloth, buttoned-down shirt, his face clean-shaven but pale. He gulped his coffee and put the mug down with a slam. "Oops, didn't mean to do that."

His eyes, red from the night before, were trying to focus on me, and having a tough time doing it in the bright fluorescent light.

I didn't say a word, not wanting to be part of his hangover.

Lulu Mae reappeared. "Want one to go?" She asked him as she reached for a paper cup.

"Yeah," he said, "since you don't have any hair-of-the-dog." He chuckled. "I've got to open the store. It's Friday morning—"

"Afternoon. Friday afternoon," Lulu Mae corrected.

"Whatever day or time it is, the sales have got to pick up or I'm down for the count."

"Traffic should be heavy this weekend because of the festival. If you slowed down at night and opened the store on time, your business would be doing better," said Lulu Mae.

"I couldn't help being out late last night. It was the 9-Ball tournament semi-finals at C Street." He stood and placed the palm of his hand proudly on his chest. "I was shooting brilliantly and the competition went into a play-off twice! My opponents wanted to toast my proficiency with the cue ball. Who was I to deny them?" He bowed from the waist and flinched. "Shouldn't have done that." He sat down again and held out his empty mug. Lulu Mae and I exchanged looks. "I'm gonna get some aspirin from the pharmacy. Be right back."

Lulu Mae went to the kitchen pass-through. "Eggs up!" When she put the steaming breakfast food down in front of me, she said in a soft voice only I could hear, "Do you know that guy?" I shook my head. "He's Conrad Jeffries, owns the antique store down the street. Called

Belle Antiques or some such. People say he was a hot shot in New York before he came down here. Likes to hang out with the locals, drink beer and shoot pool. They call him Jeff. No one in his right mind would go by Conrad down here. He'd never survive with the nickname of Connie with all the manly watermen and construction guys. He's curious is all I have to say." She shrugged as she walked away to greet a group of shoppers sitting down at one of the tables.

I savored my meal and watched the performance behind the counter starring Lulu Mae. Order slips flew off her pad, slid into place and fluttered as she whipped the turnstile around for the cook.

If I could be that efficient, I'd have the silver collections at Fair Winds done in no time… and work myself right out of my job.

Then, Lulu Mae went to the fruit basket to put the crowning touch on an order of banana pancakes. First, she cut a banana in half and carved out a wedge in the skin. In a blur, her knife made perfect slices that dropped on the steaming cakes.

"Lulu Mae, you are a marvel, a true professional."

"That she is." The antique dealer was back. He opened an aspirin bottle and swallowed a bunch of tablets. "She could hold her own with New York diner waitresses."

"It's fun watching a server who knows what she's doing," I said, trying to ignore the talking hangover across the counter.

"I'm no server, honey. I'm a waitress. Always have been, always will be."

"Looks like you're interested in antiques." Just like that, Jeff had put down his coffee, sat next to me and reached for the stack of silver reference books. "Reading about sterling silver?"

I didn't want a conversation with this guy... but wait. "Do you know anything about silver?" I said, giving him my most innocent act. I couldn't pass up the opportunity. After all, it was a man who fought with Kat last night, a man who knew about silver. The thief had taken only the single most valuable piece of silver from the church, though there were many more in the collection. If this was the man in the square last night, it made sense that he'd have drunken himself into a stupor to forget what he'd done.

"Yeah, I know a lot about silver. I'm an antique dealer, but I gotta tell you that, if you're thinking of going into the business, think again. Silver is a loser. It just sits on the shelf. People don't want to polish it and I can't compete with those companies that buy silver to melt down. Nobody cares about the intrinsic value of a piece anymore."

"Even if it's an old, unusual piece? Maybe something, I don't know, that is rare. One of a kind? Would they melt it down just for its weight in silver?"

He searched my face, trying to figure me out. I almost held my breath as I maintained my innocent I'm-asking-an-honest-question face. In a low voice, he asked, "Do you have a line on such an item?"

"Do you?" I heard my fast heartbeat banging in my ears.

He shrugged. "I hear about pieces from time to

time."

"What do you do then? Do you save it or sell it for the value of the metal?"

"I'm more of a purist. I like to find a buyer who appreciates the quality of piece."

"When you have something special?"

His answer was a simple nod.

"And do you like puzzles?" *Was I sitting next to the thief and murderer?* My breath was coming in short puffs of excitement mixed with a little fear.

He dropped his eyes and slowly raised them to the top of my head, traveling over my body. "Yes, I like puzzles, especially the ones with curly hair." *Is he checking me out? Does he think I'm coming on to him?* Surprised that he would be so obvious, I couldn't say a word. He stood up. "Gotta go. If you find something special, you should bring it by my shop. It's right on the main street. Belle Antiques... for all the beautiful things I have."

"I will."

He raised his eyebrows, his eyes still evaluating me. "You do that, Silver Girl."

Before I could collect my wits, the next scene in the continuing saga of the Cove unfolded. An overweight girl with long, straggly hair stomped through the little restaurant toward the kitchen door only to come face-to-face with Lulu Mae.

Everyone in the Cove stopped, turned and stared, waiting for something exciting to happen. We weren't disappointed when things erupted.

"Get out of my way! This ain't none of your

business," sneered the girl as she pushed her way around her into the kitchen where she screamed at the cook. "Where's Sonny? I went to the church and he ain't there. You're his mother. Are you hiding him from me?"

There was a muted reply that didn't make the girl happy. "No, I have a right to know. I'm the mother of his child, your grandchild." Nastiness coated every word. "You gotta tell me. He owes me."

Lulu Mae's whispered, "Uh, oh, Carly is trouble now." I followed her gaze toward the front of the store. Maureen was on the move. She bypassed the customers and marched straight into the kitchen. With a voice made of razor blades, she ordered the girlfriend to be quiet.

"I don't have to do what you say. You're not the boss of me!"

"In here, oh yes, I am!" The kitchen door exploded with a bang against the wall and Maureen led the girl out by the ear. Carly pulled away and yelled back to the kitchen, "I'm gonna find him and when I do, I'm gonna whip his ass." She wiggled out of Maureen's reach and made for the door. Maureen muttered the word *trash* and walked slowly back to her place at the front register, shaking her head.

Sonny was a young man with serious money pressures... with access to the church? And he was still missing? I wonder what the Chief found out. This theft might be easier to solve than I thought.

But something wiggled at the back of mind. It might not be fair to jump to conclusions, but Sonny didn't sound like the type to steal a valuable chalice and leave an intricate puzzle behind. I glanced at the clock and gasped. I was late for my hair appointment.

CHAPTER NINE

Preparation is the key to the successful presentation of a formal dinner. Always inspect the menu carefully and consider the serving options in the silver closet. Be vigilant that the pieces going to the table are in excellent condition and pristinely polished.

—"The Butler's Guide to Fine Silver" Mr. Hollister, 1898

After my hair appointment, I found the rain had cleared off and the air was crisp and clear. Back at Fair Winds, I rushed through the main house looking for Simon, the warm sunlight poured through the large windows, all scrubbed clean and sparkling. People bustled around everywhere.

Lorraine blew in the front door mumbling to herself. "I'm losing my mind. How could I forget that file?" She looked up and saw me. "Oh Abby, I love your hair."

I fluffed my shiny curls. "Those spa ladies do some magical things with my hair."

"I wish they could do some magic here." She sighed. "There's still so much to do and now with..." I could tell she was kicking herself for reminding me of Kat's absence.

On impulse, I threw my arms around her and she melted into my hug.

"Oh, thank you. I needed that," she said.

"It's going to be all right." I released her, but gave her cold hands a squeeze. "Better than all right."

She didn't seem convinced so I went to the wall and flipped on the light switch. The elegant crystal chandelier high above our heads burst into glittering light. I turned my friend around slowly so she could take in the effect of the lavish decorations in the main rooms. The majestic tree in the living room laden with shiny ornaments and tiny lights brushed the high ceiling. Around the base, a wide velvet tree skirt in all the jewel tones of the season was dotted with richly wrapped and ribboned presents for key festival people in appreciation for all their work throughout the year. The silver—everything from serving spoons to candelabras—gleamed on the linen-covered dining room table. As she took it all in, her smile widened and reached her eyes.

"And now you'd better get going. Don't you have a meeting or something?"

"Oh," she gasped. "And I'm late." She hurried down out the door then stopped and turned. "Thank you, Abby."

I clapped my hands. "Off with you!" She rushed away.

Heavenly aromas floated from the kitchen. That's where I headed since I was fairly confident that Simon would be there.

Mrs. Clark was calmly directing her staff as they stirred, simmered, iced and arranged the many sumptuous dishes on the menu. To protect against distractions and illicit tastes by those of us drawn to the kitchen, she'd set out little samples of the foods they'd prepared so far. Very clever approach, I thought. Sure enough, I spied Simon crouched by the stove intently watching the floor for spills or crumbs. I tried to get his attention, but I didn't exist in his mind until I said the magic word, *Cookie*. In a flash, he was on his feet and bouncing around my legs. I didn't disappoint him when we got down to the cottage.

I figured I had plenty of time to get ready for the evening's festivities – the party and the boat parade – which required a change of clothes or at least a layering. As I caught a glimpse of myself in the mirror, I was glad I'd kept the hair appointment Lorraine had made for me and taken a little extra time for a quick manicure. Lorraine was right, of course. The pampering made me feel better, at least a little bit. The fine ladies at the spa must have sensed something special was in the offing. They'd stood around the chair offering suggestions as the stylist worked her magic with my auburn curls. I made myself a promise that in the New Year, I'd come in and learn the stylist's tricks that tamed my hair.

I opened my closet to get dressed. I did have plenty of time, except I kept changing my mind. I put on my black velvet skirt with a sparkly top and was admiring the effect when I realized it was a bad choice. A skirt on a boat? The plan was to attend the kick-off party, then leave directly for the marina, board Ryan's boat and take our position in the Christmas boat parade. It would be past sunset with falling temperatures. I'd need something warm.

With a jolt, my mind flashed back to last night and the shivering cold of the wind, the creaking limbs over my head, the pool of blood by Kat's head. I wanted to sink into my bed and never get up.

No, that's not going to happen!

I visualized the festive decorations at the main house... and Ryan's handsome face and those incredible blue eyes. I took a deep breath, let it out and dropped the outfit on a chair.

I took a pair of winter white wool slacks and matching cashmere sweater out of the closet and put them on. Simon bounded into the room. What was I thinking... white slacks, big black dog! Who said that Labs don't shed? Whoever it was should see me vacuuming the cottage more than once a week. I dropped it on the chair with the skirt. After trying a few more options, I settled on black velvet slacks and a pearl white silk blouse with dangling earrings and a single strand of pearls that seemed to take on an inner glow against my skin.

When I saw how late it was, I quickly folded a thick sweater, wool socks, boat shoes and earmuffs into a small tote for the parade. Ready to race out the door, I caught sight of Simon standing by my discarded pile of clothes with a mournful look. *How do you always know when I'm going out?* I didn't have time to let him break my heart. "Come on, boy! You can stay with Lorraine's Chessies." In a burst of frenzied delight, he led me up to the house.

After settling Simon with a mound of treats for him and his friends, I stowed my tote and moved down the hallway toward the foyer and the main rooms. The sights and sounds and smells heralded that it was holiday time.

"Abby! I've been waiting for you." Lorraine was dressed in a rich burgundy cashmere dress that gently followed her curves and added color to her face so pale a few hours ago. I was pleased to see she had brought out a few of her family heirlooms. Her earrings were two rows of not-so-small diamonds with a single stone dangling at the bottom. Every time Lorraine moved her head, tiny flashes of light glinted around her. Above the soft cowl collar of her dress was the choker with five emerald-cut diamonds I'd only seen in a photograph framed in her library. Add to that her impressive engagement ring and her mother's diamond wedding band and she was ready to make an elegant statement as the hostess of the evening.

Lorraine put her hands on my arms and rubbed them in a comforting, consoling way. "I know the past 24 hours have been a horror for you. You're very brave to come. As I said before, what happened last night to Kat was a tragic thing." She brought her face close and her eyes bored into mine. "There was nothing you could do to prevent it. The Chief said that the evidence so far doesn't support premeditation. For now, he is saying it was an unfortunate accident."

"But somebody killed her. She didn't slam her head into that stone pedestal on purpose."

"It might have something to do with the legal definition of murder. He knows these things. They still want to talk to the other person you saw, but, as of right now, they're treating it as an unfortunate accident."

"But—"

"But nothing. The situation is now *his* responsibility. We should be supportive but we can't dwell on what happened. The Chief will figure it out, okay?' Reluctantly, I nodded.

"I know it will put a damper on the evening, but these people deserve some recognition and enjoyment. Help me make them feel welcome here at Fair Winds."

I nodded again, fighting tears. The memory of the shadows moving in a deadly dance on the brick wall of the courthouse haunted even my awake moments. I hoped that time would make them fade and take the horror away.

"I'm reminded yet again that life is short and not meant to be lived alone. After everything that's happened, it'd be so easy to roll up the driveway and sit in my house. But you encouraged me to do this and look..." She swept her hand around to take in all the decorations and preparations made by the staff. "Fair Winds has come alive again. I can't tell you how it warms my soul." She enveloped me in a hug and whispered, "You were so right." I could hear tears in her voice. "Thank you, Abby."

Dawkins cleared his throat. He was being polite but I suspected he was a little embarrassed by our exchange. Our public display of emotion might have been too much for him. "Excuse me, Madame, but perhaps you want to express your gratitude at another time. Your guests are arriving and..." He gave me a sidelong glance and... was that a little knowing smile? "And there is a gentleman asking for Miss Abigail."

Lorraine flicked away a teardrop, straightened her outfit and gave me a wink. "You're right, of course, Dawkins. It's time to party."

As she rushed to the front door, Dawkins said to me, "If you'll follow me." He led me to Ryan standing by the Christmas tree looking like the best present ever.

CHAPTER TEN

Sterling silver is made up of 925 parts of silver and 75 parts copper added for strength and durability. Only sterling flatware— knives, forks and spoons—used in each place setting should be called silverware. Anything else pretends to be the real thing.
—"The Butler's Guide to Fine Silver" Mr. Hollister, 1898

His cocoa brown hair had lost some of the highlights made by the summer sun, but his skin still had the healthy glow of someone who spends time on the water. He turned toward me as if I'd called his name. His eyes outlined by long, dark lashes sparkled from across the room. Then he smiled and I was mesmerized. Dawkins gave me a little push into action and I met Ryan in the center of the room.

Suddenly I felt painfully shy. Was it because he was so handsome or, that up until that moment, I hadn't realized how many people –volunteers and their guests – were in the large living room and all those pairs of eyes were on us?

He didn't miss a beat and gave me a peck on the cheek. "You look lovely," he said. "It's nice to see you wearing something other than jeans."

Surprised by his comment, I laughed. The ice was broken and I could be *me* again.

"You look pretty terrific yourself. Who would have thought that a blue and green plaid jacket would look so good?"

He made a few small moves to model the jacket that fit him like it was made for him, broad shoulders, nipped in at the waist. "I want you to know that this isn't just any jacket. It's a Black Watch tartan dinner jacket. I didn't want to go over the top so I paired it with charcoal gray slacks."

I acted duly impressed while I noticed that his deep blue eyes had green flecks brought out by the colors of the jacket. "I'd say it's a winning combination."

"So would I." I wasn't so sure his comment was limited to his wardrobe since he winked at me. "I was admiring the ornaments on Lorraine's tree." He leaned close. I caught a whiff of his subtle but intriguing cologne as he whispered, "I was really coveting her collection of Christmas in St. Michaels ornaments. She has every one since the festival started."

I looked at the huge sea of green pine needles almost obscured by a wild array of decorations. "I'm sorry. There are so many. Which ones?"

He pointed to a grouping of delicate flat metal medallions honoring symbols of the area like the Great Blue Heron, a gaggle of Canada geese and a St. Michaels harbor scene featuring the tour boat called the Patriot. "The 2013 ornament has a lantern to celebrate the 200th anniversary when the townspeople fooled the British. But I think this is my favorite." He fingered the one marked 2011. "I really like the artist's rendering of the Chesapeake Bay Log Canoe."

"Canoe? With all those sails?"

"It was adapted from the canoe used by the Native Americans living in the area and used to harvest oysters. When the hull was full, the captains would race to the market towns because the first boat to arrive got the best price for its catch. Now, racing log canoes is a very serious sport on the Chesapeake Bay with a grueling summer schedule. This is the only place in the world where they sail." He sighed in appreciation. "The artist really caught the grace of the boat." Then, his voice developed an edge. "And that's the one I don't have. I think someone might have *borrowed* it from our tree." He glanced around furtively. "Do you think I might...?"?"

I gave his hand reaching for the ornament a light slap. "Don't you dare. You'll have to get your own, that's all. And, Mister, if I find this one has gone missing, I shall report to the Chief that you're a thief."

"Thief? Who's a thief?" I'd recognize that voice anywhere. Harriet Snow had finally made it inside the main house of Fair Winds. And, being a world-class gossip, the wrong person heard the word thief.

"Why, Harriet, we were just kidding about sneaking one of the decorations off the tree." My little laugh sounded like a Jane Austen titter.

The petite woman didn't smile as she looked back and forth been us while not a curl of her short white hair moved. She smoothed the front of her red satin blouse all the way to the skinny gold belt at her waist atop a green velvet skirt and said, "I don't think

Lorraine would appreciate that. There's already been an unfortunate death. We don't need a thief in our midst, too." She turned to me and narrowed her eyes, making the wrinkles around her eyes even deeper. "That girl worked here, didn't she? What do you know about what happened?"

I tried to look as innocent as a newborn babe. She kept staring. I caught Ryan's expression out of the corner of my eye. He wasn't buying my innocent pose, but thankfully, he didn't say anything. At least I'd learned that Harriet hadn't caught a whiff of the chalice theft, at least not yet.

She raised her chin a little. "I think there's been enough violence." She looked at me with surprise. "It does seem to follow you around, Abby. I've noticed that. Maybe I should say something to—" She began to scan the room when she raised one eyebrow and exclaimed, "Oh!" A single word, drawn out and running right up the musical scale. "There's Mrs. Frampton... from the Hamptons... and the City." She leaned into the center of our little group. "And by the City, she means New York City, don't you know." I almost laughed aloud. Imagine Harriet making fun of someone acting superior to those around her. The woman had no idea what kind of impression she made on other people. Harriet raised her hand and waved. "Oh, Rennie! Over here."

The sophisticated-looking woman peered around the room for a way to escape, but finding none, joined our group. "Harriet, my close friends call me Rennie. You really should call me Florence."

"Oh, but I do so like the nickname *Rennie*. It's so

distinctive," chirped Harriet.

Rennie realized she wasn't going to change the older woman's mind. She sighed and looked around the group and said hello without making eye contact with anyone. Her blonde hair was so smooth that every strand seemed to know its place and stayed there, just like the fashion ads. A long, whisper-thin scarf of fine silk in a festive red print accented the deep V neckline of her black taffeta cocktail dress.

Harriet made introductions all around.

Rennie's eyebrows shot up when she heard my name. She turned slightly to exclude the others in the group. "Oh! Are you the one who is working on Lorraine's silver?" I nodded. "Well," she said, holding her hands together rather primly at her waist. "You'll have to come and give me your opinion of my silver. I had it shipped from storage, but now it seems we won't be here for the holidays so I won't need it. I'll use it another time."

"Oh, but you will be here for the Shoebox Christmas Exchange, won't you? Your name was included in the drawing." Harriet edged forward slightly to become part of the conversation again.

The woman from New York heaved a big sigh. "Yes, I'll be here for your little whatever it is."

Without missing a beat, Harriet turned and took the arm of the quiet, balding man standing behind her. "And this is Bennett Snow, my husband, of course."

While the woman from New York gave him a quick nod, scanning the room for a way to make her getaway, Harriet said, "Rennie, don't you think that Abby here should get on with it so she can have a husband, too?" She patted my arm.

I could have fallen through the floor right to the basement. My eyes flicked over to look at Ryan, hoping I wouldn't see him sprinting to the door. I relaxed a little when I saw him chuckling quietly.

Without thinking about how her comments made me feel, Harriet continued in a concerned tone. "Speaking of husbands, I don't believe I see yours, dear. Is he here?" She made a quick sweep of the room, her head pivoting around.

"No, he isn't," Rennie said in an almost defensive tone. "Robert is in Chicago. I didn't go with him, of course. Who in her right mind goes to Chicago in December unless it's on business?"

"Quite right," agreed Harriet. "Though he does seem to travel a lot for someone who is retired... and what did you say he does again?"

She was quick to clarify. "*Semi*-retired. He's wrapping things up with the corporation, but it will take some time. We moved down here from The City so he could be out of the cold when he comes home. We're not ready to wither up in Florida. We'll base out of our home in the Hamptons next summer, of course."

Harriet brought her eyebrows together, staring at Rennie. Like a dog with a meaty bone, Harriet went on. "And will he be home for the holidays?"

Rennie gave her a curious stare. "Why, of course." Her words had a shaft of ice in them. "We'll be in the Turks and Caicos together, with friends." She looked around the group. "I hope you all have a lovely holiday."

Then she walked away with a little attitude in her hips that sent the hem of her dress dancing.

Ryan orchestrated our escape. "If you'll excuse us, Abby and I were just about to..."

"Yes, we were." I caught on quick. "If you'll excuse us. Enjoy your evening." Ryan and I scooted away.

"That was close," I whispered to Ryan. "I thought she was going to interrogate us about..." I bit my tongue. Better not talk about what happened last night.

"About what? Us?" he said with a grin.

I bit my lip lightly, worried that he was looking for an excuse to disappear. I looked and caught the corners of his mouth twitching to keep from smiling. I relaxed and said, "Yes, us... as if there is an *us.*"

"There could be..." The smile faded and his face darkened. "Harriet brought up the woman who died last night. Mysterious circumstances, I hear. She worked here, didn't she? Do you know anything about what happened?"

I took a quick breath in surprise. I hoped he wouldn't probe so I said quickly, "The one thing I do know is that you're not much of a gentleman or else I would have a glass of eggnog."

He held his hands up in surrender. "Okay, okay. Eggnog, it is. Dawkins was telling me about his recipe..."

We started to wander over to the enormous punch bowl when the Pastor dashed up to me, "Abby! We have to talk." He gave Ryan a quick nod and drew me aside with his hand firmly holding my arm. "Do you have anything to report?"

"Um, no. Nothing." I fought against his jittery sense

SUSAN REISS

of urgency. It was almost contagious. "Has your janitor shown up yet?" I remembered his angry girlfriend in the Cove and wondered if *she'd* found him. It wouldn't surprise me if she gave him a black eye.

"No, Sonny is still missing in action." His eyes twitched around us making sure that no one was sneaking up to listen. "I can't believe this is happening. What have I done to deserve this? I don't know what we're going to do."

"Don't give up just yet. There's a plan for scoping out all the venues of the Christmas in St. Michaels Festival tomorrow." I wondered if Lorraine and the Chief would still include me after what happened last night. I'd find out later. Meanwhile, the pastor was waiting for some reassurance. "Look, Edward and I have evaluated the situation and feel confident that we'll find the chalice." He looked away in impatience, but I wasn't sure it was because of our slow progress or the mention of Edward's name. "Pastor, at first, I wasn't in favor of you sending someone to assist me, but Edward was very helpful in deciphering the first document."

"He always is," the good Pastor mumbled.

"Yes, he was," I insisted. "I'm glad you sent him. I thought we might—"

He interrupted me to make an announcement that was more important. "I can't stay. Must get back to the church. So much to do."

Ryan appeared at my side as the Pastor rushed through the crowd. A skinny man, he almost bounced off a man with a protruding stomach like Santa's. When he reached the foyer, I half expected this self-proclaimed

103

important religious leader to the community to give the Queen's wave, but he snatched up his coat and dashed out the door.

"He's a little weird, isn't he?" I made sure to keep my voice low.

"I think he's more of a nervous type. The least little thing gets him rattled unless he's leading a service. It's surprising, but he's good at the faith part of his job. The sermons are insightful, his delivery is uplifting, not condemning. I don't think he is wired to be an administrator though." Ryan lowered his head close to my face. "He seemed agitated while he was talking to you." His eyes narrowed. "Is something going on?"

I jumped back a little and said with an innocent smile, "No! I have no idea what you mean." I wanted him to think of me as a normal person, not someone who got tangled up in other people's lives and odd situations. I'd met so many men who ran away from women like that. I didn't want this one going anywhere.

"Abby?" He stretched out my name the same way Gran did when she suspected I was up to no good.

A middle-aged couple who knew Ryan stopped to say hello. Listening to their comments on the tree and all the decorations, a sad thought crossed my mind: Kat would have loved this. She worked hard to make everything beautiful and was cheated out of her moment in the spotlight. It was so unfair.

While Ryan continued his conversation, I got that uneasy feeling that someone was staring at me. I looked around as Stewart, the chair of the church finance committee, came toward me, walking in a straight line, and stopped so close I could smell his breath, heavy with liquor. He cocked his head so he could watch the room while he spoke to me out of the side of his mouth.

"What's happened?" He asked. "I saw you talking to the Pastor. You can tell me."

I took a small step back. "Good evening. Are you enjoying the party?"

He scowled, then straightened up and smiled. "Yes, it's a lovely party. So nice of Lorraine to entertain the volunteers before a busy weekend." He dropped the smile and spoke very clearly. "Hopefully, Santa brings us a special present."

"We'll have to wait and see, won't we?" I looked over Stewart's shoulder and found my escape. "Oh, look who's here, Edward! Shall we say hello?" I made my way through the crowd and gave him a peck on the cheek in greeting. He looked a little pasty but he'd had a shock this afternoon. It was obvious that his church was important to him and I hoped he'd forget what happened with Kat and the chalice, and move on to have some fun tonight. "I'm so glad you could come and see Fair Winds at its best." Ryan joined us and we made small talk about the weather, the party and the weekend events while Stewart gave up and took his worries to the bar.

Edward watched him walk away. "Stewart is a good man, but he worries too much and about the tiniest things. To him, it's always about *the numbers*. Difficult way to live."

"Well, tonight is all about fun." I took Edward's arm and steered him toward Lorraine. I thought they might look nice together and have some fun.

Edward smiled, but when he saw her talking with someone by the grand piano, his body stiffened and then he stopped. "She's talking with Josephine." His voice sounded like coarse sandpaper.

The woman was short and trim. Her dark, wavy hair shot with gray clipped short made an attractive frame for her face. As she chatted gaily with Lorraine, she seemed like a pleasant person. Then I realized that there was something about her... a gesture, an expression... that gave me the impression that beneath her soft exterior, there was a backbone of steel. She was not a woman I'd want to tangle with. "Could Rennie be...?"

"Yes." Edward bit off the word. He pulled away from me. "I think I'd better go. It's getting late."

I couldn't hide my surprise. "Edward, it isn't even six o'clock yet. Please stay. Lorraine—"

"Lorraine is talking to Mrs. Quinn and I don't care to..." There was pain in his expression. "I was head of the council for several terms, serving my church in any way I could. This year, *she* ran against me... and won."

I could barely hear his last words. He took a strangled breath. He put his hand over his mouth, coughed and seemed to calm down. "I'm afraid it didn't end well."

"Maybe—" I started to say.

"No, this isn't the time or the place to patch things up." He flashed a warm smile. "I think you should rejoin your young man who is looking a little lost and let me get on with my evening. You're a good girl, Abby. Please convey my gratitude to Lorraine. Good night."

He gave a little nod and walked away.

Confused by Edward's reaction and feeling a little guilty for abandoning Ryan, I went to salvage the evening.

"Edward left suddenly. Abby, is everything okay?"

"Yes, everything's fine," I said, probably too quickly.

"Well, I'm glad you're back," he said with a smile, but his deep blue eyes looked clouded. "I'm not used to having my woman run off with another man."

I laughed. "*Your* woman? You work fast. At this rate, we'll be looking at preschool options for our twins before the night is over."

It was a joke, but it was on me. He shrugged. "Would that be so bad?"

"Um, well..." I fumbled around for something to say to hide my surprise. "I can't believe you're jealous of Edward. He's old enough to be my grandfather. Surely, you don't see him as a threat?"

He raised his eyebrows and smiled. "You never know."

I glanced up to the heavens. "Please, spare me from a green-eyed man."

"They're blue."

"I know." I winked.

"I wasn't completely bored while you were flirting with Edward." I punched him lightly on the arm. "Ow, I didn't deserve that." We laughed together again. Then, his smile fell away and he angled his body toward me. He turned his face away trying to disguise what he said for my ears only. "Listen and learn about your new hometown. See that man over there?" He gestured toward a tall man, over six feet, with a prominent waistline that bulged beyond the edges of his suit jacket. "That's Grant Mathias, the president of the St. Michaels Business Association. I've been watching him in action, flitting from one store owner to another. Right now, he's talking to Conrad Jeffries, probably trying to rope him into some scheme or other of his."

I studied the two men talking by one of the tall windows. "I met him this morning at the Cove."

"Grant?"

"No, the other man. He was in the grip of a serious hangover. Reminded me of one of those guys in a country-western song." Jeff glanced over at me and gave a little nod in greeting.

"It looks like he remembers you," Ryan sounded like he was on verge of real jealousy.

I nodded back and notice that the man's gray suit fit him perfectly. The light rose color of his shirt added a festive touch and warmth to his face. A gold watch chain and fob draped across his vest added to his prosperous image. "Looking at him now, I never would have guessed this was the guy with the massive hangover I met in the Cove this morning. He said he was an antique dealer."

"Yes, he is," Ryan confirmed. "Before Grant corralled him, Jeff was telling me—no, boasting about how he'd donated some antique things for use in the Tour of Homes."

"That's nice."

"Abby, an antique chair and a lace tablecloth don't make a big supporter of the cause," he said.

"What do you know about him?" I asked.

"I know he used to work with one of the big auction houses in New York and came down here with their appraisal team once or twice a year. About two years ago, he came down and stayed. Opened a little shop, but I don't think it's doing very well."

"It isn't according to what he said this morning." My attention switched to the other man. "What do you know about Mr. Mathias?"

"He came here from Michigan, I think. Said he always wanted to run a store. Now, he has one and bought a building, I think in town. He volunteers a lot of time to the business association and has some big ideas for our little town. I also know never to put him and the Pastor together."

"Oh, that sounds ominous," I said, now keenly interested. "Why?"

"Something happened and it was ugly."

"Tell me more." He looked at me, surprised at my request. "If I'm going to live here, I should know something about the civic leaders, right?"

He tilted his head and seemed to examine me for a moment, then he went on to explain. "It's what happens too often in a small town. Probably a misunderstanding blown out of proportion. The Pastor doesn't like Grant's style. He can be brusque sometimes. He always thinks his ideas are the best and should be adopted right away. The Pastor doesn't like to move quickly. Grant dabbles in real estate and asked for some kind of historic-district exemption for one of his properties. When it was turned down, he thought it was because of something the Pastor said. They probably could work it out if they would talk to each other, but they'd rather nurse their prejudices and hurt feelings."

"Typical men," I muttered. Thankfully, Ryan didn't hear me above the dull roar of the party.

He turned and touched his index finger to his lips. "Why do you really want to know?"

I continued to look at the dealer and the businessman. "Oh, no reason. Do you realize you still haven't brought me a drink and I'm parched?"

"Well, if you'll allow me." He extended his arm and I took it. We worked our way over to sample Dawkins's bowl of eggnog. Ryan and I agreed that the blend of flavors was out of this world. Dawkins appeared and we tried to pry the recipe out of him, but he resisted mightily.

"We'll have to leave soon to get on board my boat for the parade. Want to eat something first?" Ryan asked.

"Want to eat something? Are you kidding? I'm not leaving until I have a bite of everything. Wait until you see the spread. Dawkins and I worked carefully to match the best serving piece with each item. We used one that isn't often found on the table." I hustled him to the dining room across from the main living room and in the entryway he stopped in his tracks.

"See? Mrs. Clark and her staff have been working for days," I said excitedly.

He nodded, his eyes wide as he took in the brimming serving dishes that filled the expanded dining table. Nestled with each item was a silver serving piece, everything from a mustard spoon for the grain mustard served with the roasted Brussels sprouts to the silver tongs for the fresh shucked local Choptank oysters.

I steered Ryan over to the cheeses, patés and breads. "We cheated a little with the lavash." I pointed to the crispy little pieces of flat bread that looked like crackers. "We used sugar tongs, but don't tell anybody."

"And here it is." I pointed to the display of cheese. "Mrs. Clark put Stilton cheese on the menu just so we could use the Stilton cheese server."

"It looks like a little shovel," said Ryan.

"Exactly." I reached for a plate. "You push the narrow part with the rounded edges into the soft blue cheese, pull out a plug and gently tap it on your plate." I demonstrated. "Voilà!"

"Very clever." His eyes roamed over the buffet until they landed on one of the special additions to the table. "What is that?"

"That, my friend, is honeycomb. Mrs. Clark made arrangements with the Chef at the Inn at Perry Cabin in order to offer it tonight."

He led the way farther down the table to the plate holding the honeycomb surrounded with bite-size pieces all swimming in a little sea of golden honey.

"And how am I supposed to eat that? Wait, I know! You are supposed to hold it so the honey dribbles between my lips, right?" He worked his eyebrows, barely hiding a smile.

"No, silly. You take a little bit, chew it and when all the honey is gone, you can eat the wax or dispose of it."

He laughed. "I like my idea better."

"You would." I started putting a little bit from each serving dish.

"I see you even put the centerpiece to work. It's magnificent."

The silver piece was set on a large mirror. The center section held a silver basket surrounded by eight lighted candles. Around the outside, four baskets lined with crystal bowls held candied fruit and delicate orchids.

"It's called an epergne," I said.

"A what?"

"It's pronounced a-pairn."

"A purrn." His face screwed up in such a funny way that I laughed out loud. "Great, now the woman is laughing at me."

"No!" But the more I tried to be serious, the more I laughed. "Okay, let's try it again. Say a-pair, put the accent on the second syllable and tack on an n at the end. It's French!"

"That figures. I'm a Spanish guy myself, especially after Mrs.—no, Madame Roland threatened to flunk me in high school." He took one of the chocolate-covered strawberries that were as big as a baby's fist, and grinned with pleasure as he took a bite.

"The piece dates back to the mid-1700's and was originally designed to save precious space on the table since all the dishes were put on the table at the same time."

He chuckled. "You mean they ate family style?"

"I guess you could say that. They put exotic fruits, nuts and sweets from the Far East within easy reach of the guests so they only took one at a time instead of loading up a plate and leaving some." He took another strawberry and I giggled. "People served themselves, just like you're doing. A beautiful silver piece with a serious function."

"It looks like we're not the only one admiring the silver." He gestured toward the woman standing at the far end of the buffet table. Mrs. Rennie Frampton was checking out the patterns and hallmarks of the different pieces of sterling. She even was taking serving pieces out of the various dishes.

"I can understand having an interest in silver, but that's just rude," I whispered. "She looks like she should know better."

"Abby, we don't have time for a cat fight. Grab something to eat. You'll get your chance another time."

Reluctantly, I picked up a plate and took a sampling of Mrs. Clark's creations while I kept an eye on the impolite guest, hoping I'd get the chance to call her on her bad manners.

It seemed like I'd taken only a few bites when Ryan announced it was time to go. We handed our plates to a waiter and Ryan went to get his coat while I went to pick up my tote with the warm clothes inside.

As I opened the closet at the end of the back hall, I heard voices. They didn't sound like staff. Their voices were low as if they were hiding. I tiptoed closer and listened.

"No, I haven't talked to Millie yet." The man sounded like a little boy caught by his mother.

"Why not?" A woman shot back.

"I just have to find the right moment," he said.

"Grant, the right moment is now."

So, Grant Mathias, the hot-shot business leader, was made meek by a woman, but who?

"I know, but—"

She didn't want to hear his excuse. "This is *your* dream, Grant. Not mine."

"I know, Rennie, but you're part of the dream now."

Well! Miss High-and-Mighty now what, though I wasn't worried. She was just the kind of woman who could take a man apart. I crept a little closer so I could catch every word.

"Remember when you first told me your vision, back when I was just a customer in your store?"

"You were never just a customer, honey."

Hmm, seems like Mr. Frampton should stay home a little more often.

"That's sweet, Grant, but this is business. You described a quaint village of antique shops, decorating services, all for the upscale homeowner."

"And you agreed that we should get rid of those t-shirts flapping in the wind in front of stores filled with overpriced tourist stuff." His disgust was clear. "This town is so much more than boating and good restaurants. It has such potential and we're squandering it."

"Now, we have a plan to take advantage of the potential here in St. Michaels."

"Thanks to you, we have a plan. We're doing things to make it happen."

"I'm doing things," she corrected. "You need to do what I tell you, when I tell you."

His ego sagged as he said in the voice of a naughty

little boy caught by his mommy, "I know, I know. I'll talk to her."

"Please, Grant darling. So much depends on it," she cooed.

"I will." His voice was strong with determination. "I'll do it on Monday, after the festival. Just for you, my dear heart."

"Good." Her stiletto heels clicked on the floor as she moved around. "We'd better get back to the party before they miss us. It wouldn't do for them to find out what we're doing before we're ready. Now, give me a kiss... no, on the cheek. You don't want to ruin my makeup."

I scampered down the hall. The lovey-dovey talk with a man who wasn't her husband made me sick. Anyway, I didn't want them to know that I knew what they were doing... at least some of it. Such a grand plan to turn a little village into a town of antiques and decorators without the knowledge or support of the local leaders.

Wonder what they'll think when they find out?

The important thing was that she was knowledgeable about antiques and might know the right person in New York who would pay a king's ransom for the antique chalice. I'd follow up tomorrow. Right now, I had a date with a boat parade.

I burst out of the front door and looked around for Ryan.

"Over here, Abby!" I followed his voice and found he had the car running with the heat at full blast. I got in the car and a little bark from the back seat greeted me.

Simon!

"No, no, this is a bad idea. Simon has never been on a boat. He'll be happier here."

"I saw Dawkins and he led me to the kennel. Trust me on this, Abby. Share adventures with your dog and he'll be your best friend forever." Ryan said warmly, "It will be great."

And it was.

We got to the marina, boarded the boat and I panicked. "I haven't been on a boat in forever. I don't know the first thing about what to do."

"I can single-hand her, but I'd appreciate the help of a first mate, if you'd like to try," he said.

I drew up my courage. "Okay, tell me what to do, but don't blame me if she sinks."

We laughed and he reviewed the safety information about life vests, the radio and all. Even Simon got his own life jacket. We motored out to join the group forming up just beyond the harbor with minutes to spare. There were boats of all sizes and shapes lining up: sailboats, motorboats, and Chesapeake Bay workboats like the ones I saw competing in the docking competition during the Tilghman Island Day celebration when Ryan and I first met. Voices of carolers drifted over the water from the direction of the Chesapeake Bay Maritime Museum. We took our place in the parade behind The Patriot, the large sightseeing cruise boat based in St. Michaels. Santa Claus was standing at the bow waving to all the people along the shoreline.

Simon sat proudly on the bow like the admiral of the fleet. I snuggled in Ryan's foul weather coat that was so warm that the December breeze felt refreshing on my face. Watching all the boats decorated with lights and bows and wreaths. The holiday spirit was infectious and eased out my thoughts about Kat and the terrible memories from the night before.

After making the circuit in the harbor and watching Santa move to land and mount a fire truck for a procession through town, we motored out to the river under a canopy of countless points of light high above.

CHAPTER ELEVEN

A craftsman of a sterling silver piece strives for exquisite proportions. He combines shape and design to fulfill a specific purpose. Its decorative form silently conveys the personality and character of the family and was chosen with great care.
— "The Butler's Guide to Fine Silver" Mr. Hollister, 1898

The next morning, Lorraine met me at the kitchen door.

"I can tell from the glow on your face that you had a good time last night. I want to hear all about it, but..." She hesitated.

"More bad news?" My chest tightened.

"No, no, nothing like that. The Chief thinks that because of what happened at the courthouse, the thief might leave the chalice out in the open for us to find. Like *no harm, no foul.*"

"Yeah, except Kat died."

"I know." She patted my arm so I wouldn't get riled up. "His men are stretched to the limit with all the visitors in town, and it would raise fewer eyebrows if *normal people* cruised through some of the events instead of officers."

"And you want me to..." I waited for her to complete my assignment.

"Go on the Tour of Homes." She rushed on before I could say anything. "You'll visit some houses in the historic district of St. Michaels, nonchalantly look around and, if you spot the chalice, take it, but carefully. There might be fingerprints. That's all." She smiled as if it wasn't a big deal. "... Except you'll need to change into something a little nicer than jeans and a sweater."

I was about to protest and then I remembered Kat. We had to catch the person responsible for Kat's death, so I agreed with one caveat: I had to have some more coffee.

A little later and dressed appropriately, I drove to town and zoomed into a precious parking space. My parallel parking was getting better as I spent more time in St. Michaels. When I saw the gift-and-everything store owned by Grant Mathias, I checked the time. Perfect, there was a little time before the tour started. I dodged the traffic and went inside. What I saw made me lower my head and pretend to concentrate on a display of scented soaps by the door. I raised one to my nose and peeked over my shoulder to see Rennie in a lush fox jacket and filmy silk scarf talking to Grant over the counter.

"And what is this great idea?" She looked at her watch and frowned. "I don't have a lot of time. I have to pick up a quick gift before the shops close for the parade. Make it quick."

I moved over to a tall bookcase to browse the shelves of books so I didn't miss a word of his grand idea.

Bobbing with excitement, he straightened his red tie tucked inside a dark sweater with reindeer prancing around the waist. "One of the new stores could have model trains! Kids love model trains."

"Kids don't buy antiques, Grant," she said flatly.

"But their parents and grandparents do."

"Especially when their kids break something," Rennie murmured.

"The store could carry other toys and... and some antique toys. They come up at the auctions sometimes. We could pick one of the slow weekends in the fall or winter and have Model Railroad Day. All the store owners could wear those red print bandanas and make it a town effort... sorta like the Wine Fest in the spring. What do you think?"

"I think you should let me do the thinking." She tapped her manicured index finger on her chin, careful not to touch her newly applied lip gloss. "Like my idea to bring vintage books into your shop -- leather covers, preferable – and displayed according to color."

"Rennie, I only questioned that because I thought I'd have to learn about the book trade and stock only valuable titles." He shook his head. "It requires a lot of knowledge and capital to do that."

"Well, that was silly." She moved close to face him and ran that index finger down his chest a little bit. With a little shake of her head, her long, silky hair rippled down over her shoulders and down her back. "I have so much to teach you."

His eyes ate her up. "Like what?"

She held his gaze for a moment, then stepped away

to pace the area in front of the counter. "Like the latest trends in decorating. People want other people to think they're rich. Rich people have libraries. So, regular people – copycats – line their dens with bookshelves and load them with nicely bound books by the yard. The interior designer color coordinates the bindings and it gives just the right impression. It can be lucrative if it's done right and I know how to do it right."

"It's really happening, isn't it?" A smile spread across his face, excitement lit up his eyes. "Imagine, Antique Row right here on Talbot Street in St. Michaels."

"It's not going to happen by itself, Grant. I've put my reputation on the line. Don't let it all go to waste. You have to do your part. Talk to the store owners and, to use your little railroad idea, get them all on board. This train is leaving the station come spring and the beginning of the tourist season. And be sure to replenish the yard of books you sold. An empty shelf—" She turned and pointed to the books and saw me instead. "Oh, it's you." There was no honey in her words.

"Oh, hi! Just doing a little shopping."

Her eyes narrowed and she jingled her car keys. "I have to go." In a flurry, she was out the door.

Grant turned around and jumped a little, surprised to see me. "Oh! I didn't see you come in." *You should put bells on your door,* I thought. "Good morning," he said in a cheery voice. "How may I help you?"

"Oh, just looking for a gift." I realized with a start that I should do some real gift shopping soon. *What in the world can I get for Lorraine, the lady who has everything? Not now, I won't think about that now.*

As if he read my thoughts, he took a step toward me and wet his lips, "If you tell me about the person, I could make some suggestions." The man was trying a little too hard to make a sale.

"Oh, that's very nice." I said quickly. "No, thank you, I'd just like to look around." I wandered around the shop trying to put together what I'd overheard at the party, about a quaint village with antiques for the upscale shopper to replace the t-shirts and overpriced stuff for tourists and their conversation about antique trains and books. They were planning a radical change for St. Michaels. I didn't see any evidence of how and when they were going to take over our little world, as we knew it. I needed a more direct approach. I went over to the counter where he was working on the computer. "I think I saw you at the party last night at Fair Winds."

He looked at me out of the corner of his eye without moving his head. "I was there along with a lot of other people."

"Yes, it was a very large party. There was a man who left early looking upset. Might have been a member of the clergy – black suit, white collar. Any idea what that was all about?"

"Tall, skinny as a toothpick?" I nodded. "That's the Pastor. He always looks upset. If there really was something wrong, I say he deserves all the trouble coming to him."

I raised my eyebrows in surprise. "That's…"

He waved away my concern. "Don't mind me. He and I have a history, that's all. Now, did you find a gift for your friend?"

I blurted out a line from the message left in place of the chalice. "Thanks to Ladyman, we are like the Hatfields." My eyes were riveted on his face ready to catch even the smallest twitch of recognition.

Mr. Mathias looked at me as if I'd lost my mind. "I'm sorry, what did you say?"

There was no telltale sign in the man's eyes or in his expression. I was headed down the wrong path here. "Oh my, look at the time. I'm going on the Tour of Homes and they're about to start without me. Happy Holidays!" I escaped from his shop.

And ran straight into the next event on the festival schedule. Not content to have one Christmas parade with the boats in the harbor, St. Michaels did it all over again right down the main street. People were lining up along the curb complete with folding chairs, thermoses of hot drinks and cameras. Both children and adults wore holiday headgear like flashing stars, reindeer antlers and red Santa hats. It was all very festive and very crowded. I tried to work my way along the sidewalk, but spectators were claiming their spots and they didn't want to budge.

"Oh, hello dear." It was Harriet bundled up in a puffy down coat and red earmuffs. Her hand, wearing a red mitten, clamped on my arm like a vice. "Look who's here, Ben. It's Abby from Fair Winds," she said to her dutiful but silent husband huddling up behind her. "Isn't it nice that you've come for the parade. How was the boat parade with Ryan last night?"

Did I really see her eyebrows wiggle with intense interest? Time to get away before she asked me for a moment-by-moment report. "Actually, I'm on my way to the Tour of Homes..." I pulled my arm away gently. "And I'm going to be late."

Harriet was slow to release my arm. "Be sure to visit the house with the violinist. That's our neighbor." I saw an opening in the crowd and moved toward it. She raised her voice so I'd hear her as I left. "Be sure to tell her we said hello."

Thanks to Harriet and the spectators, I was in danger of missing the first house on the tour. Finally, I worked my way up to a skinny alley between two buildings not far from Grant's store and hoped it didn't lead to a dead end. In no time, I was a block off the parade route. All I had to do was navigate between parked cars to get to the park where Simon and I played during our first visit to St. Michaels. I had the place to myself... except for the two people standing beside a red Mercedes sports car. A couple standing close, then closer still. He leaned in to kiss her, but she put her hands on his chest and gently pushed him away. Quickly, she looked around, searching for any unwanted eyes. She raised her hand and caressed his cheek, then turned and got into her car.

Rennie and Grant. Snatching another private moment together.

But not so private. I saw them... and so did Millie, that poor girl crying in the corner at the Cove. From the look on her face before she melted into the shadows, she had snagged her heart on Grant. *Good luck with that, dear Millie,* I thought. *He's got his eye on a bigger prize.* I wondered what the elusive Mr. Frampton would think of the game his wife was playing behind his back.

I scurried along so Rennie wouldn't see me as she

drove away. There was a lot to think about as I turned down the street to the first house on my Tour of Homes.

When I walked into the brick home, I found myself part of a small group of women with one man nudged into a corner, probably dragged along by his wife. A prim lady dressed in an emerald green suit with a name tag identifying her as a Hostess stood at the front of our little group. I tried to move to past her on my quest for the chalice.

"One moment, dear. We're about to begin." She turned to the group tucked into the small entry, choosing to ignore my groan that escaped when I realized that I had to stay with the group if I wanted to see the house. "Good morning, everyone, and welcome to the Cannonball House. William Merchant, a prosperous shipbuilder, built this house, which is on the National Historic Register, around 1807. As you move through the house, notice the fine pine floorboards that run the full length of the house, front to back, most unusual for homes of that time." She gestured up the steep stairway. "The long banister to the second floor was carved from one solid piece of wood. In 1813, moments after Mr. Merchant's wife came down the stairs with their baby in her arms, a cannonball fired from a British ship in the Miles River penetrated the roof and rolled down the heavy wood staircase leaving burn marks on the steps. Shaken but not hurt, they retired to a safer place. This happened during the War of 1812. Now, if you'll follow me."

The hostess led us through the living room, then the dining room. Period antiques were everywhere, including an 18th century Chippendale chair and a Sheraton desk with sliding doors. But there was no silver in sight. I slipped out the door and moved to the next house on my map, far ahead of my tour group.

Along the way, I saw an unkempt-looking young woman pushing an old stroller toward me. Carly, Sonny's girlfriend who'd caused a commotion at the Cove.

I slowed down as she approached me. "Hi. Aren't you Sonny's girlfriend?"

"What of it and who's asking?" she snarled, her dirty hair snapping in her face. Her fake leather coat was too light for the cold and the fabric strained at the seams.

"I was in the Cove when you were looking for him. Did you find him yet?"

Her eyes narrowed as she examined me. "You know anything about where he is?"

"Me? No, but if you find him, you might tell him the people at the church need his help this weekend with all the festival events."

"Yeah, well, I need him a whole lot more than they do." Without another word, she pushed past me. I didn't get a glimpse of the baby. At least she'd wrapped up the little one against the cold. Maybe she wasn't so bad. Maybe she'd gotten into trouble with the wrong kind of guy – someone who would steal altar silver from a church.

A group of carolers in period costumes came around the corner singing with gusto. The women wore long dresses and shawls. The men sported high hats and carried lanterns. The bells chimed the hour and I hurried along to the next house on the schedule.

The hostess at the cozy 125-year-old house was not a dictator like the first one. I was free to wander from room to room on my own. In the background, I heard the running commentary about the owner's love of music and antiques. Old oil paintings hung on the dining room walls.

"The paintings were done by the owner's grandmother," explained the hostess.

It's nice, I thought. *Someone decorates with old things that mean something instead of the best their money can buy. That thought would fly in the face of Grant and Rennie's grandiose plans for St. Michaels.*

"The Santa Claus quilt," continued the hostess, "is a family treasure displayed proudly every Christmas, along with a collection of English caroler figurines placed throughout the house."

I stopped in mid-step. *English* carolers. *English* chalice. Putting the chalice with the carolers seemed like a logical place to hide the treasure in plain sight. I backtracked through each room looking closely for the shine of silver.

Nothing. The momentary surge of excitement deepened my feeling of disappointment as I walked through the cozy country kitchen and absent-mindedly picked up a cookie. Outside, I took a moment to collect my thoughts and appreciate the well-tended garden. It was neat, organized and pleasing to the eye. Why wasn't life like that? I found it hard to believe that the thief who had caused such havoc and misery would put the chalice in plain sight for me to find. If I saw him, I'd—

"Oh, my dear, you've broken your cookie," exclaimed a hostess in a red and green apron. "Stay right there. I'll get you another one."

I looked at the cookie fragments in my hand and the pile of crumbs at my feet. I understood why Kat went to the courthouse square. She'd told me herself in the library at Fair Winds when she told me the value of the chalice. She said if she had a windfall of $15,000 to $20,000, she'd move back to her beloved mountains. When she overheard my argument with the pastor about where to go, her desire to move must have tempted her to cross the line and violate the law. To lose her life was too high a price to pay for that moment of temptation.

"Here you are, dear. I brought you two." The hostess handed me the cookies on a brightly colored napkin.

If only we could rectify Kat's situation so easily, I thought as I walked away fighting back the tears.

CHAPTER TWELVE

When a silver piece is selected, inspect it thoroughly. Even a tiny speck of tarnish can ruin the effect of a piece. No matter the time or place or intended use, a silver piece should gleam. Nothing will match its effect.

—"The Butler's Guide to Fine Silver" Mr. Hollister, 1898

As I walked down the street, I noticed that every front window of every historic house had a lighted electric candle. Somehow, those little lights made me feel comfortable and safe. Wasn't there an old saying about leaving a light in the window so someone could find her way home? The story or poem escaped me, but I remembered that Gran always left a lamp on in the living room window if she went to bed before I got home. Oh dear, emotions were coming in waves. I took a deep breath of winter air and moved along to the next house on the tour.

"Welcome to the Harrison House," another volunteer hostess chirped. As I wandered through the small house, it was obvious that the owner was not afraid to use rich colors. The warm cranberry walls accented with white woodwork were striking. It probably made an impression on me after living in white-walled rentals for several years. I scanned the built-in shelves painted bright white that covered one wall. There was no room for a silver chalice because there were dog figurines everywhere. Actually, they were pairs of dogs sitting opposite each other with their heads turned toward me so I got the full view of their faces. They weren't exactly cute, not like Simon, but there were a lot of them.

"Ah, you noticed the Staffordshire dogs, I see," said the hostess.

"The owner must have collected those dog figurines for a long time."

She laughed. "Oh no, they're on loan from a local antique shop. If you were interested in purchasing any of them, I'm sure it could be arranged."

"Which antique shop would that be?"

"I'm sure I don't know, but I could find out, if you'd like to come back tomorrow."

"I might do that, thank you." A violinist – Harriet's neighbor, I guessed – played a Christmas piece in the breakfast room off the kitchen, but I was in no mood to listen to music by Johann Sebastian Bach.

Outside, I tightened the scarf around my neck against the wind and headed up to the main street as the sounds of a brass band and fire truck sirens grew louder and louder. The street parade was well under way. Closely packed in the procession were floats, a brass band led by baton twirlers, an equestrian team followed by pooper scoopers, clowns that delighted the kids but always scared me and fire trucks from all the nearby jurisdictions.

"Hope there isn't a real fire somewhere," I murmured to the person who came up beside me.

"Don't worry, they have it covered." I'd recognize that deep voice anywhere.

"Hello, Chief. I'm glad you have everything under control," I said with a smile.

His chest rose and fell as he took a deep breath and sighed. "I don't know about that." He touched my arm and drew me to the back of the crowd lining the curb. "Have you found anything?"

"Not really, but Grant, the business association guy, strikes me as a sleazy character and I'm getting a bad feeling about that antique dealer who goes by the name of Jeff. Do you know him?"

"Not well. He's a little slippery when it comes to talking about his past. Why?"

I shrugged and looked at a passing float with a beauty queen freezing in a prom dress, but smiling and waving at the crowd. "I don't know. Call it a gut feeling."

"Ah, now you're a big time detective with gut feelings." He laughed and it was infectious.

"I still have another couple of stops to make. We'll see." I checked the tour map and realized that my next stop was in the neighborhood on the other side of the street.

He adjusted the belt holding his gun. "Everyone else has come up empty as well. I'm starting to get worried."

"Maybe there's something you can do?"

"What?"

"Get me across this street so I can get to the next house."

"Come on." He grabbed my arm and guided me through the crowd, past a mounted equestrian team and over to the other side.

My destination was at the end of the street, The Mary Sylvester House. The hostess was wearing a hand-knitted sweater covered with every Christmas symbol imaginable. She waved me in as she continued her spiel.

"In 1872, Mary Sylvester bought the lot for $25 and the following year, she and her husband built a small house for $275. The owners have maintained the rustic simplicity of its exposed beams above your heads. Avid cooks, they've extended their kitchen to accommodate a large professional stove, hundreds of utensils and dishes plus their working collection of more than 500 cookbooks. Along with the dining room, these two rooms occupy almost all of the first floor of the original house so it is a warm, welcoming place for entertaining."

Entertaining. At Fair Winds, entertaining means silver. Maybe there was silver here, too.

I found the dining room and slowly perused the built-in shelves that covered one whole wall. They were loaded with things, but nothing as prominent as the chalice. As I walked out the door, I paused to hear the hostess say, "The German prayer on the main gate to the garden reads 'Protect this house from weather and wind and don't let boring people in.'"

It was obvious the owners were far from boring and I hoped maybe someday I'd have a chance to meet them.

The next stop was the Alpine Village. Inside the

private home, the rich mahogany of a grand piano dominated the living room. The ever-present hostess graciously moved me into the next room, transformed into a miniature wonderland of castles, homes, shops and churches, nestled on a mountainside that rose more than five feet high. A model train made its way around the buildings and over a frozen river where tiny residents skated.

The train reminded me of Grant's idea for a toy shop that Rennie didn't think belonged in their grandiose plans for St. Michaels. I wondered if the residents would allow such a change in their little town? *Not my decision, but it did seem a shame to alter the character of the main street so much.*

"Lovely, isn't it?" The hostess stood next to me. "Each of the Gothic cathedrals has stained glass windows. It was amazing that each miniature building was fashioned by the owner out of paper and cardboard, needles and beads. And every one is a replica of a building found in Central Europe," she explained. Fascinated by the scene, I almost forgot to look for the chalice, but soon realized that it would have towered over the enchanting village. Enchanted, though disappointed, I thanked the volunteer hostess and moved on.

Two more houses on the tour were filled with antique quilts, decorated mantels, clocks and shelves of carved decoys. No silver. No chalice. What a waste of time.

Lorraine and I were to meet in front of the traditional nativity display in the middle of the town. The sidewalks were crowded with revelers, chatting and not looking where they were going. Moving along with the crowd, I spotted two little girls up ahead walking with their mother. Knitted caps, pulled tight on their heads, were trimmed tinsel haloes. They held their white angel robes high off the ground, revealing jeans and warm socks underneath. Mom must be their guardian angel. They veered off toward some pageant or event somewhere and I saw Lorraine up ahead.

"Did you find anything?" she asked.

I shook my head. "You?"

"No. But I haven't checked the Nativity scene yet. Come with me."

The wooden figures were almost life-size and very traditional. Their carved faces were tranquil. We scanned the arrangement of the three Wise Men hoping to find a special gift, but everything was made of wood.

"Maybe in front of the Manger?" There was nothing nestled in the straw.

"Now what?" I asked.

"I don't know." She tightened the scarf around her neck and nestled into the warmth of her coat. "I have to tell you that it's a good thing this festival happens only once a year. I'm worn out."

I hadn't thought about it before, but I too must be running on adrenaline. *When this is over, I'm going to sleep for a week.*

"It's silly for us to try and take both cars through this mess. My car is parked at the First Pres. The pastor was kind enough to offer me a special parking space. I'd rather sit in a warm car inching our way through town than fight through the shoppers to get to yours."

I agreed and we headed toward the church. As we moved along, I realized Jeff's antique shop was only a few steps out of our way. What a curious man. Shouldn't an antique dealer be quiet, refined, and maybe even a little pretentious? He shouldn't be a pool-playing, beer-drinking hustler. *Hustler,* I thought. *Interesting that the word hustler came to mind.*

"Do you mind if I make a stop first?" I asked.

Knowing not to ask questions during holiday gift-giving time, Lorraine agreed, "But Abby, you really don't have to buy anything for me."

I squeezed her arm buried in the thick warmth of her coat. "I know. I'll see you at the car."

"Come into the Fellowship hall. I think they're having a little reception right about now and a glass of eggnog sounds delicious, though I don't think it will have a secret ingredient, if you know what I mean." She winked.

"Probably not. Enjoy. I won't be long." In a moment, she was lost in the crowd.

There was a break in the traffic so I dashed across the street. *Wouldn't it be funny if the chalice was sitting on one of Jeff's dusty shelves with a handwritten price tag taped to its base?*

The Belle Antiques shop sign with its flaking paint hung above my head. Shouldn't a good antique store err on the side of sophistication? *Drop those preconceived notions right now. If I judge things as I think they should be, I'll miss something.* I looked at the sign again. Flaking paint could mean it was old, maybe an antique. A sign like that might be better than one with gold-leaf lettering.

People might think it was too expensive and move on. I felt like my perspective was more balanced and I went inside.

There was the usual bell on the door, but this one was different. It didn't clatter like the ones at the drugstore. It tinkled, which was in keeping with the holiday and the atmosphere of a store selling valued old things that might be expensive or might not be. A scented candle of apples and cinnamon added to the festive feeling.

"I'll be with you in a minute." The voice I remembered from the Cove yelled out from the back of the shop. "Feel free to look around."

So I did. A quick scan confirmed that the communion chalice was not on public display. It could be in the back room, but I certainly wasn't going back there to investigate. There was a lot to look at in the main part of the store and the selection of antiques might tell me something more about the proprietor. The merchandise was a hodge-podge. A table lamp had a Tiffany-style shade. Could it be the real thing? Delicate china cups and saucers sat on lace doilies. The man might be gruff but he knew how to display fine things. A couple of hanging crystal chandeliers, though not as large or elegant as Lorraine's, added extra light and atmosphere to the store. An old manual typewriter was on a student desk. I pushed down on a key and found it took a lot of effort to make the letter strike the paper. I couldn't imagine how someone could write a report, let alone a book on it. If I had to use it, the book wouldn't get done.

A thick brown fur rug made me want to slip off a shoe, take off my sock and bury my toes in it. Against the wall stood a large walnut secretary with dozens of cubbyholes that were all too small to hold a chalice. I opened the door of a cabinet that was large enough to hold the chalice. The sound of footsteps made me flick it shut and jump away.

Jeff's attention was focused on wiping his hands as he walked in. "Sorry about that. Had to finish up…" He looked up. "Oh, it's you, the silver girl from the Cove."

"Yes, it's me." My voice sounded like a squeaky mouse. Being alone with him made me nervous for some reason. I tried to calm down so he wouldn't suspect anything. I took a breath and tried to sound normal. "You did invite me to come by your shop. I was in the area so here I am."

"Here you are." He stood and looked at me, just looked at me and, for some reason, it made me very nervous.

I glanced around. "Nice shop you have." The words tumbled out and I hoped he would stop looking. And he did.

"Thank you. It isn't much by New York standards, but it's home.

"May I ask, where did you get the name for the shop? Belle Antiques is very clever."

"You're being polite and I appreciate it. The name is cheesy, but, for my clientele, they think it's chic. Chic, in this business, means *must have* to the customer and more money to me, the seller." He took a step closer and lowered his voice. "I'll let you in on a little secret. I named the shop after a horse."

"A horse you had as a kid?" I was confused.

"A horse I laid a bet on that won me a packet of money so I could open the shop. Figured the nag deserved some recognition."

"Belle. That's a good name for a racehorse, I guess." *I never understood why someone would throw money away at the race track in hopes of making a killing. For me, the odds were against me winning anything worth the risk.*

"Except it was only part of the horse's name. *Southern Belle* was too cutesy and too rebel sounding. *Belle Antiques* works for me, but the hordes of customers it was supposed to attract have failed to show up." He peered at me. "You didn't come here to listen to me prattle on about the origins of my shop's name. I bet you'd like to see my silver and you don't want to come right out and ask."

"You're right, I came to see your pieces of silver," I said quickly.

He cringed. "Ouch, you make me sound like Judas."

"No, no, nothing like that." My words tumbled all over themselves. How could I scope out his shop if he suspected me suspecting him?

He looked at me as if he was appraising a piece of furniture then relaxed. "All right then. This way, Silver Girl." He led me toward the back of the store to a tall glass cabinet that stood floor to ceiling. On each of the glass shelves was a gleaming array of silver pieces, everything from a few dinner forks in random patterns to an elegant teapot. I pointed to an unusual serving piece designed for a specific purpose. "I see you have a hooded asparagus server. It's one of my favorite oddities among silver serving pieces."

"Why? It's really functional. The flat area was designed to slide under some asparagus then tilt the end up so the spears rolled in the hooded part where they would be secure. To serve, tip it forward and the spears rolled gracefully onto the dinner plate."

"I know it gets the job done really well, but it still looks strange."

"Unusual," he corrected me. "In the antique business, we say 'unusual' and that can add a premium to the price."

"I see."

"But that isn't the only asparagus server." He unlocked the cabinet and pointed to a silver serving fork that looked like it was on steroids. "I have an asparagus fork." The four tines were wide and flared out with a small hood down at the handle. He lifted out a silver piece that looked like sugar tongs and handed it to me. "Bet you don't know what this is."

"The curved part at the ends tells me it's not for sugar cubes. It looks like it could pick up one cigarette, but I've never heard of a cigarette server."

He chuckled. "That's taking a creative approach, but there is no cigarette server." He took it in his hand to demonstrate. "It's an individual asparagus spear server if you want to pick up one at a time." He held it up to his mouth. "Or you could use it to nibble on one spear in a very dainty way." His demonstration made me laugh.

He returned the piece to its place and locked the cabinet, "You're really knowledgeable about the pieces you have," I said.

"It comes from experience. I've been in this business for a long time, too long. It's been a good ride, even the grueling auction work with a major house in New York, but it's getting too hard. I'm ready for something big to come my way so I can do what I want, go where I want." He looked at me with concern. "Are you okay?"

I could only nod. A chill ran over my skin as I heard his words, *I'm ready for something big to come my way.* They were almost the same words Kat had said to me in the library on the night she died. Did the chalice come his way so he could have a chance to move on with his life? Were the puzzles his way of tweaking the noses of the Pastor and his congregation? I wouldn't put it past Mr. Conrad Jeffries and his skewed sense of humor to play a joke like that and laugh all the way back to New York.

"Hey, are you sure you're okay? You're shivering."

I stretched my shoulders up to my ears and dropped them. Feeling more in control, I said, "Sorry, I may be coming down with a cold." The bell on the front door tinkled. "You have a customer. I'd better let you get back to work. Thanks for showing me around."

"My pleasure. Come back anytime. Hey, maybe you'll buy my shop."

I doubt that will happen, but I would like to look through your stock, I thought.

I sprinted through the crowds to the church and made my way to the Parish Hall. As I crossed the parking lot, I saw Miss Cunningham, the pastor's secretary from the church, heading in the same direction. Her hand-knitted watch cap was pulled down over her ears, leaving a few wisps of her dishwater blonde hair showing. I hurried to catch up.

"Hello! What a crazy day it is in town," I said.

She smiled and agreed while she was examining me with those big eyes that made me feel a little like a bug.

She offered to show me to the room at the far end of the hallway where I'd find the eggnog bowl and Lorraine. As she opened the door, we heard a blood-chilling scream. She took off running. Who knew that Miss Cunningham could take off like a shot? I tried my best to keep up as she rushed into a nearby classroom.

An array of women sat around a lighted Christmas tree in the corner with horrified looks on their faces. All except for one. Rennie Frampton was standing in the middle of the semi-circle of women, retching.

Miss Cunningham went up to the hysterical woman, put her hand on her arm and asked, "It's all right, dear, I'm here. What is the problem?"

That was the cue for everyone to jump up and start talking.

With her arm firmly placed around Rennie, Miss Cunningham raised her other hand high in the air. "Ladies, PLEASE!" Her declaration was enough to shock them into silence for a moment. "Everyone, sit down. NOW."

As they scurried back to their seats, she turned back to the woman, who was only hiccuping but still a little green.

"That's better. Now, tell me what's wrong. Are you sick?" With a blank stare, Rennie slowly shook her head no. "That's good. Tell me what upset you so much."

Rennie started to pull away, rapidly shaking her head, but Miss Cunningham held on to her. "That's fine. Can you show me?"

Rennie slowly raised her left arm and pointed her finger at a shoebox turned upside down close to the other boxes under the tree.

"Is it something in the box, dear?" Rennie nodded once and tears threatened to flow from her brimming eyes. "Now, now, I told you I'll handle it and I will." She turned to an older woman with kind eyes. "Mrs. Walters, would you take Mrs. Frampton to the ladies room so she can freshen up, please?" The older woman rose, put an arm around Rennie's waist and walked her out of the room.

When Rennie was gone, the spell was broken. The other women, about twelve of them, started talking at once and getting up out of their chairs until Miss Cunningham's voice cut through the noise.

"Everyone sit down and stay down." Every woman obeyed and there were many looks of surprise. "Thank you. If I can have quiet for a moment while I see…" She walked over to the box and scrutinized it. I took two steps toward her, but her arm shot out and I stopped in mid-step.

She nudged the upside down box with the toe of her shoe. One woman let out a squeal that made us all jump. Miss Cunningham gave her a disapproving look and the woman silently lowered her eyes to her lap.

With a little nod of approval, our new fearless leader turned and knelt down. Very slowly, she reached out with both hands and picked up the box. When its contents tumbled out, everyone shrieked.

A dead animal – maybe a squirrel run over by a car – was scrunched inside a baggie that was sitting in a little pool of blood.

Without a second thought, I pulled out my phone and called the Chief. Under normal circumstances, I might be overreacting, but there was nothing normal about this particular time at this particular church.

When the Chief arrived, he made the mistake of asking, *What's going on?* Everyone felt it was her job to give him the details. Pastor Francis, after seeing the Chief's car pull into the parking lot, came into the room and walked up to Miss Cunningham.

"What's going on here?" he asked as if it was her fault. In response, she pointed at the box on the plastic bag and its gruesome contents on the floor.

He jumped away and started shouting. "That's disgusting. Who brought that in here? He looked around the circle of ladies expecting one to step forward to take responsibility and punishment but nothing happened. "Tell me this instant, what happened?"

All the church ladies started at once, including Harriet Snow, who had the Pastor by the arm.

"Really, sir, I want you to know that I never planned for something like this to happen. To think that someone would ruin a simple gift exchange between the ladies of our church – well, it's almost too much to bear." She released her hold on him and staggered to a chair.

The Pastor was walking in circles, trying to follow the stories being shouted at him until he was dizzy. The

Chief walked into the middle of the confusion, planted his feet, raised his hands high above his head and roared, "Quiet!"

Startled by the order, everyone fell silent.

I stood off to the side with Lorraine and watched while the Chief calmed the women and got the details he needed. I watched Miss Cunningham, who had shrunk away to stand along the wall, out of the way. Moments ago, she became a leader when everyone else was frozen in shock. As soon as men had entered the room, she was the easily intimidated secretary again. The change was amazing and I filed it away.

Wouldn't it be funny if the spineless person was the thief?

Once the Chief pieced together all the facts and observations, the story of what happened was quite simple: Harriet Snow had organized a gift exchange among members of the Woman's Club of the church so they could get to know one another better, especially the newcomers. I had to admit, it sounded like a good idea: each person would draw a name and two weeks later put a gift for that person under the tree. Everyone was to put things that told about the recipient – a special interest magazine, some needles, pieces of fabric for a quilter, for instance – in a wrapped shoebox. As each woman went through her gift, she was encouraged to talk about her interests, hobbies and background.

Rennie's gift was road kill, though she was sure it was a rat. The Chief confirmed it was only part of an unfortunate animal run over by a car and shoveled up off the road and put into a plastic bag. It didn't matter really. The message was clear: You are dead meat here. Go away!

Sweet and unassuming Mrs. Allenson, who had drawn Rennie's name, was appalled by the contents of her gift shoebox. She professed her innocence to anyone who would listen. The Chief discounted her as a suspect almost immediately. He couldn't imagine such a fastidious older woman handling, let alone wrapping up body parts and giving the package to someone as a present. He was proven correct when an officer found a *New York* Magazine, a Frank Sinatra recording and a big red apple in the trash. Mrs. Allenson explained that Rennie wouldn't take the time to talk to her so she put together things about New York City.

"What else could I do?" she whined.

Later, the Chief confided in me. "Whoever did this has a devious, calculating mind."

"Do you think it was the thief?" The thought sent chills up my back. "Do you think he's zeroing in on a new victim?"

The Chief took a little too long to say, "I don't think so."

CHAPTER THIRTEEN

Afternoon tea is an elegant tradition to provide sustenance during the long afternoon interval between luncheon and dinner. Present the tea using an elegant silver service which includes a teapot, waste bowl for used leaves, sugar bowl and cream pitcher on a silver tray. This service helps create the right atmosphere to honor an invited guest, acknowledge a special event or share the warmth of camaraderie.

—"The Butler's Guide to Fine Silver" Mr. Hollister, 1898

The night air was cold and I was grateful for the thick scarf wrapped tightly around my neck as we walked several blocks to the church. It seemed like everyone around had driven into town for the Choir Concert. Lorraine warned me it was a popular event for residents of the Shore and many visitors said it was the perfect way to start the holiday season. She said the church would be packed so we both had our phones in case we were separated. We joined the throngs lining up to enter the church.

Standing near the main doors hung with large pine wreaths was someone with a very familiar face. Mr. Luther, a frail old man with smooth ebony skin, stood leaning heavily on his cane. Several months ago, when I came to see Lorraine in St. Michaels, I met Mr. Luther and learned of his family's long history with Fair Winds and Lorraine's family. He'd offered some sage advice then that proved very important. Perhaps he would surprise me again with some insight into what was happening at the church. "Good evening, Mr. Luther."

"Well, well. It's nice to see you again, Miss Abby." He was bent over as if carrying the weight of the many years he'd lived, but his smile hadn't changed. It was wide and honest and brilliant even in the soft light. "Yes, you are a lovely sight for these old eyes." As I moved, he saw me catching a whiff of his sweet, spicy aftershave. "I splash on a little Bay Rum for special occasions. Hope it isn't too strong."

"No, not at all. It reminds me of my dad when I was a little girl. He always said it was the only brand for a sailor."

"That's because a sailor made the first concoction," he said. "You know, those men would spend months on board their little ships without having a real bath. You can imagine the smell so one of them soaked some bay leaves in his grog – rum – and then rubbed it on his skin. That's how you get the spice of the bay leaf and the sweet scent of rum."

"What a great bit of history. Wonder if my dad knows?"

"You can tell him when you visit for the holidays."

"I won't be flying out to California this year," I said quietly. "Besides, he has two other daughters now."

Mr. Luther held up his index finger gnarled with

arthritis. "A man never forgets his first daughter – the one who stole his heart forever. You remember that."

"Yes, well, I can tell him the story when we talk. I'll be spending the holidays here keeping Miss Lorraine company and working on her silver collection."

"I know those pieces well." He waggled that finger at me again. "Remember, I spent many hours as a boy and young man polishing all those pieces. Why, some days it was like the done pieces were jumping back into the unpolished pile." We laughed together then his face tightened into a serious expression. "And you have a sad situation to put to rights."

"Lorraine says it's in the Chief's hands now, but I've been looking all day for some clue…"

He held up his hand. "Don't look with your eyes, Miss Abby. Look with your heart and you'll find people who think they know what's best for everybody else and they'll lie and cheat to make the world the way they want it. They stomp on the Golden Rule – Do unto others as you would have them do unto you. It's in both the New and the Old Testaments of the Bible, you know. Keep it in mind as you search for your answers."

He leaned on his cane and winced. "Now, help this old man to a seat if you would, please."

People were kind to open a path for us and we made our way inside. At once, the aromas of the season swirled around us. Fragrant evergreens, cinnamon-scented pine cones and sweet-smelling flowers were everywhere. Garlands adorned the tall Gothic windows. A manager scene complete with the Magi, shepherds and an angel was set up near the entrance so people could appreciate the delicate wood carving of the key figures and get into the spirit of Christmas right away. Kat would have enjoyed seeing the manger set so close to the front door. She'd said it was the key to setting the mood for the season. That's why she had created an island in the center of the foyer under the massive crystal chandelier at Fair Winds so everyone would see the symbol of Christmas as they walked into the party. When I looked toward the front of the church, my breath caught. The stately pine tree that stood to the side of the altar was decorated now. It was laden with hundreds of lights, many colored balls – both silk and shiny and ribbons and bows. High above, at the very top was a brilliantly lighted star. The altar itself was awash in holly heavy with bright red berries, graceful pine boughs and snowy white Christmas lilies. They reminded me that Kat wanted lilies for decorations at Fair Winds and had to drive to Annapolis to get them. The local florists must have sold their whole stock to the church. Kat, so committed to making things the best they could be. She was so disappointed in the love and trust she'd placed in her husband that she must have committed herself not to disappoint her clients.

As I maneuvered Mr. Luther through the crowd, we passed close to Jeff and Grant, who were so deep in conversation that they didn't notice I overheard snatches of what they were saying.

"Delivery." "New York." "Antiques." "Orders."

Orders? Was Rennie taking orders for specific types of antiques, scouring the Shore for those items and shipping them up to New York?

The momentum of the people carried us along down the aisle. When Mr. Luther was settled safely in a seat at the end of a pew, I turned around to see that Jeff had left, but Rennie was standing close to Grant, facing in opposite directions as if the crowd had pushed them together. She seemed very calm after the horrible fright of unwrapping a Christmas present containing a dead animal. I could see only Grant's face and it was clear he was listening to something she was saying. After her rude behavior in the dining room and their little tryst during the party at Fair Winds, it wasn't a big leap to guess they were up to something. I tried to get close to them, but I was moving against the flow of the incoming crowd. Just as Rennie walked away, a small break in the throng let me see her run her index finger over the back of Grant's hand in an intimate way. No question that they were up to no good, at least no good for Mr. Frampton.

There was nothing else to do but look around and take in the festive atmosphere. Yards and yards of garland hung across the front of the balcony and a Star of Bethlehem made of white roses hung in the center. I bet Dawkins would be glad he didn't have to hang all that greenery from the top of a very tall ladder. My smile sagged as I remembered Kat and her heartfelt wish to go home to her beloved mountains to live. There would be no holiday delight for her son, now an orphan.

"Abby! Over here." It was the soft, rich voice of Edward.

I worked my way over to him and said, "You're looking better tonight and, if I may say, rather debonair."

150

His dark gray suit and pearl gray shirt complimented his silver hair. "The sprig of holly in your lapel adds just the right touch."

"Oh, that's Miss Cunningham. She thought the church leaders, both present and past, should have something special." I smiled. "Well, what do you think?" He was almost giving off sparks of excitement. "What do you think of our little church all dressed up for the Christmas celebration?"

We talked about the decorations and the architecture that made the sanctuary feel so warm and inviting. "It's too bad there's one special thing missing." I gave Edward a meaningful look and he knew I was talking about the chalice. "I hope it's all right."

He smiled. "Remember what I always told Laura when she worried. I'll say the same thing to you. I'm sure it will be all right. The Lord is keeping it safe, I'm sure."

The crowd jostled us and the Chief bumped up against me.

"Did I hear you say it will be all right? Are we talking about what I think we're talking about?" he asked.

"Yes," I said with confidence. "It's a long story, but Edward is always right."

A lady – a very short, very old lady – pushed her way between us and laid a gloved hand on the Chief's arm. "Is that you?" From her shrunken position, she strained her neck to look up into his face. "Of course, it is," she said with renewed confidence. She held her small needlepoint purse in her two hands and announced, "I need to speak to you," she said decisively. "I need to speak to you about my dogs." Her paper-thin voice was difficult to hear in the commotion going on around us.

"Dogs? Well, I think that might fall under the purview of the county animal control—"

"Don't be impertinent." She sniffed. "I mean my Staffordshire dogs."

He gave me an *I'm lost* look, so I jumped in. "Do you mean those porcelain figurines of dogs that come in pairs?" She gave me one emphatic nod. I remembered seeing some on a shelf in one of the houses on the tour.

"And therein lies the problem." She waited.

The Chief looked lost again. He was very good at chasing down the bad guys, but seemed to be undone by this very wrinkled lady.

"And what would that be?" I asked.

Her mouth screwed up as if she tasted vinegar. "Someone told me that my dogs were the newer variety, not antiques. I explained that my grandmother had collected them as a girl then left them to me. But she wouldn't listen. Told me my grandmother had lied to me." She pressed her lips together to maintain her ladylike manner, but, unable to contain her anger, she shook her purse hard. "Then the woman made what seemed to be a generous financial offer for my dogs."

She lamented, "It's so expensive to live nowadays with medications going up all the time. Some extra money is always welcome. I certainly didn't expect to live this long."

The Chief straightened up and frowned. "Did she pay you?" he asked. He was very close with his mother and grandmother and was always on the lookout for people trying to take advantage of them. The scams targeted at senior citizens were everywhere, from unneeded house repairs to insurance fraud. Maybe this was a new one... and on his turf.

"Yes, she paid me, but not what they're worth. After I took the money, I talked with one of my great-grandsons who is so good on the internet." She paused.

I wasn't sure if she'd lost her train of thought or was out of breath. "Would you like us to find you a chair?"

She patted my arm. "No, dear. I'm fine. It's just so disturbing." She took in a ragged breath and continued. "He did some research and showed she was wrong. Daniel sent me copies of the information in the mail." She turned to me. "I don't have a computer. Never saw a need. But now..."

"What would you say the difference in price is between the antique dogs and the newer ones?" The Chief asked.

"Some of the new Staffordshire dogs that they call vintage sell for as little as $49. The true antique Staffordshire dogs sell in the hundreds – three, four, five hundred – but the better ones that are rare go up as high as almost $800 a pair."

"And you believe that your dogs were the antique ones," said the Chief.

"Yes." The old lady gave him a sharp nod of her head. "Yes, I do."

"Well, that's unfortunate. If you want to try to reclaim the money—"

"I don't want the money!" She declared as raised

her purse and jerked it down hard as if on a tabletop. "No! I want my dogs back."

"How many pairs did you have?" I asked.

"I only had eighty-four left," she said with a sigh.

Eighty-four?! Both the Chief and I stared at her in shock.

"There used to be more, but some broke over the years and I gave each of my granddaughters a pair when they graduated from college. So, there are only eighty-four pairs left."

I did a quick calculation in my head. Figuring an average of $500 per pair. The stranger had cheated her out of more than $42,000. I looked up at the Chief in surprise. His sharp, angry expression told me that he'd come to the same conclusion.

"Mrs.—?" he said.

"Mrs. Bolinsky." She raised her chin a little. "Mrs. Myron Bolinsky."

"Alright ma'am, I'd like to come and visit you on Monday if I may so we can talk about your dogs."

Her smile spread slowly over her parchment skin. "So, you are interested in my dogs after all?"

"Yes, ma'am."

"Good, I thought you would be. Now you can find me a chair." He walked with her so she'd be safe and comfortable and to take down her information.

Antique dealers! Always out for the quick buck. When Gran died and I inherited the house and all the antiques, everyone was willing to buy what I had, right then…cash on the barrel head, ma'am … but getting a fair price was more difficult than I expected. It took me a long time to find a reputable dealer to appraise the pieces that didn't have a deep emotional value and arrange a sale. If I had that much trouble, an elderly woman was an easy target. I was seeing red and it wasn't because of the festive season.

I wonder. An ocean of people swirled around me. I rolled up on my toes looking around for the conspirators I'd seen earlier, Rennie and Grant. *How could I work the mention of Staffordshire dogs into a conversation?*

No time. The Pastor was moving toward the microphone to begin the evening's festivities. I finally spotted Lorraine sitting in the middle of a pew with friends. She signaled for me to join her, but the way was jammed with people. Across the sanctuary, Ryan waved, but it was impossible to move against the current of incoming visitors. I settled for a weak wave in response. People in a pew toward the back scrunched together to make room for me.

Choir members wearing tan and green robes arranged themselves in front of the altar under a dramatic stained glass window that soared to the rafters. They broke into a gospel song and the concert was off to a rousing start. Another choir performed in red robes, while a more traditional group stood solemnly in gold robes. Guitars, drums and, of course, the sounds of a majestic organ accompanied the singers.

While the choir from yet another church moved into position for their performance, people in the audience were shifting in their seats and chatting. A snippet of the conversation going on between two women behind me caught my attention.

"Now, Doris, we don't even know for sure that *it* is really missing." My ears perked up. Were they talking about the chalice? *Wait, do I know that voice? Please, I hope I didn't sit down right in front of the talkative Harriet Snow.* I peeked over my shoulder to see a brunette sitting behind me instead of the gossip who wore her white hair in tight pincurls.

"We'll know if the Pastor doesn't use it for Christmas services, won't we?" I could hear the smirk in her voice.

But how did these women even suspect that the chalice is missing? I thought the Pastor and his staff were going to keep it under wraps. I could have turned around and confronted the gossips, but I was tired – tired of the treasure hunt, tired of people who were absolutely sure about something they knew nothing about.

"Oh, look!" Though Doris lowered her voice, her excitement made her words carry so everyone around us could hear. "That's the girl who's working on Lorraine Andrews silver. I'm sure it's her. I can't mention any names, but the person who told me about her is in a position to know. I bet she's involved."

"But do you think..."

"Of course. She's a natural choice. She's an expert on silver. I'm sure she knows where all the good pieces are in the county."

It was happening as Kat predicted. People believed I was a thief. I felt myself sinking down in my seat so I straightened up. I wasn't going to let these old biddies get to me.

They kept on jabbering. "I wonder if there's any connection to that poor woman's death. She worked at

Fair Winds, you know, right along with her."

That did it. I wasn't going to make a scene and ruin the concert, but I wasn't going to sit quietly while they skewered me. I got up, gave the busybodies my sweetest, most insincere smile and moved out of the row.

I felt a little light-headed. Maybe it was all the bodies in a small space or the events of the past 24 hours. I needed some air. I passed the children's Christmas tree decorated with chains of brightly colored paper and paper stars and went through a side door. Outside, the cold air made my skin tingle and a couple of deep breaths revived me. In the soft moonlight, I saw that I wasn't alone. The ivory-white headstones shimmered in rows by the church. Somehow, the scene wasn't scary or eerie. It was nostalgic, the way they say a cemetery should be. I never found comfort visiting a grave. When Gran and my dad took me to my mother's grave a year after the accident, a lady in a big hat said my mother was sleeping in the ground under the headstone. Her remark set me back several months in my recovery.

But tonight, this scene wasn't about dead bodies. It was about lives lived. Those stones stood in remembrance of the people who'd lived and died here, where they married and had their children and buried some of their babies. Where they loved and dreamed, laughed and cried. I'm sure they hated and cheated as well, but in the spirit of the season, I only wanted to think of good things.

That's why I felt sad. I was missing the good things Gran and Aunt Agnes had given me. At this time of year, sweet smells, lighted candles, Dreidel games and special

Hanukkah songs filled our home. Maybe next week I'd go to Annapolis to look for a menorah.

With that decision made, I felt much better and strolled down the ramp to the brick walkway. It was too cold to stand in one place, but the weather was invigorating if I moved around.

Close to the corner of the church, I realized I wasn't alone.

The gentle tones of a man's voice caused me to pause. "It's a beautiful concert. Everyone is happy. Please tell me you are." As he paused, I listened for a response, but a passing car drowned it out.

He continued. "It's hard now doing the things that meant something to us. So many things don't matter when new people come in." He paused again for a moment. "I feel such pain. I'm not sure I can go on with this, but if we're to be together... The pain in my chest takes my breath away. I can't."

My senses went on alert. I didn't want to intrude on a private moment. But if the man was having chest pains? A heart attack required quick action. Maybe I could help.

I rushed around the corner, but there was no one there. Did I dream it? No, I was sure there were people there. Maybe the man's friend took him inside or to the ambulance parked on the side street, standing by in case there was an emergency at the large concert gathering. I took a step to follow them, then stopped. There was a lot of help around. They didn't need me. I chuckled. I didn't even know who they were. I was involved in enough drama and certainly didn't need any more.

Shivering, I retraced my steps and went back inside to loud applause, warmth and friends.

CHAPTER FOURTEEN

The traditional silver teapot is designed with a squat reservoir to allow the tea leaves plenty of room to steep in the hot water. It is shorter and smaller than the companion coffeepot in the silver service because tea was often quite expensive.

—"The Butler's Guide to Fine Silver" Mr. Hollister, 1898

Back inside the church, people were on their feet, clapping and cheering as each of the choirs took a bow. I thought they were going to blow the roof off the church when the choirs came together and sang the song, "We Wish You a Merry Christmas." One more surge of applause followed the last notes. As if exhausted by all the good cheer, people picked up their coats and started filing toward the door. I was standing off to one side looking for Lorraine when I felt someone come up close behind me. The Chief whispered in my ear. "It seems we have ourselves a crime wave." I turned around. "First, we lose something special." His eyes roamed around to see if anyone was listening. Someone must have acknowledged him because he smiled and waved. "Then, there's our lady with the dogs. Don't worry, I'll take care of that. But it seems your friend Edward got it wrong when he said the chalice was safe and everything would be all right."

"What? Oh no..."

He lowered his voice. "A choir director found an envelope addressed to the Pastor stuck in his sheet music."

I felt the blood rush down to my feet and I staggered.

"Abby, Abby? Are you okay?"

I leaned against the Chief to steady myself. "I'm fine. I think it's just the heat and all these people." He peered at me from under his thick eyebrows. He wasn't convinced.

"Truly, I'm fine. Tell me, what was inside the envelope."

"What you'd expect, another letter. This time there's no mystery about what the thief is trying to say."

"Why?"

"It's straightforward, in your face, written using words cut out of a newspaper."

"That's good. Maybe he's done playing games," I said, feeling more confident.

The Chief squinted at me and asked, "Why are you so sure it's a man? A woman could have pushed Kat."

"No, it was a man. I'm sure of it." I closed my eyes to visualize that moment in the courthouse square. It was hard, but I bypassed the emotion and focused on what I saw. "His shadow was taller than hers."

"Could have been a play of the lights or a tall woman," he countered.

"No, I don't think so. Plus his shadow head didn't have long hair."

The Chief shook his head. "What about Josephine Quinn from the church? She has short hair that could make her look like a man in silhouette. So do a lot of people, Abby."

"Mrs. Quinn isn't as tall as Kat—" My voice caught, but I wasn't going to break down here, in front of all these people. I tightened down my emotions and continued. "And I don't think it was a woman wearing one of those knitted watch caps to hide her hair. It would have distorted the shape of the head." A shudder ran through me. "And then there was that wail after she fell. No, it was definitely a man."

The Chief put up his hands. "Okay, okay, you've sold me."

"Tell me about the message he sent this time."

"Like I said, there's no puzzle here. His words are clear and so is his meaning."

"Which is?"

"He is one angry man," the Chief said, shaking his head. "He called us idiots. He blamed us for going to the wrong place... and he blamed the pastor for what happened." The Chief rushed on. "I'm not showing this note to preacher man. No telling how he'd react, but somehow I have a vision in my head of him leading a group of men carrying blazing torches and pitchforks down the street, ready to burn down the town until he finds his chalice."

I had to suppress a giggle because I could see it so clearly. Beneath that mild-mannered exterior, Pastor Francis could become a loose cannon. "This could turn into a serious situation very quickly."

The Chief nodded slowly. "You're not kidding. So, I think we're going to sit tight and wait for what he said will be his last missive. He's going to give us one more chance to be reunited with the chalice."

"Reunite? That's a strange word to use."

"Hey, I'm just telling you what the note said."

"I want to see the letter. Where is it?"

"Whoa there, little sister. I gave it to the forensics boys who are still in town after what happened at the courthouse. I figured this is our best shot at getting fingerprints or DNA. Nobody touched the letter but the Pastor—nobody but the thief. We have a chance of finding the person who took the chalice—" He caught himself.

I added, "And who hurt Kat."

He nodded sadly. "I hope the experts find something."

This whole situation was draining: the mental challenges – trying to work out the puzzles and the motivation of the thief plus the emotional shock – losing Kat. I noticed people were starting to look at me, even stare. I felt my face growing hot. I licked my lips and tried to pull them up in a friendly smile. People noticed and some returned my smile, but not all of them. Searching for a thief turned killer while keeping up festive appearances was hard.

The Chief's eyes flashed with determination. "We're going to catch this sicko, period." Then his expression fell away as if he couldn't look at me.

"Wait, what is it?" I asked, suddenly nervous.

He shrugged and shook his head all at the same

time. "Nothing, it's nothing." His words sounded dull.

My eyes bore into him, looking for a sign of what was wrong. "There's something else, isn't there?" I gasped. "Lorraine?"

He reached out and grabbed my arms. "Abby, Lorraine is fine. It's nothing like that." He gave me a reassuring squeeze. "We're meeting in the Pastor's office. That's daunting enough. We might even scare up a cup of eggnog." He patted his slim waistline. "Not that I need the calories. This time of year is always a challenge for me."

"It is for all of us. Lead the way."

I followed the path he carved through the crowd. People were everywhere, caught up in little groups, talking and laughing. A blast of warm air hit us as we walked into the parish hall. Lorraine was waiting by the door. I was so relieved to see her that I almost threw my arms around her. Somehow I swallowed the urge and only took her hand and squeezed. She gave me an inquiring look, but before she could say anything, Stewart rushed up to her and grabbed her hands and held them tight.

"Lorraine, I'm so glad I found you." Her eyebrows shot up in surprise and shot a questioning glance my way. I gave her a little shrug and she turned her attention back to the short man with the round glasses. She started to say something about the concert, but he interrupted her. "I need to talk to you. May I come to Fair Winds? Can we talk there?"

Mystified, she nodded. "Yes, yes, of course. Anytime. What..." But he had faded back into the crowd. "I wonder what that was all about," she said to me.

"No time now. We're being summoned."

At the door to the Pastor's suite stood the man of the hour, gesturing for us to hurry, then he turned to accept congratulations from parishioners and visitors alike. Knots of chatting people slowed our progress and the delay was building up pressure behind his genial mask. If we didn't get to him soon, I feared he might explode.

Somehow, the way opened up and when we were safely in his office with the door closed, his smile fell away and his face darkened.

"Ruined! My last Christmas in St. Michaels Choir Concert, ruined!" The Pastor stood on the other side of his desk, beating his fist on the top of his high-backed chair for emphasis.

Assistant Pastor Paul ran his finger inside his white clerical collar as if it suddenly felt tight.

Lorraine, wanting to bring a little peace to the outraged man and the uncomfortable atmosphere said, "I thought the concert was lovely. Everyone enjoyed it."

"Of course they enjoyed it," he shot back. "They didn't know that the invisible thief who has haunted our days and nights sent another crazy puzzle for a choir director to find in his music. A *visiting* choir director, for heaven's sake. I had a terrible time explaining that, believe you me." He turned his back on us and raised his face to the ceiling as if looking for a divine source of strength.

"Everything is fine there," said the Chief. "You did

a good job. I know the man and he thought a treasure hunt at Christmas was a clever idea. He's thinking of suggesting it to his reverend."

A long groan was the only response from the Pastor.

There was a knock at the door and Paul moved to answer it.

I could just glimpse Edward's face through the small opening.

"I dropped by to congratulate you and the Pastor on a beautiful evening. And, I was wondering, since the chalice hasn't turned up yet, is there anything else I can do to help?"

The Pastor planted his feet and put his hands on his hips. "No!" he bellowed. "Edward, go away. Paul, close the door."

Reluctantly, he did and leaned against the door. "Don't you think you were a little hard on him—?"

"No, I do not. This is my last Christmas in St. Michaels Festival as Pastor and it should have been glorious. Instead, it will cloud my entire tenure here. And dealing with that man doesn't make it any better. He has been nothing but trouble as president of the council, always fighting me every step of the way."

I had to say something in Edward's defense. "I think you're being a little unfair. He worked with me in deciphering the first puzzle. It was complicated and—"

The church leader had lost all patience. "A game— that's what you thought this was all along. You should have found the chalice instead of playing with clues like this was a game. I'll have you know this is a very serious business. If you had approached it with the attention it required, we would have our silver chalice back where it belongs..."

I could feel it coming and I said silently, *Don't say it, Pastor.*

"And a woman wouldn't be dead and her son crying at Christmas."

Shocked gasps filled in the room. Certainly, I was not going to accept the blame he laid at my feet, but I was not going to lower myself to his childish bullying.

I took a deep, deep breath to steady myself and met his challenge. "This isn't a game and it never has been," I declared. "Those things aren't puzzles for us to figure out. I think they're messages to the church—messages to the congregation and to *you*." I probably put too much emphasis on the reference to the Pastor but I was barely keeping a lid on my anger. "You're hearing the message loud and clear, but choosing to ignore it. You were the one who should have been in the courthouse square. He wanted to talk to you. Since I saw what happened and you didn't, let me be clear. The thief – the man we're dealing with – is unhappy and desperate. My greatest fear is that if you don't listen to whatever it is he's saying to you, he will destroy your precious silver chalice."

The Pastor placed his hands on the back of his chair with great care and leaned toward me, his eyes narrow slits. Pronouncing each syllable clearly, he replied, "I don't believe you."

"You don't? Consider this. Do you know why Kat went to the courthouse?" The Pastor didn't respond, no one did. "She went to get the chalice away from the thief. She wanted, needed a windfall of cash so she could leave the Eastern Shore. She told me so herself. I think she overheard our argument about the House Divided letter and decided the courthouse was the logical place to go. She figured that chalice was her ticket out of here. All she had to do was get it away from the thief and –"

The Pastor scratched his nose and said, "That's all nice speculation, but the fact remains—"

I cut in to finish the sentence. "The fact remains that a woman is dead because the thief would do anything – *anything* – to keep the chalice so he can deliver his message to you and the congregation. Since you've opted not to tell your parishioners, he's talking directly to *you*.

"But if you're *not* listening, if it doesn't mean anything to *you*, why *not* destroy it? Why should it exist as a temptation for somebody else, somebody like Kat who wants it only for the money? The chalice disappears forever, the thief fades away and there is no justice for Kat. She was foolish and what she did was wrong, but she deserves justice. I will not let you deny her that."

In the cold silence of the room, I turned to the Chief. "Please get me a copy of the last message as fast as you can." Then I looked back at the Pastor, my eyes drilling into his. "*I* want to end this horror. *I* want closure for myself, for Kat and for your church. I can and will see this to the finish." I moved around the young pastor still standing by the door, opened it and walked out.

CHAPTER FIFTEEN

Hot chocolate requires extra consideration before serving. Due to the density of the chocolate, it tends to sink to the bottom of the pot. Use a chocolate muddler to agitate the drink before pouring it into a shallow chocolate cup in order to offer it at its best advantage.
    —"The Butler's Guide to Fine Silver" Mr. Hollister, 1898

On the way back to Fair Winds, not a word was said about the choir concert or what happened in the Pastor's office. Lorraine was pleasant as she reminded me about my appointment to look at Rennie's silver the next day. I squelched a groan.

When we arrived, Lorraine insisted I come in for a cup of hot chocolate. Worry was written all over her face. Not wanting to add to her stress, I agreed and was pleasantly surprised to taste hazelnuts with the rich chocolate flavor in my glass mug.

She saw my reaction and smiled. "It's Frangelico. It adds something special and the liqueur will smooth out the rough edges from the evening."

Just what I needed. I raised the mug again and took a deep drink just as Dawkins appeared at the door.

What now?

"I'm sorry to bother you, Madame, but a man insists that he must see you."

She winced. "The Pastor, again?"

"No, this time it is someone with manners who is willing to wait to be announced, rather than barging into your home. This gentleman is waiting in the foyer. He says his name is Mr. Greer, Mr. Stewart Greer."

Both Lorraine and I groaned.

"You'd better bring him in, but Dawkins…"

"Yes, ma'am?" A look passed between them. "Yes, ma'am."

Stewart walked into the room still wearing his overcoat and holding his hat in his hands. He was hesitant about everything – where to stand, where to look – everything.

"Stewart," Lorraine began. "What a surprise."

"Um, you said I could come and see you."

"Yes, I know. I didn't expect it to be so soon and…" she glanced at her watch. "so late at night."

He took a step toward her. "But it can't wait. It's important."

"Alright," she said quickly to calm the man. "Why don't you sit down and tell us what is going on?"

He sat on the edge of the seat cushion at the far end of the sofa. His eyes darted from the floor to me and back again.

Lorraine caught it and said, "You can speak freely in front of Abby. She's as involved in this church business as I am, even more so." She gave me a tiny smile as she prepared to deal with Stewart.

The man's demeanor hinted that he'd like to shrink down to the size of a feather and float away. The word *meek* drifted through my mind again, the same word I'd thought about when I first saw Millie sitting at that big table in the Cove, crying. Too bad the age gap was so wide. These two people seemed made for each other. It was a wistful thought but...

"Stewart?" Lorraine prompted. "Why have you come?"

He started to speak but had to clear his throat to make any sound come out. "I-I know, I mean I think I know who took the chalice... and why."

Both Lorraine and I perked up but tried to remain nonchalant, so we didn't spook him. We sat and waited. Lorraine had to prompt him again before he continued.

"I don't like pointing fingers, but I feel it must be done." His resolve was growing stronger.

"I think you're right, Stewart. Tell me, who..."

Stewart interrupted her when he blurted out. "It's Paul, it's Pastor Paul." He drew his head back like a turtle trying to disappear into his coat. "I'm sorry, but it's true."

We exchanged a quick look and Lorraine continued. "Why do you think it's him?" The little man seemed to be lost in his thoughts. She prodded, "Does it have something to do with what you said that first day when the chalice was discovered missing and we were all gathered in the sanctuary?" Still nothing, so she pushed on. "I think you asked Pastor Paul, 'What are we going to do?' You said the church couldn't take another loss. What did you mean by that?"

The little man trailed his hand through his thin, gray hair just as he had that day when this all began. "I don't know..." he started again. "That's the reason I'm here. I found he's created a special account and is slowly moving money into it."

Lorraine shrugged. "Isn't that part of his job to act as an administrator? It sounds like that would be something he would do."

"Under normal conditions it would be, but there is nothing normal about this account. He never reported the existence of this account to me or in any of our committee meetings."

"Maybe it was an oversight," I suggested. "There seems to be a lot going on at your church. Maybe he just forgot." I liked Paul. It seemed that he was dealing with more than enough second-guessing and dictatorial attitude from Pastor Francis and bearing up well. Stewart's insinuations smacked of piling on.

"We have checks and balances in our system to flag questionable actions such as this. I instituted them when I assumed my post as chair of the finance committee."

"What do you think he's doing?" Lorraine asked.

"The bank contacted me directly to discuss the possibility of misappropriation of funds."

"What?" I almost came out of my chair. Of all the people I'd met connected with this church, Pastor Paul was the last one I'd even consider doing such a thing.

"It's true. He created the account, did not report it to me or any member of the committee and..." He took a deep breath and let it out slowly with a pained look on his face. "And he is the sole depositor to the account. I fear that the person who can manipulate funds might also be capable of stealing our chalice."

"Forgive me, Stewart, but that seems like quite a leap."

"I agree, especially when you're talking about Paul," I added.

Lorraine put out her hand to signify that I should wait and listen. "But it's still worth exploring. Tell me, how much money is gone from church funds?" asked Lorraine.

"Well..." Stewart stammered.

"How much has he taken?" I asked.

"Well..."

"Stewart, if you're uncomfortable telling us, then you should have a conversation with the Chief. He—"

"NO!" Stewart pause and looked down. He was surprised to realize that he had come to his feet. He took a moment to compose himself, sat down again then began again. "No, I don't mind telling you. There are no funds missing as of now, but money has been shifted."

I settled back in my chair, relieved.

"Don't you think you're making an assumption?"

"Mrs. Andrews, it may sound like I'm making something out of nothing, but in proper accounting practice, it is a serious red flag."

Lorraine relaxed. "I'm sure you would know better about such things, but I still think it would be a good idea to talk to the Chief. He should have this information considering everything that's going on."

Stewart shook his head in rapid little movements and hunched his shoulders. "No, no, I don't think

I should be the one to talk to him." When he saw the confused expression on Lorraine's face, he said, with a wrinkled brow, "He doesn't know me as well as he knows you. I think it would carry more credibility coming from you." He rushed on. "I can give you all the information he'll need..."

She took a slow, deep breath through her nose and straightened slightly. "Before you do that, let me raise the issue with him." Her tone was calmly confident, but I could see she was uncomfortable with the man's request.

She rose gracefully from her chair. "Thank you for coming, Stewart, and letting me know about this situation. I'm sure someone will look into it." She extended her hand. "Dawkins will show you out."

How did she know that he appeared at the door waiting for the guest to leave without looking? Their connection was becoming a little unnerving.

When the little man was safely out of earshot, Lorraine asked me what I thought.

"I think the whole situation sounds off. Stewart might be throwing suspicion on Pastor Paul to divert attention from himself. I can't figure out what's going on there."

"I'd like to know the real reason why he doesn't want to talk to the Chief. I'll make a point to bring it up the next time I see him."

Lorraine just looked at me and shook her head. "I don't know what to say. This situation keeps getting stranger and stranger."

"Do you believe him?" I asked.

"I don't know what to believe."

"Maybe it's all an act, being so timid. For all we know, he could be the thief and is trying to divert suspicion away from himself to someone else."

"That sounds plausible, but no one suspects Stewart. Until now. We're the only ones even thinking about him."

I shrugged. "You're right. What a sad little man. What are you going to do? It's late to be calling the Chief."

She confirmed the late hour with a look at her watch. "You're right. I think this tidbit can wait until morning."

CHAPTER SIXTEEN

It is believed that the word sterling dates back to the reign of Queen Elizabeth I when British currency became known as pound sterling. The word referred to a silver coin known as a star-ling referring to the small star on it.
—"The Butler's Guide to Fine Silver" Mr. Hollister, 1898

After my declaration the night before, I knew I had to do something, but I wasn't sure what. Lorraine made herself scarce sensing that I needed to work this out for myself. Waiting for Simon to finish his business outside, I stood at the window sipping my morning coffee without even one goose for company on the Miles River, I remembered a conversation with the Chief about Jeff, the antique dealer. My gut told me that something wasn't right about the man, but I couldn't put my finger on what it might be. There was only one way to find out.

I dressed in a nice pair of slacks, jacket and feminine blouse, even put on a little makeup, and drove into town. Destination: Belle Antiques.

"Thank you," I said to a customer leaving the shop who held the door open for me. I slipped inside without the bell announcing my arrival.

Jeff was walking into the back room of the shop, speaking to an unseen someone. "There goes yet another happy shopper leaving empty-handed."

"What we reap from this trip to New York will make up for all your tightfisted customers," a woman said.

I knew that voice, a flat New York suburbs accent with an overlay of sophistication which, to my ear, sounded awkward. I knew the voice, but couldn't figure out why Rennie was in the back of Jeff's shop and on a Sunday morning. Was she having an affair with both Jeff and Grant while her husband was out of town all the time? It wasn't long before Jeff joined her and kicked the swinging door closed so I couldn't see them, but I could move closer to hear what they were saying.

"...you're right." He conceded some point to her in a friendly way. So they knew each other, but how well? "I want to load the van tonight so I can leave for the city early in the morning."

"Ha! That will be a first, you up early in the morning. You know, you should find a good woman who will keep you away from the bars," Rennie suggested.

"I do just fine with the ladies," Jeff shot back with a wicked tone.

"I mean... oh, what do they say around here? *You're a mess.* Yes, that's it. You need to find someone to clean up your act."

"I don't need any help, thank you. I have no trouble—" He paused.

She gasped a little. "Don't be crude. You know what I mean."

Rennie was flustered. That was a first.

"Instead of wasting time analyzing my love life, you'd do better to look to your own."

She went on the attack. "Why? What do you mean?"

"Well..." He dragged out the word and she rose to the bait.

"Tell me, what have you heard?" She sounded like she was going to blow a blood vessel.

"I caught the little show you two put on behind his shop." He said with a hint of amusement. He seemed to enjoy irritating her to get a reaction. "You can trust my discretion, of course." His tone had a sweetness one could trust only if a person was comfortable sleeping with poisonous snakes. "But if I saw you two together being all chummy, there might be one or two others who—"

"Who did you see?" she demanded. "Who was there?"

"Really, Rennie, this isn't a big city where you could lie down on the sidewalk and people will step over your body to go about their business. This is a small town with lots of eyes and people who care about what they see."

She paused. Then the old, confident attitude was back. "Nobody saw us. I don't believe you saw anything, either. Besides, you know what I'd do if you breathed a word to anyone... *anyone*."

"Yes, ma'am. I have an idea of what you're capable of and I am not interested in testing you. Me? I'm happy drinking beer, playing pool and running your antiques to New York."

"Good. Shall we get back to work? Before you load anything, I want to run down the list of things they've requested. Remember, these are *my* contacts, *my* friends. They've made commitments and I will not have them disappointed."

"Yes, ma'am." Jeff said it with a soldier's salute in his voice. "Why don't you read them off and I'll make sure they're all here. That will make it easier to load."

I pawed through my purse and found a piece of paper and a pen. It wouldn't hurt to make a copy of her list. I juggled my things so I could write using my purse as support. *It's a good thing the Chief can't see me right now. He'd tan my hide.*

As if conjured up by my thoughts, the front bell tinkled and the Chief walked in. I backed into the corner behind a sofa so the Chief wouldn't see me. Just as I crouched down, Jeff came through the door to the back.

"Well, the local constabulary has arrived. Have you come to arrest me, Chief?" said Jeff with his usual rash, careless abandon.

"I don't know, should I? What have you done?" countered the Chief, only half in jest.

"Nothing you should know about." Jeff laughed to lighten the mood.

The Chief laughed with him, but it sounded insincere to me. "I just came by to see if anybody's tried to sell something for quick money, something that may not belong to them. With the holidays and all, people could always use a little extra cash. Wouldn't want folks tempted to do the wrong thing."

"I know what you mean. It hasn't happened to me,

but I've heard about it from other people."

The Chief's voice took on an interested note. "Other people like who? People here in town or in Easton or—"

Jeff snickered. "Oh no, nobody around here. I was talking about New York. Some dealers have that happen all the time and some of them take the goods. Not me. Not there and not here. I don't want to get on your wrong side, Chief."

Ha! I wanted to jump up and tell the Chief to check out the back room… but I kept my mouth shut and stayed in my hiding place. I didn't have enough information yet. After I had Rennie's list, he'd listen to me. He might even forego the tongue-lashing I knew I'd get if he found me hiding behind a Victorian sofa with worn red velvet upholstery. If he found me now, I'd never hear the end of it. I stayed in place and kept quiet.

"Anybody approach you with something that doesn't match up with who they are, you call me, okay?" said the Chief.

"Yes, sir." That soldier's salute was in Jeff's voice again. Was life just a big joke to him? Having fun, right this very minute seemed more important to him than staying out of trouble.

"You keep in touch, Jeff, and Merry Christmas." The bell tinkled and the Chief went out to continue his rounds while Jeff pushed through the door to the back room again.

I heard him say, "That was close."

"He's not a problem for us," Rennie insisted. "All these goods were gotten fair and square."

"I'm not so sure about that, my dear."

A note of superiority entered her voice. "Everyone received payment and that's all that counts. Buying and selling antiques is so far beyond that man, he wouldn't recognize one if it was under his nose. Besides, this is just one small step in our overall scheme of things."

"Yeah," said Jeff. "You and your boyfriend are really making things happen. I saw Millie the other day in the Cove. She couldn't keep the tears out of her coffee."

"First, he's not my boyfriend and second, if Millie had bought into the vision and agreed to switch from selling t-shirts and touristy stuff, her rent wouldn't have jumped and she'd still be in her retail store space."

Jeff pushed something that scraped across the floor. "I don't have time to debate the pros and cons of what you two have planned. Let's go over your list so I can load this stuff."

"Not necessary," she said coyly. "While you were out there chatting with the police, I matched the pieces to my list. It's all here. Just get it to the city in good condition and we'll have our money.

"Oh, I have to run. That girl who is working on Lorraine Andrews's silver is coming over to the house in a little while and I have to get ready for her."

I looked at my watch and saw she was right.

"This Abby person doesn't have any real credentials from what I can tell. I want to test her with my silver to see what she knows. If she's as dumb as I think, it might work in our favor. I have a former client in the city who will buy just about any piece of antique silver I bring her as long as it's in a few specific patterns. And Mrs. Andrews has pieces in those patterns. I checked them out during the party at Fair Winds the other night."

"You never miss a trick, do you?" said Jeff with a mixture of awe and disgust.

"I try not to. Call me when you make the delivery. And Jeff, drive safely and stay off the booze at least until you're on your way back."

"Your concern for my welfare warms my heart, Rennie. Who knows, I might give Grant a run for his money... along with your husband."

"You are a horrid man, truly horrid," she sputtered. "Good-bye." The outside door slammed.

Time for me to leave, too, but how was I going to get out of the shop without the telltale bell on the door giving me away? Who knew how long it would be before another customer came in? I had a better idea.

Silently, I stood up. The pins and needles in my legs made me want to cry out and my feet were numb. Gingerly, I made my way to the front door. I waited for a moment to prepare myself like an actress for my little bit of subterfuge. If he didn't hear the bell when I opened the door, I could escape unnoticed. If he heard the bell and came into the shop... well, I knew what I had to do.

I grasped the door handle, turned it and pulled. I heard Jeff coming so I danced around so it would look like I was just coming in.

"Hi, Jeff. Thought I'd pop in for a minute. I'm still shopping for some holiday gifts."

"Come in, Silver Girl. You're always welcome. Looking for anything in particular?"

"No, not really. It's the kind of thing that I'll know

it when I see it."

"Gotcha. The store is yours." He swept his arm around in a wide arc. "Look to your heart's content. I have to finish up something in the back. Let me know if you need anything."

"Um, I know you have some wonderful things out here in the public part of your store. I bet you have some real gems in the back. Think I could take a peek?"

He stepped in front of me, blocking my way. "No."

I was so surprised by his response that I stepped back. "I'm sorry, I didn't mean…"

He cleared his throat and smoothed his hair back, all charm again. "I'm sorry. It's just that my back room is a mess and I'd be embarrassed for anyone to see it."

You weren't embarrassed to have Rennie see it, I thought. "Even if it's just me? I wouldn't tell a soul."

He shook his head. "No, let's do it another day after I've cleaned it out a little."

Cleaned it out. Interesting.

Disappointed, I looked around the store and tried to put some enthusiasm in my voice. "That's okay, there's enough here to keep me occupied. You go back to what you were doing and I'll poke around."

After he went in the back, I had to fight the urge to race out the front. I forced myself to wander around from one cabinet to another to give the appearance of shopping. On a shelf in the third cabinet, something caught my eye. I should say it was two somethings.

Jeff emerged from the back, "Ah, you have a good eye. You spotted the one cabinet in the whole place that has some nice things. What do you like?"

"Those two dogs there." I pointed to a pair of porcelain painted poodles. "Are they Staffordshire dogs?"

On his guard, he peered at me from under half-closed eyelids. "Yes, but I thought your specialty was silver," he said slowly. "Most people don't know about the dogs."

I said without missing a beat, "A friend of mine collects them. They're really not to my taste, but she loves them. Maybe—"

"Sorry," he said, as he opened the cabinet. "These two puppies aren't for sale. They're on their way to a new home." He took one out and cradled it against his arm, picked up the other one and closed the cabinet.

"Oh, that's too bad." I made a show of looking at my watch. "Oh, I'm late for an appointment. Got to run. Thanks anyway. I'll have to come back." I scooted out the door, but not before I saw a wary expression cross his face.

I worked my way around the building so I could see the back of his shop. I ducked behind a bush which gave me little protection against the wind that was whipping around. I was tempted to leave but I needed to confirm that Jeff was packing up. If people saw me hiding there, they'd probably call the police, which might not be a bad thing.

I pulled down on an evergreen branch to get a clear view of the back door. A white panel van was pulled up to it and all its doors were open. I was starting to shiver when Jeff came out of the building with his arms full of something wrapped in a quilted pad, the kind used by a moving company. He stepped into the vehicle and moments later went back into the shop empty-handed. Jeff was packing up. Based on what Rennie said, he was moving antiques to buyers in New York. The chalice may or may not be in the van. I was almost certain that Mrs. Bolinsky's dogs were bedded down someplace inside.

It would be a mistake to confront Jeff myself. I'd learned my lesson more than once. I did the next best thing. I pulled my cell phone out of my pocket and called the Chief. The call rang and rang then went to voicemail.

"Chief, it's Abby. Please call me as soon as you can. I think I know where the chalice might be and, if I'm right, it will be on its way out of town very soon. Call me!"

I couldn't stand the cold anymore so I scribbled down the van's license plate number and made my way back to the main street and away from his store.

CHAPTER SEVENTEEN

Both British and American silversmiths have created a vast array
of designs for silverware and silver hollowware. The pattern
for an established house most assuredly was selected years ago.
New additions may join the collection as pieces are developed
for specific uses. Make certain if a new pattern is introduced, it
complements the established one.

—"The Butler's Guide to Fine Silver" Mr. Hollister, 1898

I jumped in my car and took the St. Michaels Road towards Tilghman Island, past the Bozman turn and McDaniel. Along the way, the Chief returned my call. I filled him on what I saw.

He listened patiently, then asked, "And how do you know all this?"

I gulped and hoped he couldn't hear it. I rushed on before he could say anything. "Does it really matter? The point is that something is going on at that shop, probably something illegal and I think Jeff is right in the middle of it, up to his eyeballs.

I'd hoped for an excited reaction, but the phone was silent. Maybe I'd lost the signal. "Are you there?"

"Yes, I'm here, trying to make sense out of all this.

Abby, the man has a right to move merchandise in his vehicle, Abby. He is in the antique business."

"I know, but Rennie... Mrs. Frampton was talking about—"

"Were you sneaking around, young lady?" He was not pleased. "Eavesdropping got Kat into big trouble."

"Well, I—"

"When was this?"

I felt like I was digging myself into a hole, but I couldn't lie. "I was in the store when you were there." I cringed, waiting for the explosion. He didn't disappoint me.

"What? You were in the store when I was there today?"

I held the phone away from my ear. "Yes." I said, weakly.

"I didn't see you. Where were you?" He demanded.

"Behind the Victorian sofa." It would have been easier confronting Jeff than having this conversation with the Chief. He was silent for so long I began to wonder if he'd hung up. "Chief?"

"I don't want to talk about this now... but we will discuss it another time."

"The information about the antiques? But they're—"

"Your antics. Abby, if they... you could get yourself hurt." I heard him sigh, long and low. "Okay, did you do something useful like get the plate number of the van?"

It felt like the sun broke through the clouds. "Yes, yes, I did." I fumbled with my phone trying to bring up the app where I'd recorded the number.

"Abby, if you're driving and I think you are, pull off to the side, stop and read me the number. Don't do it while you're driving," he ordered. "We've got enough problems without you being in an accident."

It was the least I could do, for both our sakes. I stopped on the shoulder and gave him the number. "Are you going to chase him down and search his van?"

He sounded exasperated. "No, that's illegal and violates his Constitutional rights."

"But I'm sure Mrs. Bolinsky's dogs are in there. At least you can get them back for her."

"I need probable cause to do a search and seizure," he announced.

"But—"

"But," he continued. "If we have reasonable suspicion to start an inquiry, it might lead to probable cause."

"I'm not following all that, but you've got to stop him."

"I'll see what I can do." There was a lilt in his voice that reassured me and probably made guilty people very nervous. "And don't you do anything as foolish as hiding behind a sofa, you hear me?!"

"Yes, sir!"

Just past Sherwood, I followed my GPS directions to a brand-new two-story home that looked out of place on the Eastern Shore. In my opinion, it belonged in an upscale suburban community outside a big city. But it was an appropriate home for Rennie. The woman rubbed me the wrong way the night of the Christmas in St. Michaels Kick-off Party at Fair Winds. I couldn't justify her inspection of Lorraine's silver and now, this was supposed to be a test of my knowledge of silver.

Settle down, I told myself. *You promised Lorraine you would be polite and share information. I wonder what Lorraine would say if she knew what I'd overheard.*

By the time I stood at her front door, I plastered a smile on my face.

Rennie's greeting was warm and she showed me around the first floor. Showed off, was more like it. She walked me through the living room and study.

As we wandered around, I commented, "That incident at the gift exchange was horrible." She didn't respond. "I felt badly for you."

"Small town, small minds," she tossed over her shoulder. "In here, you'll see we put in a granite fireplace surround that almost covers the wall. It gives the family room a cozy feeling, don't you think?"

We looked at the sunroom through glass French doors because it was too cold to go out there. Then she led me to a gourmet kitchen that took my breath away. It was so well equipped that it begged for a chopping block piled with fresh vegetables, steaming pots of soup and pastries in the oven. Instead, everything was shiny clean and cold. She spared me the garden room, mud room, laundry room, maid's quarters and four-car garage but made sure I knew about them.

As we doubled back toward the dining room, I asked as I looked around, "Your husband isn't home?"

"No, I'm afraid he's wrapping up things so we can enjoy the holidays together."

Her answer sounded a little automatic as if she

used it often. "I don't believe I know what he does?" If Lorraine heard my feeble attempt at innocent curiosity, she would roll her eyes or fall over laughing. Fortunately, Rennie wasn't paying that much attention.

"He's in business." That was the extent of her answer.

"Ah, what kind of business?" I asked sweetly. That fake Southern belle was coming out in me again.

Her clicking heels stopped on the stone floor. She turned and said with barely controlled politeness, "Business that requires him to travel a great deal. Now, did you come here to look at my silver or not?"

I laughed off her terse attitude. "Of course. Lead me to your pieces of silver." She did not respond to the Biblical reference the way Jeff had. Considering what I saw in the town parking lot when she was talking with Grant, talking and more, the comment suggesting betrayal was appropriate. I felt sorry for Mr. Frampton. I resolved that I'd be very nice to him whenever we met and not judge him by the nasty woman he'd married.

"It's all in here." I followed Rennie Frampton from the Hamptons into their dining room.

In the center of the room was a large round piece of glass set on a stone pedestal swamped with all kinds of silver pieces. There were dinner knives and forks, a bonbon dish, a six-piece tea service and much more. I made nice comments, but her flatware pattern was nothing special. There was one interesting item, actually it was three matching pieces: a roast carving set with a serious knife about 14 inches long, a fork with long tines and a matching knife sharpener that I picked up to find surprisingly heavy. It was unusual to find all three pieces with their original blue protective pouches in a collection. Rennie didn't notice my interest. Her attention was on something else.

"This piece brings back fond memories." Her voice was soft as she picked up a knife with a long blade that came to a point at the end of the cutting edge. "This was the knife we used to cut our wedding cake. I thought it was an extravagance at the time. When we got married, we didn't have much. Bob—" She caught herself. "Robert hadn't started his business venture yet. We could have used the money on regular things for the house, but my grandmother insisted. Now, I'm glad she did. It will stay in our family, of course. When our boys get married, they'll use it to cut their wedding cakes. I'll be sure of that," she said with a little nod of certainty as she put the knife back on the table.

Rennie's softer side surprised me. It was sweet that she valued her grandmother's effort and felt the importance of family traditions. Not everyone had to have a high quality collection like Lorraine's or even the variety in Aunt Agnes's inventory. With a jolt, I remembered that this woman had sneered about how this visit would be a test of my knowledge. Okay, Miss Conniving Lady from New York, if you can make this a test, I should conduct one of my own.

"Any sporks in your collection?" I asked.

"Any *what?*"

"You know, ice cream forks. Do you have any of those?"

She recovered quickly. "No, I have no need for

them. I try to serve more exciting desserts than ice cream."

Well, la-di-dah. I guess Mrs. Frampton from the Hamptons wasn't as knowledgeable as she pretended to be.

I went back to work looking through her pieces to hide my reaction. She wandered around the table, trying to act nonchalant. "I imagine you talk to a lot of people around town, I mean the ones who have more substantial homes in the area. Do they all have sterling silver, especially the serving pieces and hollowware -- and by that, I mean tea sets, coffee pots, gravy boats, platters, pitchers, that sort of thing."

That's okay, Rennie. I know what you're talking about.

"If they have these big homes, they must entertain often so they have these things, right?"

"I've only been here for a short time, so I don't know many people. Lorraine is the one to ask."

"No, that's not necessary. I'm only trying to gauge the interest. Perhaps you know someone who might be downsizing or moving? Someone who might be interested in selling some of those things without the hassle of going to New York?"

"I can't think of anyone right now." After what I overheard in Jeff's shop, it was clear they'd found people who were willing to sell their possessions but I wondered how involved she was. "Do you do that kind of work?"

"Work? Oh, I don't work, not really. My life revolves around my husband and his activities. I have to be ready to throw a few things in a bag and fly off with him to..." she shrugged. "Wherever... California, Las Vegas, Mexico. I only had a few days' notice before we left for London. So, you see I have to be flexible." When she saw me redirect attention back to the silver, she quickly added, "But I still have my contacts in the City."

"New York?"

She looked at me as if to say, is there any other city? "I used to do interior design work for my friends."

I thought of Kat. If she'd been as clever as Rennie, would she still be alive?

Rennie sat down and carefully arranged the long silk scarf of purples and blues draped around her neck. "It started when they asked for my opinion about a fabric or sofa for their own home, in the city or the Hamptons. When they started referring me to people I didn't know, I thought it was appropriate to charge a little something, for my time, to cover my travel expenses, that kind of thing."

She glanced around, but I was sure she wasn't seeing the crown molding or crystal chandelier. She was someplace else, someplace more favorable, more advantageous to her lifestyle. "I had a year-round pass to the sample rooms of all the designers." She looked directly at me. "The *important* ones. And I loved going to the auctions of the *important* pieces." She touched her chest in delight. "I'd get all dressed up, stroll through the private viewings with a glass of champagne and talk with *important* people. It was heaven."

"How did you fit that in with all the traveling?" I asked.

"I'd tell my husband if I had to be in the City. He understood."

"But now you're here in St. Michaels," I said.

Her shoulders sagged. "Yes, I know."

"The pace is different. You'll have time to enjoy things. Since you're interested in interior design and art maybe you'd enjoy painting watercolors."

A look of horror flashed across her face. "Please!" She reset her smile and continued. "Now that the house is built and all the decorating is done, my life isn't slow, it's dead. I thought more would be going on. When Robert suggested we build a home here, away from the cold, messy weather in the City, I thought it was a good idea." She shook her head. "Now, I don't know."

"There are many interesting people here. It takes a little time to find them, get to know them, that's all."

"Oh, I haven't given up my friends or business contacts in the City. In fact, I may do a little something from time to time. Nothing major. Just something to keep my hand in." She gave me a super-sweet smile. "If you hear of someone who wants to sell something worthwhile – not flea market junk – but a real antique piece, you'll let me know, won't you? Maybe something from Lorraine's silver closet...?" She raised her eyebrows to ask the question.

How did she know about the silver closet? It's a good thing it was locked during the party or who knows what Rennie would have done. My smile was a mask to hide how I truly felt about this woman: she made me sick to my stomach. "I'm sorry, I don't think she is selling anything right now."

"Too bad." She rose from the side chair with the silk scarf rippling around her. "Just keep it in mind."

She moved to a wooden cabinet with burled walnut inlay on the doors. "Now, I want to show you something special."

She opened it as if it was Ali Baba's cave. The two pieces she placed on the table were truly treasures. Quickly, she added two more. The silver pieces looked like the turrets of a stone castle complete with windows and flags flying from the top.

"Aren't they wonderful? My sons play games with them. There was Camelot, Capture the Castle and oh, I don't know. The boys are so creative, even when they were young."

I reached out and touched the open metal work of one *castle* that was about ten inches high. "Where did you get them?"

She waved her hand as if batting away my question. "I think they were in my mother's cabinet. I have no idea where she got them."

"Then you don't know what they are?"

She shrugged, "They're curiosities. I used them for table decorations." Her expression was serious. "What do you think they are?"

"Since you're a member of First Presbyterian, you wouldn't know." Gently, I lined up the pieces.

"Know what?" Her eyes darted from the pieces on the table, to me and back again. She hated being in the dark.

"These are spice boxes used in the Havdalah ceremony."

"The what?"

"Havdalah marks the end of the Sabbath – the

Jewish Sabbath – and the beginning of the new week."

Rennie's mouth fell open. She had no idea what her boys were using as toys.

"A fragrant spice like clove or a sprig of a sweet-smelling plant is put inside and passed around so everyone can enjoy the scent. It's part of the wish for a good week."

"Wait, my mother... Why would she have them?"

"There are two possible answers to that question: either she thought they were unusual and liked them or... there is a Jewish connection in your family?" I said it for effect and I wasn't disappointed.

She gasped and shook her head hard. "That's not possible. No. My family has always been Protestant, members of one denomination or another."

I wasn't going to go into the history of Jews forced to convert to Christianity. Instead, I brought up a topic that was sure to interest her.

"You might want to put these spice boxes in a safe place. They're quite valuable."

Her eyes went wide. "They are?"

"I'm no expert on spice boxes, but some of the modern artistic designs like those in the shape of a pyramid, a walnut, even an ancient sailing ship sell for $200 to $400. The older silver pieces like these date back to the mid-1800's to 1900 and sell for a thousand dollars or more."

"Really?" She looked at her children's playthings with new respect. "Thank you, Abby. I know just the person who—" She stopped abruptly. "Why don't you finish looking at the other pieces while I put these away?"

I noticed the spice boxes didn't go back in the cabinet. They went on the table by the door.

CHAPTER EIGHTEEN

Fine sterling silver is not limited to the dining room. Accessories for the library are designed to manage every eventuality. They include a silver page turner, page holder, letter opener and the paper clip. Remember, the crowning touch of every desk – the silver inkwell – requires constant attention so the ink does not damage it.

—"The Butler's Guide to Fine Silver" Mr. Hollister, 1898

It was nice to spend an evening at home for a change. Well, not home as in my cottage, but with Lorraine at the main house. After stuffing ourselves on a dinner of leftovers from the party, we settled in the library with Lorraine at the desk this time, working through her Christmas card list.

"I can't believe how many friends you have," I said in honest surprise. "And they've all sent you a card? I didn't think people sent Christmas cards anymore. I hope we can make it through this whole list. "

"I know, it's exhausting. I haven't seen some of these people in years, but I guess we have to keep up the tradition. I hope I ordered enough cards."

"It's a good thing you had them print the return

address on the envelope or we'd be writing until Valentine's Day. Let's get started." It was good to hear laughter again in this room.

There was a lot of cross-referencing and address updating to do. My eyes were growing heavy. Simon snoring in front of the fireplace made it harder to concentrate. Visions of pillows and a thick down comforter danced in my head. I was grateful when Lorraine declared we were done for now. As I was about to wake Simon so we could go back to the cottage, he jumped up and ran barking out of the room. Lorraine and I looked at each other, mystified by the dog's behavior. It wasn't long before we heard footsteps coming down the hallway.

Dawkins led a young man, dressed in the navy-blue uniform of the St. Michaels Police Department, into the library then went to stand quietly behind Lorraine's chair.

"Good evening, ma'am. Miss Abby," he said with a trace of nervousness.

The dying embers of the fire crackled in the silence.

With a sharp intake of breath, Lorraine stood. "Something's happened. What is it, officer?"

"Ma'am, it's nothing. Well, it is but it doesn't affect you directly." He scratched his head. "Well, I guess it does." It was obvious the officer was a new recruit.

"Out with it, man," demanded Dawkins. What's happened?"

The young man stood up straighter. "A murder, sir. I mean there's been a murder, ma'am." he blurted out. We all stared at him as he tried to get hold of himself.

After rubbing his nose and clearing his throat not once but twice, he sounded a little calmer. "Yes, ma'am, and the Chief sent me to fetch Miss Abby."

"We already know about the murder," said Lorraine, looking first at me then at Dawkins.

He turned to me. "He'd like you to accompany me to the station."

I looked at Lorraine, lost. "Why would he want me? I've already told him everything I saw. What more—?"

"He said I was to say that he needed some information and that you were to come with me... um, now." The officer looked at his shiny shoes, almost embarrassed.

All thoughts of a warm bed flew from my brain as I slipped my feet into my boots. "Well, I guess if he needs me, I have to go."

Lorraine jumped up again. "I'll go with you. Just let me get my coat and I'll meet you at your car." She rushed around the desk, but stopped when she heard the next thing the officer said.

"Ma'am, Miss Abby is supposed to ride with me in the police unit."

Tiny pinpricks of worry moved over my skin. It took me a moment to shake it off. "Of course, officer. We'll follow the Chief's instructions."

Lorraine was on the move again. "I'll follow you in my car. Dawkins?"

"Of course, madam." He rushed out of the room.

"Everything will be fine, Abby," she said as I put on my coat with Dawkins' help. "We'll be right behind you. Don't you worry about a thing."

Hearing Lorraine tell me not to worry made me worry all the more as I rode in the back of the police car. Finally, I gave up asking questions since the officer wouldn't give me any information. I had no idea the ride to St. Michaels could feel so long when I wasn't sure what I'd find on the other end.

We walked into the station, which was ablaze with fluorescent lights. A horde of people were moving around intent on various tasks. The officer touched my elbow and escorted me to the Chief's office. He was on the phone, but gestured for me to take a seat.

When he hung up, I said, "Chief, if this is about Kat and the other night, I—"

"Well done, Jamison. That will be all," he said to the officer. "Abby, thank you for coming." He sounded very official.

"Of course." I sat up in my chair, definitely on my guard.

He opened a file folder, read for a moment, then asked me, "Your full name is Abigail Adeline Strickland. Is that correct?"

My chest tightened. This is how a visit with other police officers had begun months earlier... when I was suspected of murder. "Yes, sir."

He leaned back in his chair and massaged his temples. He didn't want to have this talk, but I couldn't begin to guess what had happened or why I was involved. The next few minutes were filled with the noise of ringing phones, hushed conversations and people moving around outside his office. I thought I heard somebody crying, but I couldn't be sure.

Finally, he dropped his hands on the top of stacks of paper on his desk and, filled with resolve, said, "Miss Strickland, where were you tonight?"

I blinked and stared at him.

"She was with me, all night." Lorraine filled the doorway. "And I demand to know why you're treating her like a criminal and asking her such a question."

The Chief shook his head, the loser in this battle of wills. "Ma'am, I—"

"Don't you *ma'am* me, Chief Lucan. You send a uniformed officer to my home and take Abby away in the back of a police car... like a common criminal." Her voice was climbing in pitch and volume. She took a deep breath, moved a chair up to his desk and sat down. More controlled, she went on. "I would like to know what is going on... and I shall sit here until I do."

He knew when he was bested, but he had to conclude the formal interrogation. "Miss Strickland, where were you tonight between the hours of 7 and 9:30." Lorraine started to sputter but the Chief held up his hand for her to stop.

"I was at Fair Winds all evening, working in the library." I wished I didn't sound so wobbly.

"And Mrs. Andrews can vouch for that?" He continued.

"Yes, sir, and so can Dawkins, though he wasn't in the room with us the whole time. Chief, I—"

"All right, I'll need you to sign a statement to that effect before you leave."

"Yes, sir."

Then the Chief put his elbows on his desk and his

head in his hands. "I'm sorry. I have to do my job."

Lorraine and I looked at each other then she said in a soft voice. "I'm sorry too. My behavior was appalling. I—"

"No. Let's just move on. I need your help in identifying certain pieces." Lorraine and I exchanged looks again and silently agreed. "Come with me please."

We followed the big man through the crowd of people – some in plain clothes, some in uniform – and it felt like they were all stealing glances at us. I never felt so exposed. It didn't help that we had no idea what had happened. He took us into a small room and pointed to plastic bags marked Evidence on a desk. Inside each one was a piece of sterling silver. To the side, there was a stack of other silver pieces, all carefully sealed in bags as well.

"Can you identify those pieces for me, please? Start with those in the center," he directed, pointing to five bags with large silver pieces inside.

When I took a closer look, I wanted to be sick. I recognized the telltale stain on the gleaming silver surfaces. It was dried blood.

CHAPTER NINETEEN

Always hold a piece of sterling silver with a clean cloth to prevent the unwanted introduction of oils from the human hand or fingers. Substances and fingerprints mar the appearance and finish of a piece.

—"The Butler's Guide to Fine Silver" Mr. Hollister, 1898

Lorraine walked in behind us. "Sorry, I saw someone I know and wanted to say hello." She put her purse down and pulled off her gloves one finger at a time. Looking over the collection of silver, she laughed. "Oh my goodness, Chief! Either there's been a big silver heist or you've caught the bug to collect silver."

She took one look at my face and her smile disappeared into a look of concern. "What? What is it?"

I sat down as the Chief filled in the details. "I'm afraid there's been an attack, and someone is dead."

Lorraine's hand went to her throat in horror. "Who?"

"Robert Frampton."

We looked him in surprise and said in a chorus, "He's out of town."

"How do you know it's him?" I continued. "Rennie

says he's always out of town." I looked at Lorraine for confirmation. "I don't think anyone has ever met him."

"Well, one person knows him… and has identified the body as that of her husband."

Rennie's screaming words reached us from down the hall. "I demand to see the Chief this instant. You have to…" The Chief closed the door so we couldn't hear her rant.

Lorraine collapsed into a chair in disbelief. "What is she doing here?" She gasped. "You mean she killed him?"

The possibilities started surging through my mind. *Did Mr. Frampton come home and surprise his wife in the arms of another man? Did Grant lash out and kill him? Did he hear she was fooling around? Did he come home and confront her. Did they argue and she… But why all the silver in evidence bags… and why did so many of them had blood on them?*

"I don't understand, Chief, but tell me what you want me to do," I said, trying to stay focused.

"Mrs. Frampton called 911 and dispatch called me after they sent out the duty officers. When I got to her house, it was chaos. The victim – her husband – was on the floor of the dining room, bleeding from…" He waved his hand as if waving away the details of the scene we didn't need to know. "Mrs. Frampton was screaming, 'She killed him, she killed him,' pointing at Millie. And Millie was shouting, 'It was her. I saw her through the window. She killed her husband because of Grant.' I have no idea what she was doing there or…" The Chief opened his eyes wide and shook his head a little. "what

Grant has to do with any of this...yet. So, they were both standing there with blood on their hands, tossing accusations back and forth. Frampton said she heard some voices downstairs, came into the dining room and found him on the floor with silver knives and forks sticking out of him. She said Millie was there, leaning over him.

"Millie says she saw Mrs. Frampton stab her husband. She was outside looking in the window, Lord knows why. Then, she said she came in and tried to save him by pulling out all the silver things and tried to stop the bleeding." He shook his head. "My officers didn't know what to do so I told them to bring 'em both in."

"Millie's here, too."

He nodded with a pained expression on his face. "I separated them, but when they realized they could hear one another through the walls, they started yelling so loud a man couldn't think."

"How did you get them to quiet down?" Lorraine asked.

"I said I'd take them down to the harbor and throw them in if they didn't shut up."

"Interesting approach," Lorraine said with a smile.

"It worked. That's all I care about. I started doing the paperwork and realized that I don't know what to call these things. Those aren't regular forks and stuff, so I thought you could give me their proper names... for my report."

A smile started to grow on my face and the Chief wouldn't look at me. "That's not all, is it? You dusted them for prints and found mine, didn't you?" He looked away and I sighed. "This is getting to be a habit. If someone is killed with a piece of sterling, the police come charging to my door."

He held up his two beefy hands in defense. "They were there, all right. Just doing my job."

"Let me fill in the blanks. I was at Rennie Frampton's house this afternoon at her invitation. She pulled out her silver collection and had me look it over. Of course, I touched many of the pieces. Okay?" I was kind of pleased with myself. I was getting better at dealing with the police.

"Now, let me see what we have here." I laid out the five bags with the bloodied pieces inside. It gave me an eerie feeling to see the three-piece carving set I'd seen just hours ago. "This is a roast carving fork." Its long tines were covered with dried blood. "And this is the matching carving knife."

"I'm confused. You called it a *roast* carving fork and knife?"

"There are two carving sets. This is the larger one. The knife is about 14 inches long. The other type of carving knife is only 10. This fork is substantially bigger as well."

"That explains it. No, don't ask. Next." He made a note on each bag with a marker.

I hefted the knife sharpener and he labeled the bag.

"Oh, oh dear." The knife in the bag I picked up next made me sad.

"What's wrong? Are you okay?" Lorraine was quick to react.

"Yes, it's just that this was their wedding cake

knife. Rennie said she would make it a family heirloom. I hope..." I looked at the Chief.

He shook his head. No, he wasn't going to give me any more information. "What about that last thing? It looks wicked, if you ask me."

The tines of the fork in the last bag flared out like the end of a trident. I showed it to Lorraine for confirmation. "A lemon serving fork?" She nodded in agreement.

"My lord, there's a sterling thing for everything."

"Just about," I said. "What about the other pieces in the pile?"

"No need to go through them right now. You've identified the ones that were next to the body. That's all I need right now."

I grimaced, looking at the elegant pieces. "She stabbed him with *five* pieces? Isn't that overkill?" Appalled at the word I used, I stumbled to make it right. "I mean..."

"No need. But I think you're right. One of them went after him with five pieces of silverware."

"Or maybe it was both of them," Lorraine suggested.

The Chief rubbed his face. "Just what I need, a conspiracy."

"Do you think one of them took the chalice?" I asked, my mind racing with possibilities.

"Or he took it and they killed him for it." Lorraine added.

"Oh, I don't need these crazy ideas."

Lorraine stood up. "You have to admit, Chief, that a lot of crazy things are happening around here. Don't forget the dead animal someone gave Rennie at the

Christmas exchange."

"How could I? That's one we'll be talking about for a long time. Just wish I knew if it was a prank or connected to this." He gestured to the silver murder weapons all lined up and labeled on the desk. "Maybe the medical examiner will tell us something. The body's already on the way to Baltimore for the autopsy."

"So fast?" I asked.

"I've got two possible suspects. I can only hold them for 24 hours, then I have to charge one or both of them with probable cause or let them go. And I haven't got enough yet and I'm worried if I release them, they'll kill each other in my parking lot. I need more information and fast."

Lorraine paused. "Chief, could his death have something to do with what he does... or did for a living? No one seems to know what that is."

"I do. Had to find out so we can reconstruct his movements. She called him Robert, but his name in business was Bobby Gee."

"No, not the—" The Chief nodded. "Well, I'll be."

"What? Wait. Who?" My head bounced from one to the other trying to figure out what was so obvious to them.

"Bobby Gee, the professional bowler who went on to start up a chain of bowling alleys around the country," the Chief explained with a grin. "They call... called him the King Pin. He traveled all over the country promoting the game. Even made it to Europe. They called him Bobby Gee because he always said 'Gee, that was a great shot' after he threw a strike."

Stunned, I looked at Lorraine. "She made it sound like he was some special entrepreneur jetting to London and Paris. Why, the little..."

The chief said with regret, "I bet he was more comfortable with a beer and a hot dog than a glass of champagne and hors d'oeuvres."

Lorraine pursed her lips. "Same old story. She was trying to make him into something he wasn't. Poor man."

The Chief opened the door and we were face-to-face with Rennie. Her hair was wild and her face was twisted in pain. Mascara had dried in clumps under her eyes from crying.

"What's *she* doing here?" she screeched. "You're all against me. That woman killed my husband. Why won't you believe me?"

The officer wrestled her down the hall and into another room. My heart went out to the new widow, unless, of course, she was a murderer.

The Chief had to raise his voice to be heard over the yelling match that started up again. "There they go again. I swear this job makes me crazy sometimes."

We said good-bye the best we could and left him to his work.

CHAPTER TWENTY

Proper equipment is vital in polishing silver. Use one cloth to apply the polishing compound. Use a second cloth, dry and soft, to raise the shine. Use a large cloth because your hands should not ever touch the silver during the polishing process. If there is contact, you may need to begin the process again.
—"The Butler's Guide to Fine Silver" Mr. Hollister, 1898

I wanted to sleep late the next morning. These late nights and all the emotion were taking a toll on me. But Simon had other ideas. He wanted to go out and he wanted to go out NOW!

"Okay, okay!" He danced around my feet as I stumbled to the front door. "If you knock me down, you might never get outside." He ignored me, completely caught up in his little game. By the time we got to the door, his tail was wagging so hard I thought it would come off and fly around the room. I threw the dead bolt lock and he charged into the fog-shrouded morning.

As I was about to close the door, something white caught my attention out of the corner of my eye. A white envelope was stuck in the door knocker, addressed to **Abby** in bold black block letters. Probably a message from Lorraine. She knew I wanted to sleep late this morning, wrote a note and had someone put it on my door.

When I tore open the envelope and unfolded the paper inside, it was obvious that it didn't come from Lorraine. Rage and resentment leapt off the page and punched me in the face. I let go of it and watched it flutter to the floor.

All I wanted to do was wash my hands... and resolved to do just that after I called the Chief. My fingers were shaking so badly that I had to punch the buttons more than once. After he assured me that he was on the way, I scrubbed my hands red. Then I stepped carefully as I went back into my little living room, staying as far away as possible from the poisonous message on the floor.

It wasn't long before there was loud barking and a sharp rapping at the door. The Chief had arrived and Simon was thrilled. Somehow the big man got through the door without letting the dog gallop inside. With the door safely closed, we stood together looking at the paper as if it was a curious animal at the zoo.

"Tell me again, you found the letter on the door in an envelope." I nodded. "It was addressed to you."

"Yes, the envelope is there on the floor, too."

He pulled a pair of latex gloves out of his pocket. "You looked at the message, dropped it on the floor and called me?" I nodded. "And nobody else has touched it."

"Nobody, except the sender."

"Good. Maybe we'll get some prints. And you think it's from the thief?"

"Oh yeah. Wait until you read it." He held it so I

could read the message without touching the paper.

The first lines, written in plain English, appeared as individual words cut from a newspaper and pasted on the paper to make sentences.

"Dear ABBY,

You pretend to be a smart modern woman but you're nothing but a broken reed. It's YOUR FAULT. You let them follow the wrong path and you let a woman die. Now, you are so WEAK that you are distracted by a man dead in his own house. It has nothing to do with me and my business with you and the congregation.

You are weak, so I must be strong and do what is right.

Abby, this is your LAST CHANCE to atone for your sin and restore the chalice to the people. You must come by the time the clock strikes the day you were created. If you fail this time, it will disappear into the flames to which you have condemned me.

I barely noticed the sequence of pictures and numbers that appeared below the message. All I could see were the harsh words in capital letters: ABBY, YOUR FAULT, WEAK and LAST CHANCE. *Who are you... and what gives you the right to blame me? I didn't ask to play this foolish game that turned deadly.* The words echoed in my mind. *I tried to do the right thing, to get the chalice back where it belongs. Who—*

"Abby? Abby?" The Chief looked and sounded worried. "Abby, it doesn't mean anything. Pay no attention to it."

"I can't ignore it. Now, it's personal," I declared, as

I reached for the paper.

"Oh, no." The Chief pulled it out of reach. "If it's personal, you're no good to me or the case. You should go back to Fair Winds. I'll handle this."

"No," I snapped. "You can't tell me to go home. I'm all you've got for solving the puzzle right now." I searched his face, his brow creased with concern. "I did the others and got them right. I'll do this one, too. Let me make a copy and I'll call you when I'm done." As I led him to my scanner, I was burning to teach the thief a lesson and hoping I could pull it off.

The Chief waited while I dressed then walked me up to the main house. Lorraine met us at the back door, all aflutter. He had called to tell her what had happened. Just then, an officer arrived. If the thief was bold enough to cross the property of Fair Winds, the Chief wanted to make sure we had some protection while we hunkered down inside.

"Brandon won't come into the house unless you need him. He'll just patrol outside." The Chief looked at Dawkins sharply. "Make sure all the outside doors are locked."

Lorraine started to protest, but one look from the Chief quieted her.

"This situation is escalating. Just because he says in this letter that he had nothing to do with last night's murder, do you want to trust that? I don't, especially after what happened to Kat." He turned to me. "For now, young lady, you stay up here and if you go out, you don't go out alone. Understood?"

I couldn't believe we were hostages of a nameless

shadow who made up puzzles we were supposed to figure out. I stared into space seeing all the messages he'd left for us.

"Understood?" he repeated.

Jarred out of my daze, I nodded. "Yes, I understand... but I'm not happy."

"You and me both." He held up paper and envelope in his hand. "I'll get this to the forensic guys. Pretty soon they're gonna ask for their own offices. Abby, you sure you want to work on the puzzle— Wait." He looked at his vibrating cell phone and took several steps away before he answered it. I took a few steps toward the kitchen for coffee, but his raised hand stopped me.

When he finished his call, he came back to us and announced, "Change of plans. That was Baltimore. They're bringing some things down here in connection with last night's crime and I'm going to ask for you to help." He looked at both Lorraine and me. He saw the concern on her face. "No, it's nothing dangerous. I guess you could call it technical. Figure they'll be ready for you in about two hours, figuring driving time and setup. Think you can be at the station then? Hey..." he added with a little laugh in a feeble attempt to lighten the atmosphere. "That should give you plenty of time to work out this last puzzle." I gave him a look that wiped the smile right off his face.

Back at the desk in Lorraine's library, I looked at the message. I knew I should focus on the lines of words and numbers that would lead us to the chalice, but my eyes kept drifting up to the top of the message, the part that was addressed to me.

ABBY — Wrong — ABBY — Your fault — ABBY — Last chance — ABBY — LAST CHANCE

How obnoxious can a person be? *Or misguided. If this person can steal a communion chalice from his own church and blame me because it hasn't been found...* Then it hit me. *The thief knows I'm involved in the investigation.* The thief must be close. Only a few people knew about the missing chalice and the puzzles. *You let your anger tip your hand. Gotcha!* I could feel a huge smile growing on my face as I reached for the phone to call the Chief. I could image the protests of innocence and outrage as he hauled them all in for questioning. What a zoo that would be with the Chief as ringmaster.

I was halfway through dialing his number when my hand stopped in mid-air. Just how many people knew? It shouldn't be that many because both the Chief and the Pastor wanted to limit the number of people. Slowly, I lowered the phone. Carly knew something was wrong because the police were looking for Sonny. And there was Miss Cunningham, who was spreading the word far and wide. With a wave of disappointment, I remembered that it was a call from Miss Cunningham about Sonny's whereabouts that drew Kat into the treasure hunt that cost her life.

No, the thief could be anyone. The only way to shut this down was to solve the puzzle. Reluctantly, I picked up the paper and concentrated on the part below the personal message.

"Am I bothering you?" Lorraine asked as she stood at the door after I'd been working on the clues for a long time and getting nowhere.

"It's more like saving me." I leaned back in the chair, exhausted. "I can't seem to make heads or tails of this set of clues. I told everybody in the beginning that I'm no puzzle expert."

Lorraine came in and pulled a small chair to the other side of the desk and sat down. "I seem to remember that you wanted to solve this last puzzle. I guess you should be careful what you ask for."

I leapt out of my chair and started to pace, more like stomp around the room. "Come on, you read the beginning of the message. What did you expect me to do?"

Lorraine started to say something. "I —" But I was faster, my anger like a wildfire out of control.

"Am I supposed to walk away from those accusations?"

"Maybe—" She said in a timid voice.

"How could I live with myself, live *here* if people think those awful things about me?"

She took a step toward me and held out her arms. "Abby." The caressing tone of her voice stopped me in my tracks. "No one thinks any of those things are true. Why would they have asked for your help if they didn't think highly of you?"

"They asked me because of my association with you." I suggested.

She slapped her hands on the desk and pushed herself out of the chair. "You can be exasperating! Is it your generation? You're acting just like—"

We froze. The unspoken name and the memories hung in the air between us. In the quiet, we slowly melted into puddles of sadness.

Gravitating to the large overstuffed sofa by the fireplace, we sat down and Lorraine put her arm around me. "It's too soon, Abby. You're still bruised from..." She tightened her hug. "You're vulnerable right now. We both are. So, let's catch our breath and move on gently."

I nodded weakly as she continued. "We didn't know Kat very well, but she was part of our lives here at Fair Winds. We feel her tragic loss. To be thrown into the treasure hunt and now the hunt for her murderer—"

"Chief said it wasn't murder, at least not in the first degree," I added quickly.

"I don't care what the legal definition might be. If this person hadn't taken the chalice for who knows what reason, Kat would probably be alive right now. This person is responsible somehow, in some way."

"Whoever it is isn't content with hurting one person. Now I'm being skewered," I said.

"To someone who doesn't know you, your independence and self-reliance might appear threatening."

I pulled away, stared at her and jumped up to pace again. "What am I supposed to be, some sniveling girl, pregnant at 16 with no education, under the thumb of some man? Just because I've—"

"Abby, stop it! Come and sit down." She patted the cushion next to her and after a moment's pause, I did. "You are intelligent, well-educated, with a good foundation, thanks to your Gran and Aunt Agnes. You have a great heart filled with compassion, and a will that is very brave. To sell up and leave the West Coast and come to Washington after your Gran died, and start all over again... that was an act of courage. To work tirelessly to uncover the danger I was in and to put yourself in danger; I can't describe my reaction to that. Then, after a great shock and sadness, you picked yourself up once again and came here to the Eastern Shore to heal and reinvent yourself once again." She chuckled in wonder. "And you're not even thirty years old." She took my hand. "I think you're amazing. You *are* amazing. And don't you forget that."

Hesitantly, Simon padded into the room and sat at my feet. I'd never had a dog before. He'd come into my life only a couple of months ago when a friend moved to California and couldn't take him with her. Now, I couldn't imagine living without him. He put his paw on my knee.

"See? Simon thinks you're pretty special, too."

Tears prickled my eyelids. I stroked Simon's silky head. Quiet for a moment, I could see the thought enter his mind: I have her attention, let's play! He was off in a flash and came romping back with a rope toy. I got down on the floor and we played Tug of War and Keep Away.

"That's better." But after a few minutes of playing and laughter, Lorraine said, "Abby, do you want me to tell the Chief to find someone else to work out this last puzzle?"

I let Simon win the toy and he scampered out of the room. I pulled myself up and walked to the desk. "I'd like to..." I started again. "I want to crack this thing and bring this to an end," I said with conviction. "Let me work on it a little longer and if I can't do it, I'll let him know myself."

"Okay." She stood up. "I'll leave you to it. Good luck."

I put a piece of paper over the message at the top addressed to me. I told myself there was nothing of importance there for me. That done, I took a deep breath and concentrated all my attention on what was below:

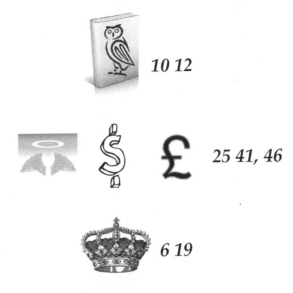

10 12

25 41, 46

6 19

I stared and scribbled and searched the internet for I don't know how long. The pictures and numbers were swimming together. I was about to admit defeat when Lorraine tapped on the door.

"Am I interrupting? It's almost time for us to leave."

I could see she was afraid to ask, so I answered her unspoken question. "No, I haven't cracked it yet. Guess I'll have to tell the Chief and, who knows, maybe somebody in Baltimore can figure it out. That's where everybody around here goes when they've got a big problem."

Lorraine didn't react, just led me to the back door where Dawkins helped us with our coats and out to the car to help the police with another murder.

CHAPTER TWENTY-ONE

The Continental style of holding a knife and fork is used during a formal dinner. The fork is held in the left hand with the tines pointed down, the knife is held in the right. A bite-sized piece is cut and conducted straight to the mouth by the left hand. Thus, it is vital that all parts of every piece of silverware are inspected carefully and any bit of tarnish is removed.

—"The Butler's Guide to Fine Silver" Mr. Hollister, 1898

We were met at the station by the young officer who'd brought me in the night before. As he led us to the stairs that went up to the inner sanctum, Lorraine made an observation.

"It's much quieter today than it was last night. Did the women finally get tired of doing all that shouting?"

"No, ma'am. They were driving the Chief crazy, so he moved them to two separate hotels and locked them in with matrons from the Sheriff's office. They're still in custody but they can't yell at each other anymore. And the Chief can think." He lowered his voice. "And that's a good thing, believe me."

We walked into a large room where several men were talking quietly. On a long table set up in the middle was a body, but this time it was only a dummy. The five silver pieces I'd identified the night before were laid out on the side with some markings inked on clear plastic wrapped tightly around each handle.

The Chief introduced a Mr. Hanley. "He's the forensic investigator in this case, from the Chief Medical Examiner's office. He has a few questions you might be able to answer for him."

The tall man wearing a vest shook hands with us and explained that our participation would be recorded in case it was needed in a court of law. Lorraine and I looked at one another then to the Chief who gave us a simple nod of his head. She gave me a little shrug of her shoulders.

"Of course, Mr. Hanley. Abby and I would be happy to help in any way we can."

He smiled, asked his assistant to begin the recording and laid out the situation. "We've asked you both here because of your background and experience with sterling silver pieces. In addition, Ms. Strickland, you visited Mrs. Frampton yesterday afternoon when she showed you her collection of silver, is that correct?"

"Yes, sir."

"We have determined," Mr. Hanley continued, "That Mr. Frampton was attacked using five pieces from that collection. At this time, we have two persons of interest. The question is who handled each piece and how."

"What about fingerprints? You found mine. Can't you tell who else handled them?" I blurted out wishing I hadn't. The sooner Mr. Hanley was done, the sooner we could solve the last puzzle, find the chalice and I could go back to the cottage and sleep for a week. "I'm sorry."

"No, you went right to the heart of the matter. Yes, there are fingerprints, but the question is which ones are in the right position to handle a piece being shown to a friend, and which are in the right place to kill a man?"

Lorraine and I looked at each other again in confusion and surprise.

"Ladies, I hope I may speak frankly, so we can get through this exercise as quickly as possible?"

I suspected that this meticulous man did nothing quickly if it had to do with a case.

He motioned us to the dummy laid out on the table. Fortunately, there were no distinguishing facial features so it looked like a stuffed sock with arms and legs. "We've marked the wounds on this made by the killer."

"Or killers," added the Chief.

Mr. Hanley agreed and went on. "We've matched each silver piece to each appropriate wound. First, we need to know, Ms. Strickland, what you remember from your visit with Mrs. Frampton and how she handled each one of these pieces. Let's begin with what you identified as a lemon serving fork."

"Well, I—" All of a sudden, my brain was in a fog, The events of the last several days, the unnerving experience of being questioned about another murder and the mysterious note left on my door this morning had made it hard to concentrate.

"Take your time, Abby. Why don't you sit down?"

Seated in a metal folding chair, I looked at the dummy, then the serving fork wrapped in plastic. I closed my eyes and tried to remember walking through the house with Rennie: the living room that seemed too formal to sit in, the family room with the stone fireplace. "We went into the dining room. Rennie had put a lot of pieces on her glass table. We looked at a number of things and I remember picking up the lemon fork. I presume that she picked it up to place it on the table."

"That's a good start," said the investigator.

He placed the fork by the right hand of the victim. *Dummy, I can't think of it as a real body. Poor Mr. Frampton, Bobby Gee. The man none of us knew.*

"This piece you identified as a wedding cake knife, is that correct?" asked Mr. Hanley. I nodded. "That seems pretty specific. Can't you use any knife to cut a wedding cake?"

"I suppose so," Lorraine said, "But part of the beauty of collecting and using sterling pieces is a hundred years ago and more, craftsmen designed them for very specific uses. Of course, there was time for elegance back then. Today, we have to plan carefully to serve the right foods to match the pieces we want to use. A wedding cake knife would be a treasured piece passed down from one generation to the next, for obvious reasons."

"I see. And Mrs. Frampton showed this to you yesterday during your visit to her house?"

"Yes, she did," I thought for a moment. "She did just that, showed it to me. She was standing on the other side of the round table and held it up for me to see."

He asked me to demonstrate, and I held the knife using both hands, one at each end to show the blade and the pattern of the handle. I was beginning to see the point of this exercise. "Rennie's fingerprints shouldn't be on the handle of the knife because she never held it by the handle. The killer would have grabbed it in her fist."

Mr. Hanley volleyed back, "Unless she took it out of the storage cabinet by picking it up by the handle." He moved to place the knife on the dummy.

"Wait, sir." Lorraine reached out for the knife. "May I?" She put it down on the table. "If I were taking this knife out of the cabinet, I would pick it up this way." She placed her thumb, index and third fingers on the handle near where it joined the blade. "I'd pick it up here because it's better balanced and there's no need to put my hand all around the handle unless I was going to use it. If there are fingerprints on this handle, you have your killer."

Brilliant, I thought. *Why didn't these trained investigators see the logic?*

"A very good point... unless that person claims her prints got on the silver when she was pulling the knife *out* of the body in an attempt to save him."

The room was quiet as we all mulled over that bit of information.

It seems I jumped to the easy conclusion. I wonder if she pulled all the pieces of silver out of the body or just the knife?

"Let's move on." Mr. Hanley picked up the knife sharpener with a sterling silver handle. "And this piece?"

Still stuck on the part about trying to save Rennie's husband, I was slow to answer. "Yes, it's part of a matching set that includes the carving knife and fork here on the table."

He turned to Lorraine. "Would you pick this up the same way you did the cake knife?"

She shook her head. "No, I don't think so. It's much heavier at one end so one would hold it by the handle." The man grunted in agreement and laid the piece by the dummy's head.

I couldn't control my curiosity any longer. "Was that what killed him, a blow to the head?"

"Patience, Ms. Strickland. We're almost done." He took up the carving fork. "What about this piece?" He asked as he handed it to Lorraine.

She took it in her left hand and turned it over so the tines pointed downward. "This is how you'd hold it when carving a roast. It's meant to stabilize or hold the meat in place while you're cutting it with the knife." She handed it back to him.

"The same way you'd hold it if you were stabbing someone." He jabbed the fork in the air and we all jumped.

"Yes, I-I guess that's right," she replied.

"Or pulling it out of the body," I added.

"Very good, Ms. Strickland." He put the fork on the dummy's face.

"Did she stab him in the face? Is that what killed him?" It made me sick to think about it.

"Yes, she stabbed him in the face. The eyes to be exact." He gave us the details straight, without emotion, as if he was reporting a trip to the grocery store instead of the violent way one person ended the life of another. "The two long tines fit over the bridge of the nose quite well." I heard someone groan as he demonstrated. That someone was me. "But that wasn't the killing blow, believe it or not." He picked up the carving knife. "The most lethal weapon in the group did the trick. I know some gang members in Baltimore who'd like this little number. The blade is about ten inches long. A very effective weapon when it's plunged into the chest cavity." I cringed. "I know you hold it one way to cut meat and, if you were pulling it out, you might grab it the opposite way. Either way would work to stab someone." He put the knife on the chest and sighed. "Chief, I think this has been a good exercise," he turned to us. "And I thank you ladies for coming in, but I don't think we have anything conclusive. This concludes the recording." He said quickly, impatient to move on to something else that was a better line of investigation.

We said our good-byes and walked downstairs. The main room of the normally quiet station was still simmering with activity. A violent murder didn't happen often in this area and I guess everyone wanted a taste of the experience. As the Chief liked to say, "There's only so much you can learn in a classroom. Experience is the best teacher." He encouraged participation. The organized chaos of so many people was distracting for me. Somehow uniforms should match, but there was an array of colors: khaki, light blue and black. Some officials wore jackets marked *Police* and of course, the blue-on-blue uniform of the St. Michaels' officers. That seemed to nudge a thought, but it was gone just as fast. Lorraine said goodbye to the short blonde-headed secretary and we bundled up before we went outside to face the wind.

As we snaked our way between parked cars,

Lorraine said, "I'm glad they kept the lighthouse design on the cars." Its bright beam stood out against the blue background color of the police car.

I started to walk away, but after a few steps, I cried, "Wait!"

Lorraine stopped and turned. "What's wrong? Are you sick? Did the—"

"No, no, I'm okay. It's just there's something about the police car or maybe it's the lighthouse there." I went back and looked at the police car again. Mumbling, I walked all the way around the car, looking at all the decals and artwork. "I thought I remembered... No, whatever it was, it is gone."

"Let's go home. Maybe it will come to you." Lorraine suggested.

I started to cross the street when she yanked me back by the arm, out of the path of an oncoming car, another blue police car. "Be careful, Abby!"

I came out of my fog and watched the car driving away. "That's it! It was in a blue pouch. I have to go back." I turned around and sprinted to the front door of the station with Lorraine in my wake, asking why a blue pouch was important.

Inside, I worked my way through the crowd of people again until I reached the staircase in the back. It was tough trying to go up the steps with all the professionals coming down after stealing a look at the dummy Mr. Hanley brought from Baltimore. "Excuse me. I'm sorry. I need to... thank you."

Upstairs, Mr. Hanley was holding an impromptu class for the officers, showing them some detail or another. Everyone was so focused on what he was saying, I couldn't get anyone's attention. I hate it when people are dramatic, but I was tired and felt like I'd been through a sausage grinder. I planted my feet and announced in a loud voice, "She didn't do it!"

Every face turned toward me. My face was turning Christmas red. "She didn't do it," I repeated quietly. As much as I disliked Rennie, I couldn't see her charged for a murder she didn't commit.

Everyone froze except Mr. Hanley, who stepped around the group and came toward me. He stopped, tilted his head to one side and examined my face in the same way he looked at his specimens and evidence. After what seemed like a long time, he continued to stare at me while asking calmly, "Why do you say that?"

"It was the blue police car that made me realize it." They all just stood and stared at me. I wasn't making any sense. I took a deep breath. "Rennie didn't kill her husband because she never touched it."

"Take it slow, Abby," said the Chief. "What didn't she touch?"

"Okay, you asked me to remember exactly what Rennie did when I was at her house yesterday afternoon." The Chief nodded. "At one point, she took out the carving set to show me."

"Yes, that's what you said before." Mr. Hanley frowned and glanced at his watch.

"That's just it. Each piece in the carving set comes in a tarnish-resistant blue pouch to protect it. Rennie took out the carving knife and fork so her prints would be on those pieces, but she handed me the sharpener.

I'm the one who took it out of its blue pouch. I slipped it out, examined it and put it on the table next to the rest of the set. Rennie never touched it. Her prints wouldn't be on it." I sucked in a quick breath. "You said Mr. Frampton was hit over the head with the sharpener. You know why my prints are on the handle but the other set of prints belongs to the killer."

Mr. Hanley crossed his arms over his chest and continued to peer at me while he considered this new information. Then, he went over to the table, picked up a file and consulted a report inside. After several moments, he closed the file and said to the Chief, "I think we'd better bring her upstairs."

The Chief nodded and gave the assignment to L.T., one of his senior officers. The man was about to leave the room when he asked, "Ah, which one, sir?'

The man shook his head sadly, "Millie. Bring Millie in."

"What about Mrs. Frampton, sir?"

"Leave her where she is for the time being."

Mr. Hanley spoke to the officer who had just put away the camera. "Would you take unpack the camera and record Ms. Strickland's statement. And I'll have a few questions as well." Then, his serious expression relaxed into a smile. "But I think you may have nailed it."

CHAPTER TWENTY-TWO

*There are two ways to serve lemon pieces: the lemon server that
has a raised edge on one side slides under a slice and is then
served; the two or three sharp tines of the lemon fork can pierce
the thick rind of the tart fruit.*
—"The Butler's Guide to Fine Silver" Mr. Hollister, 1898

It took some time to answer all the different ways
Mr. Hanley asked about the knife sharpener, but in the
end, he was pleased with my answers and observations.
He and the Chief felt confident they could charge Millie
with Bobby Gee's murder because of my information
and the fact that they found her prints on the knife, the
piece of silver that caused his death. But there were
still some important questions about why she attacked
the man and what was she doing in his house anyway.
Motive, always the key.

I waited until the investigator was busy with
paperwork to ask the Chief if we could talk privately for
a minute. He led me to a corner and I related what I'd
seen in the parking lot during the Christmas parade and
how I wasn't the only one watching Grant and Rennie.
I could have sworn it was Millie in the shadows. Then I

reminded him that I'd listened, from behind a Victorian sofa, to the conversation in the back room of the antique store. He started to breathe fire so I rushed on, suggesting that he might want to talk to Jeff about seeing the lovebirds, too and to confirm he saw Millie as well.

He said he'd look into it, but he wasn't pleased. "I really hate it when you put yourself in compromising positions, Abby," he said sadly. "I don't want you to get hurt."

"I didn't and I won't," I said brightly, more than ready to escape.

As he walked me downstairs, he said, "We have one piece of unfinished business."

Remembering the arrival of the new puzzle that morning almost knocked me over. I was about to give him the bad news when a shrill voice distracted me.

"Stop pushing. Don't touch me." It was Millie being brought into the station with her hands cuffed behind her back. Her dark chocolate brown hair hung limp around her face. Her splotchy face was drawn from lack of sleep.

The Chief raised his voice to be heard over her stream of demands. "Put her in the interrogation room."

"I don't want to talk to you! I have nothing to say," she squawked.

"Easy, Millie. We're just going —"

"We're gonna do nothing," she snarled. "I don't have to talk to you."

Calmly, he said, "That's your right, Millie. You don't have to say a thing but then we won't know why you did what you did." He raised his shoulders, resigned.

She squinted at him, filled with suspicion, then glanced at me. I could see an idea blossom in her mind as her eyes relaxed and a smile grew on her lips. It was an idea she liked very much. She assumed a haughty pose with her chin held high. She spoke in a controlled voice only tinged with attitude. "All right then. I'll tell what happened, but I won't tell you." She whipped her head around and glared at me. "I'll only talk to her."

His eyes went wide with surprise. "No, Millie. That's not gonna happen."

Her snide tone was back. "If you want to know what I did, I get to tell her and only her."

"She's not part of the police department and I don't think your lawyer—"

"I don't want a lawyer. I don't need a lawyer. It's her or nothing!" Her anger was building.

"Why do you want her? Who is she?" I admired how quickly he could switch tactics.

She looked at me and her eyes softened. "She's just like me," she said in a little voice. "She's alone, too. And Miss Lorraine likes her."

I touched his sleeve. His eyes searched my face. "Are you sure, Abby?"

I nodded and we followed Millie and the officer into a small, almost empty room. A camera hung high on the wall staring down at us. She was put in a chair on the other side of the table and the handcuffs were transferred to a holding ring to secure her in one place.

After signing a paper waiving her right to an attorney, she settled back in the metal armchair. "Ah, that's nice. Chief, you can leave us now and take all your men with you." She looked over at me and smiled. "We'll be fine, just having a little girl talk."

Looking at me, he raised his eyebrows to ask silently if I was okay. I blinked slowly in response. "But you stay on this side of the table, no matter what," he said softly. "Got it?"

I took a deep breath to steady myself. "Got it."

"I'll be right outside." He stepped into the corridor and, as he closed the door, I heard Lorraine say that she didn't think this was a good idea. With a click of the lock, the real world went away and I was left with this young woman whom I'd first set eyes on a few short days ago. We'd never been introduced. I didn't even know her last name. When I first saw her crying at the big table in the Cove, I remembered thinking there was nothing distinctive about her, that at a party she'd blend into the wallpaper. Not anymore. Now that she had gotten the attention she wanted on her terms, she was smoothing down her hair and checking out the small room painted a pale yellow and smiling as if it met with her approval.

Millie wiggled in her chair, getting comfortable, and smiled at me. "This is nice, you and me together."

I was almost afraid to say anything. *Don't think about what she did last night*, I told myself. *Maybe if I sit quietly, she'll spew out the details. The Chief will have her confession and I can get the hell out of here. Okay, here goes...*

I smiled.

It was a little smile. I hoped she didn't see my lips twitching the effort.

"Do you know why I picked you?" All I could do was shake my head no. "Well, let me tell you. We've never met, you know, formally, but I know all about you. I know you've got people around you, just like me. And you don't have a special person, one who loves you, just like me. I think you'll understand..." She pointed her thumb at the door. "And make them understand... because you're alone, just like me."

She smiled as if we were the oldest of friends. As she leaned toward me, I fought the reaction to pull back. "And I picked you because *she* hates you!" I must have looked confused because she started bouncing in her seat with glee. "Rennie, of course."

"She hates me? But why?"

"Rennie has been here almost a year and nobody likes her. You moved to the Shore only a month ago and everybody loves you. She's so jealous that you're good friends with Miss Lorraine, too." She leaned back in her chair and gave me a big smile. "I say, any friend of Miss Lorraine's is a friend of mine."

"Is that why you asked for me?"

"Yup!" The girl settled back, rubbed the arms of the chair with the palms of her hands and chuckled. "It'll make her so angry that I talked to you. Ask me anything you want. I want you to tell people it was all a mistake."

A moment ago, I didn't know what to say. Now, the questions tumbled around my mind and I didn't know which to pick first. I jumped in. "Millie, what was a mistake?"

"Killing Mr. Frampton. Heck, I didn't even know the man. I didn't want to kill him."

I thought that was all there was to it, a mistake or accident. But she wasn't finished.

"I didn't mean to kill him. I went out there to hurt her."

I knew I shouldn't react and just keep her talking, but it was hard not to show the horrified shock I felt.

Trying to keep calm, I went on. "Millie, who did you want to hurt?"

She sneered, "Mrs. Rennie Frampton, of course. You have no idea what a bad woman she is. She's mean and selfish. Yes, she's selfish. She wants it all for herself and won't leave things alone so somebody else…" Her voice trailed off as she stared off into space.

"Millie? Somebody else… like who?"

Her eyes, glistening with tears, slowly moved to meet mine. "Like me." Her lower lip came out to form a pout. "She wouldn't let me be happy. She took it away."

"How did she do that?"

Fat tears swelled and rolled over her lashes and down her cheeks. I pulled some tissues from my bag and pushed them across the table, making sure I pulled my hand away before she could touch me.

She wiped her eyes and blew her nose. "She came here from the big city with her big ideas. She dazzled him, blinded him so he couldn't see what was standing right in front of him. Me, she took him away from me."

"W-who?"

"Why, Grant, of course. Such a nice man. Warm, funny, so excited about everything." Millie drew up the corners of her mouth into a soft smile. Her eyes drifted to the empty space next to me and she sighed like a young girl in love. "So happy, but then *she* came to town and ended it all for me. I could have stood in front of

him naked, totally naked and he wouldn't have seen me.
All because of her." Millie leaned her arms on the table
and we sat quietly while she shredded the damp tissues
that held her tears. "It was all her fault. If she'd just go
away, everything would be okay again. It could happen.
Anybody who traveled so much must not like it here. I
figured it was only a matter of time. Whenever she left
town, I thought that was it, she's gone. Good-bye and
good riddance. But she always came back."

She straightened up in her chair with pride. "If she
wasn't going to stay away by her own choice, I wanted
to make sure she went away and stayed away." Without
warning, the tears started up again. "But she poisoned
his mind and he told me that I was the one who had to
go, not her." She rubbed her face. "Not fair, it's not fair."

"Millie, how could he tell you to go away? You—"

"She made him tell me that I had to change my shop
– my sweet little Ray of Sunshine Shop – change it into
some horrid store filled with old, smelly stuff. Antiques.
Who likes that junk anyway?"

*Grant, Rennie's playtoy she used to fill her time while
her husband was out of town, along with their dream for St.
Michaels were at the center of all this.*

"Your shop is your shop, isn't it?" She nodded,
moving her whole upper body. "So, how could he force
you to change it?"

All the emotion drained out of her face. She looked
at me with eyes devoid of hope. "He's my landlord. He
threatened that if I didn't change my shop, he'd raise my rent
so high, I couldn't survive. How could he do that to me?"

"You have a lease, don't you? It protects..." She

was shaking her head.

"I'm on month-to-month. Daddy's trying to buy me a little building and— Oh no!" Her hands flew to her mouth. "Daddy's going to kill me."

"Millie," I said, trying to be very matter-of-fact. "Your daddy isn't going to hurt you." I paused for a moment to let that sink in... and it did. I was surprised how much she trusted me. "Okay, what did you say to Grant?"

"It wasn't Grant, not really. It was her. She made him say those awful things. I worked it out that if she wasn't here anymore, he'd go back to being a kind, loving person again and everything would be all right. All I had to do was get her to leave... permanently."

"How were you going to do that?"

"I thought I'd talk to her – tell her how things had to be. Then she'd sell up and leave."

"But something happened, didn't it?" She stared into space again. "You were there, weren't you? You saw them in the parking lot, didn't you?" She lowered her head and rested her chin on her chest. "Millie? Is that when everything changed?" The woman gave me a little nod in response but kept her chin low. "Tell me how it changed?" Silence. "Okay, I'll tell you what I think and you let me know if I'm right." She nodded again.

"You thought they were getting too friendly and you had to do something to get her away from him." I paused but she'd didn't say anything. "What I don't understand is how you thought you were going to do that?"

Her head popped up. "Easy. Her husband is out of

town all the time and she's alone in that great big house. I went over last night and let myself in. I thought we'd sit in the kitchen having coffee or sit on her bed like a slumber party and work everything out."

Don't show your disbelief at this girl's strange idea of how the world works! I ordered myself. *Stay cool and keep it simple.*

"Millie, most of those houses have alarm systems. How were you going to get inside?"

"Easy. I got in last night and she didn't know it, did she? I picked the lock on the garage door. They're usually simple locks, not like the ones on the front or patio doors. If I could get through there, I was in. Most people don't lock the door that goes from the garage to the kitchen." She raised her shoulders. "You see, I had to learn how to pick a lock like that, the same kind that's on my little shop. When I first started, I kept forgetting or losing the keys. I wasn't used to carrying keys. We never locked up stuff out at the farm. This is the Eastern Shore, for heaven's sake. But I had to lock the shop when I wasn't there and Daddy kept getting on me about being responsible. If I couldn't keep track of the keys, he'd say, I didn't deserve my Little Ray of Sunshine shop. I taught myself how to get through the door without those stupid keys. A bobby pin, a credit card, there are all kinds of things to use. I even got myself a set of lock picks and now it's real hard to keep me out of pretty much anywhere."

This woman was a disaster waiting to happen... for a long time.

"So you picked the garage door. What if the alarm

had gone off?"

She gave me a little shrug. "I would have run off to the trees right near there. By the time anyone came, I'd be long gone."

"But the alarm didn't go off," I said.

"No, and I thought it was a sign that things were turning my way." She squeezed her arms and shoulders tight to her body and her eyes were wide, like an excited child anticipating a treat. She clasped her hands together as best she could with the handcuffs on.

"Then what happened?"

She twisted her face -- concentrating, trying to get everything just right. "I went into the kitchen where she had some lights on low so I could see everything. I was getting my bearings when I heard keys at the front door and a man walked in. He came down a hall into the kitchen and saw me there. I don't know who was more surprised, him or me. He started shouting, demanding who I was and what I was doing in his house."

Mr. Frampton. Boy, did you pick the wrong time to come home, Bobby Gee.

Her eyes seemed to glaze over and I could tell she was back in Rennie's house, seeing it happen all over again.

"I backed into a dark room, turns out it was the dining room. I was trying to get away. He followed me, all crazy."

"You were a stranger in his house."

She shrugged. "I only wanted to talk to *her*. That's when the hall light snapped on. *She* called down. He ignored her and kept coming. I bumped into something and there was nowhere to go. I reached behind me and felt something sharp. I grabbed it and held it out trying to scare him off. He lunged at me. I didn't realize I was holding a big fork until just before it went in his eyes. There was nothing I could do."

The carving fork.

She covered her face with her hands and her words were muffled. "What else could I do? I had to defend myself. Daddy always taught me that."

Not when you've broken into somebody's home! Deep breath, deep breath.

I had to prompt her because I knew that the Chief needed a detailed confession. "Then what happened?"

"It was awful, the way he was waving his arms around. Guess he couldn't see." To demonstrate, she closed her eyes tight, raised her face toward the ceiling and flailed her arms in the air. I moved back so she couldn't reach me.

"I thought I could get away, but he started coming at me again. I reached back and grabbed something else and stuck it in his hand." She snickered. "Not that it was going to do much to stop him, but boy, did it make him howl."

The lemon serving fork that looked like a small trident.

"*She* called out again. If she came downstairs, they could box me in and get me in trouble. I couldn't let that happen. She'd hurt me enough. It was time for me to hurt her. She'd taken my guy away from me so it was only fair for me to take this man away from her."

"Kill him?" I tried to keep disgust and disbelief out of my voice.

"If I had to. They say, 'All's fair in love and war.' I was in love and this was war. It worked for me." She looked at her nails and went after some dirt under one of them.

"What did you do next?"

"I looked over my shoulder and saw all these silver things all shiny in the light from the kitchen. I picked up a couple of them and went after him. One felt kinda heavy, so I hit him on the head."

The knife sharpener.

"The other had a sharp point, so I swung it. Got him on the face."

The wedding cake knife.

"But he kept coming so I grabbed a big ole knife and bam!" She made a fist as if holding the knife and thrust it forward till her arm was out straight. After a moment, her body relaxed and her hand bounced on the table. "That's when things got crazy."

Only then, Millie?

"He staggered, then fell over on his back. *She* was standing in the archway and screamed. I had to think fast." Millie put her elbows on the table and lowered her voice. "You see, she's real smart. She'd say that I killed her husband. It would be her word against mine and I knew everyone would believe *her*, Miss High-and-Mighty. No one ever believed in me." Her lips slowly stretched into a smile. "That's when I got the greatest idea ever."

"I started screaming, too. 'You killed him. I saw you. You killed him 'cause you want Grant.' Then I looked at the body on the floor with all those nice silver things sticking out and realized that my fingerprints were all over them." She giggled. "That's when I got my next best idea. 'I have to save him,' I yelled and threw myself on the floor next to his body, grabbing the silver and yanking it out. She came after me, beating on me with her fists. When she saw all the blood running out, she threw herself on him and tried to cover all the holes with her hands but there were too many of them. I didn't count, but there were a lot. She ran in the kitchen and dialed 911, I guess. I was busy putting my hands on everything. That's how both of us got so bloody. It was one royal mess, I'll tell you."

"What else happened?" I asked, trying to keep the horror out of my voice.

She shook her head gently. "Nothing, really. We yelled at each other till the police got there and well, you know the rest." She leaned back and rubbed the arms of the chair again. "I did what I went there to do. Hurt her. Make her pay. And I did."

"But Millie, I'm confused. Where was Grant in all this? Did he —"

She interrupted me with a declaration. "Grant and me, we love each other. He just doesn't know it yet."

CHAPTER TWENTY-THREE

The hallmarks that appear on sterling silver pieces made in the United Kingdom and Ireland offer a wealth of historical background. A mark indicates the purity of the silver used. A date mark letter shows the exact year the piece was made. A city mark such as a crown or anchor identifies the place of manufacture. Not least is the unique mark to identify the maker or silversmith.

—"The Butler's Guide to Fine Silver" Mr. Hollister, 1898

The door burst open and the Chief came and stood with me while officers put the handcuffs back on Millie's wrists. "Put her in the holding cell. They'll transport her soon."

As she was about to leave the room, she stopped. "You'll make them understand, won't you, Abby? She's a bad lady and it's only fair what I did."

I couldn't stop myself. "Millie, you said no one believed in you, remember?"

"That's right. They would've believed her, not me, just like they always do."

"You're wrong about that. Your daddy believed in you when he gave you that little shop."

The stunned look on her face was the last thing I saw of her.

The Chief closed the door and sat with me. "You did good, Abby. We got it all."

"One sad story."

"Her perception was her reality." He shook his head. "Not uncommon among people who do bad things."

Looking over his shoulder, I saw Lorraine standing in a corner waiting for me. She gave me a sad smile and a small nod. "Chief, you can keep this world of yours. I'm going back to my sterling silver," I said as I started to get up from the hard chair.

"Ah, not quite yet. We have a bit of unfinished business. The chalice?"

"Chief, do you think it was Millie who hurt Kat?"

He took a deep breath that made his chest fill out his white shirt. "It's a possibility, but my sense tells me she didn't have anything to do with it. We'll have to wait and see how that investigation develops."

I suddenly realized that, with all the commotion about Bobby Gee's murder, the Chief might not know about the surprise visitor we had. "Did Lorraine tell you that Stewart Greer came to see us at Fair Winds? He stopped just short of accusing Pastor Paul of stealing the chalice."

"What? I think that's pretty far-fetched, don't you?"

"Yes, but he made a fairly strong case," I said though it pained me. "He said that Assistant Pastor Paul had set up an account and has been moving money into it without anyone's knowledge."

"Before we start chasing every wild idea, let's follow up on the last message the thief left. Once we have the chalice and the mystery man from the courthouse square, we'll deal with other things. Do you have a solution to the puzzle yet?"

I groaned and dropped back in the chair. "I have bad news. I can't make heads or tails out of it." I took the printed copy of the scan out of my bag and laid it on the table. "Well, that's not quite true. I have some ideas, but... Look at these first two lines of the message."

He picked up my copy of the message, lined it up on the sharp edge of the table and tore off the top part, the personal attack against me. "It's all in the wrist," he said and balled it up and threw it in the wastebasket. "There, that's what I think of that." He came back to the table and put down the puzzle so we both could see it.

"I have no idea what a halo, handcuffs, a lion and a bee have in common?" My frustration was showing. "And then you have the numbers, twelve and thirty-one. There is one thing." I pointed at the space between the two numbers. "That looks like a colon. Could it be a time of day, like thirty-one minutes past noon… or maybe it's midnight? I don't know. It doesn't make any sense to me."

"Twelve thirty-one. Twelve thirty-one," he mumbled, thinking. "There's something about those numbers."

"Twelve *colon* thirty one," I corrected. "For heaven's sake, this is a sacred chalice. You think we'd get a little divine inspiration." While he was thinking, I listened to the muffled sounds of the investigators down the hall. Then, I started to get up again. "If you think of something…"

There was a big grin on his face. Softly, he said, "12:31 'You shall love your neighbor as yourself.' The Book of Mark, Chapter 12, Verse 31."

The air was electric. "How did you get that?"

A deep, booming laugh burst out of the Chief that shook his whole body. Then, he started to hiccup. He patted his chest, trying to get himself under control, but his broad smile stretched across his face and made me chuckle. As he settled down, he looked at his shoes. I realized that for the first time since I met him, "Lucky" Lucan – the tough, strong, macho Chief of Police for St. Michaels – was a little embarrassed… no, shy.

"How did I figure it out? My grandmother," he said.

I shook my head, trying to clear my mind. "I'm sorry. You've lost me."

"She always made me go to Sunday school and drilled me on my Bible verses. The first numbers identify my favorite verse: 'You shall love your neighbor as yourself.' If we all followed that directive, I'd be out of a job. Since we don't, I, along with my fellow officers around the world, am pretty busy. To tell you the truth, that's one of the reasons I became a police officer – to keep the honest people honest and put away the ones who don't get it, so they'll stop hurting people."

We looked at the paper together. "So, you really think..." I began.

"You have a better idea?"

"Well, no..." I said.

"Let's see if we can make it work. We've got a halo, the scales of justice, handcuffs, a lion, but I don't know how the bee fits in. The halo suggests a saint. The scales of justice and the handcuffs could refer to people working in the justice system. It fits. Mark is the patron saint of notaries and others, I think. I've heard pastors call him *Saint Mark the Lionhearted.*"

He pulled open the door. "I have a Bible in my office. Be right back."

In moments, he gently laid the book on the table and opened it. "If I'm right..." He flipped through the pages looking for the passage Mark 12:31:

Thou shalt love thy neighbor as thyself.

"So far, so good."

I looked at this experienced law enforcement officer who lived close to violence. Over the past few months, he'd shown me a little of his private side – his love of family, his caring for people like Lorraine who had loved and lost plus his gentleness with animals and victims.

Seeing him leaning over a bible somehow, it looked right. "Let's look at the next one," he said.

14 15

"There's another halo so I guess we're looking for another patron saint?" I suggested.

"Could be. A pen used to write a book?"

I was picking up the rhythm. "The artist's palette and the Mona Lisa…if we go with your idea that these symbols are associated with a patron saint…" I pulled out my smartphone and set up a search. "Maybe it's the patron saint associated of writers and painters or artists." I drilled down into a website. "Here it is. Saint John the Evangelist. Does that sound right?"

"Let's see." He turned the thin pages. "Okay, I'm in the Book of John. What are the numbers?"

"14 and 15, no colon this time."

"The thief probably figured that if we got this far, we'd know these were references to the Bible and wouldn't need the colon as a crutch. So, Chapter 14, okay. Verse 15…" His finger traveled down the page. "Got it"

If you love Me, you will keep My commandments.

"Great. The thief started this whole thing by breaking the commandment, *Thou shalt not steal*," I said. "If these are messages to the congregation and the pastor, maybe the thief believes other commandments have been broken as well."

"Makes sense, I guess."

I scrolled through an entry on my phone. "Oh, here's the connection between Saint Mark and the bee. It says that he is the patron saint for people dealing with an insect bite. That's pretty specific. I wonder—"

"No time. Let's look at the next clue." The Chief was on a roll.

265

I rubbed my forehead. *What I wouldn't give for some aspirin.* "It's been a long time since I played an instrument, but I don't think the notes are significant. There aren't enough of them. Let's see who is the patron saint for musicians." I tapped my phone's screen and the answer came up. "Saint Cecelia. Is she in the Bible?"

"No, I don't think so."

We both checked our sources—I looked on the internet and he looked in the Bible—and we couldn't find anything.

"Maybe it's something else entirely." I could barely keep the disappointment out of my voice.

The Chief was mumbling one word over and over: music. Then he slapped his forehead with the palm of his hand. "I'm glad my grandmother isn't here. She'd be telling me what a thick skull and a lame brain I have and I wouldn't want you to be hearing all that."

"What? I don't understand."

"Music… in the Bible… as in songs… as in the Psalms! Let's see what Psalms 25:5 says." He quoted:

I hate the assembly of evildoers, and I will
not sit with the wicked.

"The thief really has a problem with the congregation."

"Does it seem like it's telling a story?" Excitement crept into my voice. "Maybe this is the explanation for everything that's happened. If we figure this out, maybe we'll find the chalice and learn why he took it."

"It's the best option we have. Let's run with it."

There was a tap on the door. Lorraine poked her head in. "Before you run anywhere, I thought you'd want to know that Dawkins just called my cell. Ryan is heading toward the boat dock at Fair Winds. Were you expecting him?"

With everything going on, I completely forgot. What an idiot. "What time is it? Oh, it doesn't matter. He asked me to go on a short cruise up the Miles to see the ruins of the St. Johns Chapel and I said sure. I thought all this mess would be over, but it's not. I can't go now."

Lorraine and the Chief exchanged glances.

"Oh, yes you can," declared the Chief. "I think you've done more than your fair share of crime-busting for one day. I'll take the rest of these clues to the good people at the church. This is more their bailiwick than yours." He focused his chocolate brown eyes on me. "You've done enough, Abby. Now, get along with you." Lorraine had her keys in her hand. "And wear something warm."

CHAPTER TWENTY-FOUR

On British and Irish silver, the assayer's mark to show the purity of the silver is a Lion Passant, a lion with one paw raised. A hallmark is applied to the silver using a hammer and punch. It is a process that leaves sharp edges and metal spurs. After, a final polishing is required before a piece is offered.
— "The Butler's Guide to Fine Silver" Mr. Hollister, 1898

I didn't keep Ryan waiting very long and we were on our way under a deep blue sky and a sun that kept us warm. It was probably the last gasp of good weather before winter set in. I'd stopped in my cottage to pull on some warm clothes, a hat that came down over my ears and a thick cuddly fisherman knit sweater. I was overheated by the time I got to the dock. I assumed it was the clothing and not my proximity to this hunk of a man. He wore a heavy white fisherman-knit sweater and mirrored sunglasses to protect his eyes from the glare off the water. His hat and gloves were on the dashboard of the boat. This rugged outdoorsman must have wanted to feel the wind in his hair.

I had to laugh as I approached the dock. Ryan and Simon were frolicking.

"I hope you don't mind. I brought him a toy and some cookies."

I shrugged. "Who am I to object? Look at him. He loves it." Simon had the toy in his mouth and was racing from one end of the dock to the other at top speed.

"I thought we'd take him with us," Ryan suggested. "He's proven that he can behave on board. Even though this boat is smaller, I think he'll be okay."

"Why didn't you bring your sailboat?"

"The place we're going is too shallow and…" Were my eyes glazing over? "You don't need the details. The little boat is better. Come aboard."

He showed me where the life jackets were stowed and laid out the heavy rain jacket I'd worn the night of the parade. "Just in case you get cold." He called Simon to the boat and cast off. "We're going up the river away from St. Michaels and the Bay."

"Why do they call it the Miles River? Should it be the St. Michaels River or am I missing something?"

He grinned. "You got it right! It was called the St. Michaels River. Then a Quaker community was established in the area. They wouldn't call it the Saint Michaels River because saints were not part of their belief so they called it the Michaels. Over time, people got sloppy in their speech and the local people started saying it was the *Miles*."

Traveling the area by water gave me a new perspective. Always intrigued by the barely-marked driveways along the St. Michaels Road, I now saw where those roadways led: beautiful homes with large windows and wide porches to enjoy the water views.

At this point, the river was about a mile wide and the sky was truly a large dome over our heads because the land was so flat. I remembered with a shiver that the flatness of the land here was one thing Kat hated about the area. She was home now. Her family had taken her body back to the mountains she loved for the funeral and internment. And now, another woman was making plans to take her husband's body back to New York for a funeral. A shudder ran through me as I remembered the matter-of-fact way Millie had described her need to hurt Rennie and make her go away. Her reasoning made perfect sense to her and was horrible to me.

Ryan spoke over the drone of the engine. "I'm not going to give you a penny for your thoughts. I'm going to give you something else to think about."

How did he know I was thinking about Kat and getting distracted from the beauty right in front of me?

"Many property owners in this area, people like Lorraine, still run working farms so things haven't changed much in that way since the time of the Revolutionary War. In fact, there's a legend that has to do with silver. Like to hear it?"

Simon came over and curled up on the bench seat next to me with his head on my lap.

"Now we're ready for story time." We both smiled.

"Before the fighting started, there were lots of meetings on how to respond to the British. It took days for the mail to travel from places like Boston, New York, Philadelphia, even Baltimore so the men traveled to those cities for face-to-face meetings. They hoped that their homes and families would be safe while they were gone and, to reduce the possibility of an attack or theft, they would transfer or hide the family valuables.

"One of the property owners used a large strongbox to hold money, jewelry and the family silver, then he'd bury it somewhere on the farm. When he returned, he'd dig it up and life would go on."

I remembered the story of the family who owned the chalice originally. They too were afraid somebody might come to take it so they gave it to the church to keep it safe.

Ryan went on with his story. "There was one time—"

I gasped. "Oh no..."

"Yes, you guessed it. Before he left on a trip to Philadelphia, he buried the box on his land and didn't tell anyone where it was. In the big city, he caught a fever and died... before he could tell anyone of the location of the box. The story goes that his wife had men digging holes all over the place, but they never found it. Today, from time to time, treasure hunters will ask for permission to dig around. I'm not sure they know which farm it was. Maybe the search is part of the fun."

Oh Ryan, if you only knew. Our search for the missing chalice has been deadly.

He did a double take looking at my face. "Uh, oh. Did I say something to upset you?"

"No," I said quickly, trying to put on a happy face. "I'm enjoying our cruise. Where are we going?"

"See that marker with a reflective sign marked 7 up ahead?" He pointed to something that looked like a tripod sticking high out of the water. "On top is equipment to operate the light at night, but on top of that flat surface is a nesting place for osprey, known as the sea hawk. They come home to this area in the warm months to mate. The same nesting pair has returned to Number 7 for the past eight years, built their big nests out of sticks and raised three chicks each year. We won't see them. They've flown south for the winter."

The number 7. Where had I seen... The number seven was one of the symbols in the list of clues. It must have been important, but—

"Abby?"

"Huh? What?"

"You were a thousand miles away," he said with concern. "Is there anything..."

"Yes, Florida... sounds so nice and warm." I cuddled into my scarf.

He continued to talk about the birds, but his face showed worry... worry about me. "Osprey don't stop at Florida. They fly down the east coast of South America to Venezuela and beyond."

"I'll have to watch for them next spring if I'm still here."

"I hope you are," he said softly.

I could barely hear him over the drone of the engine, but I said, "Me too." We looked at one another for a long moment, then I broke the spell and looked away, feeling shy and yes, a little scared but thrilled, all at the same time. I looked out over the water. "Are we running out of river? It's a lot narrower here."

He throttled back the engine and pointed up ahead toward a modern bridge across the water. "It's just on the other side of that bridge. There used to be a ferry there for people living on the other side of the river who wanted to travel to St. Michaels. It wasn't an easy trip a century ago or more. It could take a whole day, even in good weather. And that was a problem for people who wanted to worship at the church in town. So, the church fathers of Christ Church wisely built a chapel – St. John's – here that was more convenient for their parishioners."

He backed off our speed again and we slipped under the bridge. On the other side, he pointed to the left.

"It's in ruins!" Partial stone walls and Gothic window openings were all that was left of the old chapel. The roof was gone and nature was slowly reclaiming the site with ivy, grasses and other native plants encroaching on the once sacred space. "What happened?

"Love happened," he said softly.

"The families who lived on this side of the river came to this chapel and they brought their children and farm workers, everybody came. That's where a teenage boy and girl met and fell in love. He was the son of farm workers that worked up and down the coast during the harvest season. She was the daughter of a large landowner. Her father went crazy when he found out she'd gone to the church to meet the boy and they were going to run off together. The kids were willing to give up everything to be together. The father went after her and took his gun."

I looked over the smooth water as we floated in the cove, a sadness bearing down on me.

"Nobody knows what happened or isn't saying.

The fact is her father shot the boy and he died. They called it an accident, but the girl never recovered. The story goes that she drowned herself in this cove rather than live with a broken heart. People couldn't forget what happened and let the chapel fall into disrepair. Now, it's beyond salvaging." I could feel the sting of tears welling up in my eyes. "But that's not the end of the story."

He came and sat next to me. I turned to him, hoping for some redeeming part of a real-life story of Romeo and Juliet.

"Since the parish stopped holding services here, two swans have come to this cove every year to spend spring, summer and fall together, raising their families. Swans mate for life and some say the swans are the spirits of the young boy and girl who have come home to be in the one place they were happy, the chapel." He shrugged, "I know it's far-fetched but I like to think it's true."

"Why does it have to be so hard when you find someone to love?" I thought of Millie, who wanted so badly to be in love that she was willing to hurt another person, even take a life. A tear spilled over and ran down my face.

He wiped it away and took my face in his hands. "It doesn't have to be... once you find the one person you want to be with throughout eternity." Ever so gently, he pressed his lips to mine.

A warm puff of air caressed my cheeks as if the spirits of the lovers approved. I moved into him and slowly wrapped my arms around him.

The boat rocked gently and Simon barked. Ryan and I jumped and hit heads. The mood broken, we both started laughing... but his words echoed in my mind.

Once you find the one person you want to be with throughout eternity.

Where had I heard that? Someone else talked about eternity. Slowly, it came back to me.

She was the love of my life. I would do anything for her, for us. We always tried to live a good life so we could spend eternity together.

"That's it!" I jumped up, making the boat rock madly.

"Hey, easy there." He took hold of my arm and gently guided me back down to the seat. "I've never gotten a reaction like that before. It was a great kiss but—"

"No, not that." I saw his face fall. "No, I mean. Oh..." And I kissed him. "That, that is very good, but right now, there's something I have to finish."

"What's so import—"

I grimaced. "I can't tell you."

He flinched back a little in surprise. "Can't tell me," he repeated. He turned slowly and looked straight out over the water, trying to make sense out of what was happening.

I bit my lip. It was way too early for me to put up a wall between us but I'd promised. "I really, really want to tell you but ... you have to trust me." I wanted so much for him to go along with me that I was almost pleading.

"Trust you," he repeated.

"Right now, you need to take me back to Fair Winds and fast."

He searched my face for some answers.

Everything was still while I waited. The boat didn't rock. Simon sat frozen as he watched us. He leaped to the deck in surprise when Ryan slapped his hands down on his thighs.

"Okay, I trust you." He went over to the boat controls. "If the lady wants to go back to Fair Winds, we go back to Fair Winds, Simon." The dog barked in agreement and Ryan started the engine.

I pulled out my phone and almost fell overboard when Ryan nudged the throttle forward. There was no question in my mind that he was taking me seriously.

Finally, all the pieces had clicked into place. I felt like I had a good idea of what was going on and I had to tell the Chief. I dialed his number but the call failed. I tried again, same thing. I looked. Barely one bar. The cell companies were upgrading the service in the area, but they still had holes to fill and I was in one of them. We tried Ryan's phone with the same result.

"I've got to get to town to tell the Chief."

"Hold on, I'll get you there as fast as I can."

I held on to the rail and to Simon as we flew over the water.

CHAPTER TWENTY-FIVE

Always handle sterling silver with care. If you do not allow ample time for the polishing process or rush the selection and delivery of pieces, grievous damage could occur.
—"The Butler's Guide to Fine Silver" Mr. Hollister, 1898

"Abby," Ryan yelled over the roar of the engine and the splashing of his super quick power boat against the water. "Tell me what's so urgent. Are you in trouble?"

I was busy holding on to Simon and trying to keep my hair out of my eyes and mouth, while trying not to bounce out of the boat. It might have been the coward's way out, but I yelled back at him, "I can't hear you."

Fortunately, he believed me. There wasn't any room for conversation because of everything going on in my head. Facts, suspicions, and random thoughts were swirling around, trying to make connections and when they didn't, they came in at a new angle. My intuition told me I was right, but should I trust it? This time, I'd give the Chief everything I had and let him handle it."

Ryan yelled, "There's Red #2. See the lighthouse at the Maritime Museum?" He steered the boat in a wide turn toward the St. Michaels harbor and throttled back. The bow of the boat settled down in the water.

"Why are we going so slow?" I asked.

His answer sounded a little impatient. "Because we're in the harbor. In the harbor, we go slow."

I nodded and looked around. Might as well enjoy the view before I talked to the Chief. *The Chief!* I pulled out my phone again. Bars! I dialed again, the call went through and he answered.

"Chief, Chief, where are you? It's Abby. I know—"

"Whoa, slow down. I'm in my office and why do you want to know?"

"Great! Don't leave. I'm on my way. We're coming in the harbor now." I clicked off and saw Ryan staring at me. He was sitting on the back of the driver's seat, his back straight. Slowly, he lowered his sunglasses to study me. Suspicion pulsed around him like a neon sign. I knew if I didn't handle the next few minutes well, it would affect our relationship. What could I tell Ryan without betraying the trust Lorraine, the Chief... everybody had put in me to keep silent?

"Look, you're right. Something's going on and I'm involved but—"

"Something bad is happening and you're working with the Chief."

"Right, but it will all be okay. Thanks to you, I think I have the missing piece for the Chief. And it's all because of something you said." I pointed toward the park. "Can you take me over there please? Right there by the ladder will be fine." *Oh, I have to get out of this boat before I blow it and tell him everything.*

"Abby, what did I say? I don't—"

"And could you take care of Simon for a few minutes? I'll be right back." I scrambled up the ladder and called out, "Thanks" as I hustled down the street toward the police station a couple of blocks away.

When I got to the police station and walked into the Chief's office, I had to sit down to catch my breath.

He stood at his desk going through the mail, waiting patiently. When he was done, he dropped the last envelope on the stack and said, "Well? What's so urgent?"

"I know who took the chalice… or at least I think I do." I huffed.

"Okay, let's hear it."

"It's a man."

"That certainly narrows it down, but we knew that from the courthouse square." He rubbed the back of his neck as if I was causing the pain.

I sank back into the chair and steeled myself against the lecture that I knew was coming my way. "Something happened at the concert that I didn't tell you about…" He opened his mouth but I rushed on. "I didn't tell you because I didn't think it was important. I thought I'd intruded on someone's private conversation, but now I think it was the thief." I recounted my visit to the cemetery during the concert and what I overheard.

The Chief sat up in his chair, put his elbows on his desk and peppered me with questions.

"You say it was a man's voice?"

"I think so. It was deep like a man's voice."

"Did you recognize it?" I shook my head. "Did

you hear the person he was talking to?"

I paused, thinking. "That's strange. I don't remember hearing anyone else..."

"Or he was talking to a woman with a very soft voice."

"No, I don't think so. It didn't sound like a conversation. It was more like a monologue. That's strange."

He stood up. "Let's go over to the church and you can show me where this happened. Maybe we'll find something, I don't know, but it's worth a shot."

He drove us to the church, each of us lost in our own thoughts. We talked about the setting where I overheard the man talking in the night. First, the Chief walked over and examined the area where I thought the person must have stood when I heard talking. There was a strip of grass running along a brick wall, but no telltale signs or evidence.

"I'm going to try to recreate the conditions when you heard the voice. First, tell me what he said."

"I think it was something like, 'I'm not sure I can go on with this, but, if we're to be together...' Then he said he was having pain in his chest."

"Okay, go stand where you were when you heard the voice and tell me when my voice sounds about right."

I scooted around the corner and took up my position on the brick landing. After a few moments, I said, "If you're talking, I can't hear you."

"Is that better?"

"Yes, but it sounds like you're yelling, not talking."

"Let me try this." He spoke again.

I cried, "That's it!" I ran down the brick ramp and found the Chief standing about halfway down looking at the brick wall. "What are you looking at?"

"The Wall of Remembrance." He was standing in front of a brick wall that formed a boundary of the cemetery. At regular intervals, there was a plaque etched with a person's name and a pair of dates. "If someone is cremated, the urn is placed in this wall instead of in a grave." He gestured toward the small field of granite markers that looked gray in the daylight. "I bet your guy was talking to someone who couldn't answer him."

Together, our eyes scanned the names on the wall... and we both gasped when we saw it.

Laura Wilkins Chandler
Beloved Wife of Edward

CHAPTER TWENTY-SIX

Tarnish is caused by exposure of a piece of sterling silver to sulfur that may be in the air, for example. Often, it is more pronounced in the colder weather when the house is closed up with little fresh ventilation and the fireplaces are in use. Tarnish can hide wear, damage or a repair as well as the natural lustre of the piece.
—"The Butler's Guide to Fine Silver" Mr. Hollister, 1898

"No-o-o..." I breathed. "It can't be." Through the anguish that gripped me, I heard his words again.

I feel such pain. I'm not sure I can go on with this, but, if we're to be together.

I thought the man was having a heart attack. His heart was breaking and now, so was mine. Somehow, I knew it was true. Edward, my friend, my helper was the thief.

"It's been there all along, right in front of me. He was angry about losing his elected position. He resented Josephine Quinn. He mentioned the changes happening around him. Why didn't I see it before?"

"What about Kat?" The Chief sounded shaken. I don't think all of his training prepared him for this.

I heaved a deep sigh. "I'm not sure, but I think

it was an accident. The Pastor was supposed to go to the courthouse to talk about the chalice. He went to the church instead. Kat showed up. I think they fought over the chalice, pulling it back and forth. Did she really just lose her balance?"

The Chief shook his head. "What a waste." I nodded. "I'm having trouble believing it. He was working with you, helping you solve the puzzles to find the thief and the chalice..." He was at a loss for words.

"I know, I know. There's one way to find out if we're right." I took my phone out of my pocket.

"Whoa there, little missy. Don't you dare call him! Have you forgotten what happened the last time you went off like a lone cowboy? Put that phone away."

The order chilled my blood. My only response could be *Yes, Sir.* I looked up at him, my voice calm. "May I suggest that I call his cell to see where he is?" My throat tightened. "We can go to him, talk to him. Find out the truth."

The Chief thought a moment but shook his head. "No, we don't want to give him any idea that we suspect him. No telling what he'll do." I shivered with the thought of what happened at the courthouse. "He might go to his house and destroy all the evidence, if that's where he put together the messages. I need to search his house."

I felt the icy chill of shock as I realized that the Chief had kicked into his official mode of investigator, officer of the court and upholder of the law. I struggled to wrap my head around what would happen now, but I had to if I was going to be part of it.

"If he did these things, we'll find evidence like cut-up newspapers, glue, large sheets of paper he used to put together those messages."

"We may even find the chalice," I added, though I still didn't want any of it to be true.

He glared at me. "There is no *we* in this. *We* will not search his house. *I* will handle the investigation, but first, I have to get a search warrant. I'm going to do this according to the book. This case is not going to be thrown out of court on some technicality or mistake I made. And this will go to court. The crime is theft, pure and simple, and I don't think the church is going to let that go. Then, there are the circumstances surrounding Kat's demise. A lot of questions there, so we'll do it right."

"How long will that take?" I sounded like I was whining.

"Probably an hour, maybe a little more." When he saw the expression on my face, he said, "Look, it's been how many days? Another hour shouldn't make a difference."

I thought for a moment. "You know, he might be here at the church."

Both of us looked around at the large stone building. Could Edward be inside right now? Could he be standing where I stood last night, listening to what we were saying? The Chief's eyes roamed all over the area trying to take in the situation. He looked at the door and windows, then swung around to check out the cars in the parking lot. Then he turned toward the parish hall.

"Instead of running all over the place, let's talk to

the one person who'll know if he is here and will have his home address if he's not."

We said her name in unison. "Miss Cunningham."

We walked into the Parish Hall and found her working at the computer. She didn't hear us come in because her earbuds were firmly planted in her ears. She almost jumped out of her chair when the Chief stepped up to her desk.

Flustered, she pulled out the wires, gathered them in a tangle and stashed everything in a drawer. "Oh Chief, I didn't hear you come in." I felt sorry for the woman who looked like she'd been caught stealing from the cookie jar while sitting in the office all alone. She was working, not playing video games or surfing the internet. Who could begrudge her a little musical entertainment? Well... No, I had more important things to consider.

Miss Cunningham saw me and, as she looked at the Chief again, the color drained out of her face. "Is something wrong? Did something happen?"

Using his soothing voice, he said, "No, everything is fine. We came by to get some information. I'm sure you have it in one of your files."

She perked up with the color coming back to her cheeks. "Of course, Chief Lucan. I'll do whatever I can to help." Though her head never moved, her owl-like eyes swung back and forth between the Chief and me so she didn't miss anything.

"First, you can tell me who is around on the church property right now. The Pastor, Paul, Edward?"

She dropped those big eyes to the desk as if she

could see a monitor covering all the rooms and hallways. She shook her head. "No, the pastors are out making calls and I'm often alone here since Sonny disappeared. I haven't seen Edward, let me see." She tapped her finger on her chin. "No, I haven't seen Edward since the Choir Concert. Is that all you need?"

"No," the Chief said lightly. "Could you give us Edward's home address, please?"

"Certainly." She reached for the church directory lodged with other reference materials between two bookends on her desk. Her hand froze and she looked at him with growing horror. "No, it can't be. Not Edward." She pulled the directory and clutched it tight to her chest. Those big eyes were becoming wet. "No, it can't be him."

I touched the Chief's arm, then went around the desk and sank down by her chair. "Miss Cunningham, we don't know anything for sure."

Then a thought struck me. "You like Edward, don't you?" She nodded, her voice strangled with emotion. "You worked closely together when he was active here at the church." Again, she nodded. "He is nice to you, isn't he?"

She took a big gulp of air and squeezed out the words, "He used to be so happy, always smiling. He is nice and kind and makes me laugh."

She's been secretly in love with him for a long time. As any woman in love, she would know when he was close by… and what he was doing. I was getting close. I could feel it. "He thinks you're nice too. He told me so."

"Really?" A small smile touched her lips.

"Yes, he was at Fair Winds the morning the chalice disappeared. He was helping me try to decipher the clues in the puzzle the thief left in the church. You called him on his cell phone. After he talked to you, he came back to the library and told me you were very nice. You called to beg him to bring the chalice back."

Her body went stiff, but I continued. "You knew Edward had been in the church… was it the night before or the morning the theft was discovered?

She took a deep breath ragged with emotion. "I was helping with the pageant costumes that night and, when I left to go home, I saw his car in the parking lot. I knew he wasn't in the Parish Hall and I saw a dim light inside the church. I went toward the church door to say hello." Her chin sagged down to her chest. "I don't see him very much anymore since the people turned their back on him and after all he's done for our church." Her large round eyes glazed with tears. "That's when I heard the crash."

She heard Edward break down the door to the vestry to make the disappearance of the chalice look like a common break-in.

"I didn't know what to do so I rushed back to my car and drove home. I thought if Edward was inside the church, he'd take care of whatever happened." The tears formed and started to leak down her face. "The next morning, when I heard what happened…"

"You threw suspicion on Sonny, the janitor," I said quietly.

"I didn't know what else to do." Frantically, she looked from me to the Chief and back to me, hoping we'd understand.

"But you started to say something there in the church, didn't you?"

"Yes, but the Pastor was going crazy. You know, you saw him. If he found out that Edward was in the church that night, why... I-I don't know what he would have done." Her whole body wilted. "The Pastor feels that Edward always puts him in the middle between the two groups within the church. One wants to keep things the way they've always been or move slowly with any changes. The other group wants to turn things upside down before next Sunday. Like two children... like two spoiled children, they want the Father to pick one over the other. The spirit of compromise has disappeared. And all the Pastor wants to do is make everyone happy until the day he retires. Believe me, he's counting the days."

"So, you decided to keep quiet. What then?" I nodded a little to encourage her to continue.

"Well, I thought if you went chasing after Sonny, it would give me time to talk to Edward, find out what happened and, if he really did have the chalice, talk him into returning it." As she looked at the Chief, her chin trembled. "I-I'm so sorry, Chief."

I jumped in before the waterworks could start again.

"You watched Edward while he was taking care of his wife when she was dying. You saw how much he was hurting and you couldn't do anything to help." Her body shook and two big tears plopped on her clenched hands in her lap. "It's been almost a year since he lost her, you were thinking, maybe…"

Her eyes rose and met mine, searching for… I don't know, possibility, hope, something to hold on to.

"You know some terrible things have happened and we want to talk to Edward. He might be able to tell us what's been going on." I reached out and covered her hands with mine. "If Edward was sick or injured, you'd want to help him, wouldn't you?" A speck of blood appeared on her lower lip where she was biting down, trying to control herself.

"Miss Cunningham, I think Edward needs us. Please help us help him."

She paused for a moment, then slowly laid the directory on the desk and turned to the page listing Edward's information. She tried to write it down for us. I took the pen from her shaking hand and jotted down the address.

"Thank you, Miss Cunningham. It will be all right."

As the Chief and I walked outside, I realized that I'd told the secretary the same thing Edward always told his wife when she was worried, the same thing he'd told me at the concert.

The Chief said something, but I missed it. "What? I'm sorry, I…"

"I said, you'll have to find your own way home. I have to get the paperwork done before I go over to his house."

"If you can take me back to the park, my ride is waiting."

CHAPTER TWENTY-SEVEN

*The rich, warm color of a fine piece of sterling is called the
patina. It can only develop over time. In reality, the patina is a
web of fine scratches on the silver's surface that comes from gentle
use. The patina makes a piece distinctive.*
—"The Butler's Guide to Fine Silver" Mr. Hollister, 1898

The Chief dropped me off at Muskrat Park. As I
started down the brick walkway toward the water, a
black, furry missile headed straight for me at top speed,
barking his head off. The joy of unconditional love
given by a dog was still new to me, but to be the object
of such affection made me feel warm all over. Then that
good feeling changed to caution then fear. Simon wasn't
stopping. He wasn't even slowing down. I stopped
and braced myself. The impact of his front paws almost
toppled me.

"You have to learn not to jump!" My words didn't
faze him. He kept jumping and barking and wagging
his tail. "Simon, stop it!" No effect. Out of desperation,
I made a threat. "I'm going to tell Lorraine. You're out
of control. She'll teach you to behave." As if I'd flipped
a switch, all four paws went down, he went silent and

plopped his behind down on the grass, his tail still wagging madly. My jaw dropped. What kind of hold did she have on him? Well, it didn't matter. I'd take it. Calmly, we walked toward the water where Ryan was waiting by the boat.

"I was beginning to think you'd forgotten all about us," he said.

"Never." And it was exciting to realize that I meant it. That warm feeling from the swan's cove up the river was coming back.

"Interested in getting something to drink, maybe something to warm us up before we head back?"

Reality came back like a cold wind gust. "Sorry, I can't. Something's come up and I need to get back to Fair Winds right away." I paused, close to giving in but I knew if I didn't get on board, I'd stay with Ryan and miss the confrontation, the explanation for all that happened. I knew everything pointed to Edward but, somehow, I couldn't accept that this mild-mannered, handsome, intelligent man caused so much havoc and a death. No, I had to hear it from him. I started toward the boat.

"Wait a minute. What's up?" The tone in his voice made me stop.

"Uh, nothing. Just have to get back."

"No, I need to understand. One minute we're hell-bent to get you to the police station. Then, you're gone so long I thought you'd been kidnapped or got a better offer. Now, you want me to deliver you back to Fair Winds… just like that, with no explanation."

"Ah, that would be right." I shrugged, feeling very shy.

"No, that would be wrong." The breeze wasn't the only thing getting colder.

"Look, I would really appreciate it if you'd take me home." I smiled but it felt so artificial. I wasn't happy. I was a little put out that he was giving me a hard time. No, to be honest, I was frightened that I was going to blow any chance I might have with Ryan -- right here, right now. But I had no choice. I had to finish what I'd started. "I don't have time to explain it all right now. Can we just go?"

"Fine, you'll have plenty of time while we head back."

"Fine." *Oh, he could be so aggravating.* I stepped on the bulkhead.

"Watch out for the splinters. The wood on this bulkhead is weathered," he warned. On board, his captain persona kicked in. He handed me his foul weather coat. "Here, put this on. It'll be cold going back." With Ryan's help, Simon got back in the boat and settled down on the deck of the boat with his paws on the side. His head swiveled around so he didn't miss a thing.

When Ryan started the engine, it sputtered. I thought I'd have to walk back to Fair Winds but it didn't die.

"It'll smooth out when it warms up. Don't worry, I'll get you back."

He cast off and we were underway. "Okay, you have my full attention."

I tried to make a joke. "And who is going to steer the boat?" I said with a little laugh.

"I can steer and listen at the same time." He looked at me without a trace of feeling or expression.

I felt like the moment we'd shared up the river was dying. What could I do? I could trust Ryan but legalities were involved. A church artifact was missing. A woman... Kat died. Someone was responsible and had to pay the price. The Chief trusted me. If I betrayed that trust and revealed something here and now that destroyed the case later... I couldn't do that. Kat deserved justice.

Quietly, I said, "I'm sorry. I can't." I rushed on. "It has nothing to do with you—"

"Except that it's my boat and my time and my date."

"No, I didn't mean it like that."

"Then what do you mean, Abby?"

I didn't know what to say so I turned my head to watch the Crab Claw Restaurant slide by and remembered the day Lorraine tried to get me to eat a steamed crab. The look of the beady eyes still gave me the shivers. I was safe until next season, since the local blue crabs had burrowed into the mud of the Chesapeake Bay for the winter. At least something was working in my favor.

As we passed the Harbour Inn, I snuck a peek at Ryan. His face was blank, but I couldn't see his eyes. He'd put on sunglasses again. Feeling very uncomfortable, I wanted everything to be resolved so I could go in my cottage, lock the door and snuggle down with a hot cup of coffee, alone.

We moved through the harbor at a snail's pace. Ryan anticipated my question. "We have to motor out at this speed so we don't hit bottom and damage the propeller. Look at the water behind us. We're churning mud which means it's shallow along here. When we came in, it was high tide. Now... well, I told you that you were gone a long time."

"Look, I'm working with the Chief on something, but I'm not at liberty to talk about it." I was making a mess of this but I didn't know how to fix it.

"Now you're into top secret stuff. Murder wasn't enough for you last time."

"No, it's nothing like that. It's... it's..."

"It's what?" He wanted an answer.

"It's confidential." I didn't want to fight with him. The sooner we got to Fair Winds, the better. "Can't we go a little faster? It must be deeper here. The Patriot is over there." It was a big boat with two levels to take tourists up and down the Miles. "I could pedal a bike faster than this."

"Rules and good manners require all boats to observe the 'No Wake Zone' in a harbor. That means we can go no faster than 6 mph."

There was no escape. Maybe if I assured him that I was okay, he would drop the cross examination. "Look the Chief knows what's going on and I'm safe. So, you see, there is really nothing to talk about." I smiled.

"Even with me?"

"I'm afraid so, I said reluctantly.

Ryan scratched my dog behind one ear. "Simon, I guess we have to get Cinderella back home before she turns into a pumpkin." He steered the boat to the left a little so some green buoys lined up on the right.

"What are those for?" I asked, trying to direct our conversation to a safer topic.

"Those buoys help define the channel so a captain knows where he's going and why. Not that this captain has a clue."

"Ryan, please don't be like this. The Chief doesn't want me to talk about it. I have to honor his wishes."

He scanned the water as we made our way through the harbor, but said to me, "You're into something again, Abby. You can't fool me. I don't know what it is but it's bad. Didn't you learn your lesson?" He took one hand off the wheel, rubbed the back of his neck and started mumbling to himself. "Investigating a murder, a MURDER, for heaven's sake. Running around, asking questions of complete strangers."

He turned to me, the anger etched on his handsome face. Anger? Or was it concern? As if hit by an arrow, I realized that he cared. He cared about me. I was elated. "What are you smiling at? This isn't funny. If you valued your own safety, you wouldn't go off and do these things. It's irresponsible."

I felt like a child who had misbehaved. But I wasn't a child. "I beg your pardon." I could feel my eyes narrow, shooting daggers at him.

"I'm just saying… you should take care of yourself."

"I do." Each word was sharp.

"You need—"

It was too late. Something about his attitude lit me up like a match. "I don't need anything, thank you. I can take care of myself." We had cleared the harbor and were coming up to one of those tall wood pilings out in the middle of the water, marked with a big 3 on a green sign. "Can't you make this thing go faster now?"

"Yes, ma'am." He turned the wheel around to the right. "Hang on." He pushed the throttle forward, pressing me back in my seat. It was sudden. It was scary. Even Simon whimpered as he lay down on the deck because it was too hard for him to stand up even with four legs.

I shouted over the noise of the engine. "Look, I'll be fine."

"Fine." He kept his eyes on the water ahead.

"Fine," I said under my breath.

We raced up in the river in silence.

When he made the slow approach to the Fair Winds dock, I tried to salvage something of our time together. "I'm sorry. It's just…

"You're in a hurry, remember? Sorry it took so long to get you here, but that's the way of the water." He held the boat close to the dock ladder so I could step out, but he didn't offer to help and didn't tie up the boat, just left the engine running.

"Thank you for squeezing me into your schedule," he said. "It was fun for a while."

I couldn't believe how frustrating he could be. Balancing someone's love and my personal need to do something was a trick I hadn't learned yet. At least I knew that this was not the time or the place to push the issue. Being sensible… or taking the easy way out, I started making my way down the dock without another word.

"Abby." Something in his voice made me turn. "Be careful."

Those two little words helped, but I was still torn so I waved and made my way up to the house with Simon jogging along beside me.

Inside, I peeled off Ryan's coat. Somehow I'd have to get it back to him. If nothing else, I could put it in the mail to avoid another argument. I threw it on a chair. I'd deal with that later. Right now, there were more important things to do. I raced into the library. This time it didn't bother me when Dawkins appeared silently like an apparition.

"Where are those papers I asked you to copy for me?" I even sounded snappish to myself.

"On the desk as you requested," he responded.

I found them and gathered up my notes as well. "I need the..." But Dawkins had disappeared. Men! Never there when you need them. Always pushing into your business when you don't.

I flipped Simon a cookie, told him to stay and raced out to my car.

CHAPTER TWENTY-EIGHT

The patina on a valued piece of sterling silver created by tiny scratches is desirable. The effects of use and damage that cut deep are destructive and may prove irreversible.
—"The Butler's Guide to Fine Silver" Mr. Hollister, 1898

I drove up to the brick rambler with a well-tended yard and a circular driveway where three St. Michaels police cars were now parked. The Chief was standing at the open door talking to someone inside. One of the officers came down the front steps as I approached.

"He's not here, Abby, but the Chief is going in. The cleaning lady accepted the search warrant. I'm getting the camera."

I sprinted up the steps and followed the last officer into the house.

The front rooms were a nice size and felt comfortable. I was working my way toward the back when a gruff voice made a demand.

"What are you doing here?" The Chief stood with his hands on his hips above the wide black belt that held his gun, holster and handcuffs. This man wouldn't be swayed by sweet talk or persuasion.

"I put together all the things that brought you here. I deserve to be here."

He stared at me for a long minute. "All right, but don't touch *anything*. If you see something, tell me. Don't go off on your own like you did before."

I flinched.

"Okay, point taken. I'll stay behind you."

He gave me a sharp nod and led the way toward the bedrooms on the side of the house.

We went from room to room – master bedroom, guest room, study. The Chief opened closet doors and cabinets. Nothing was out of the ordinary. Nothing suggested this man had researched silver hallmarks, constructed a rebus, written on large paper, nothing.

The Chief was deflating like a leaky balloon as he walked back toward the living room. I was following him just as I promised when one of his officers called out.

"Hey, Chief. There's a door behind a curtain in the bedroom… and it's locked."

We rushed down the hallway to the master bedroom and to the far corner of the room. Floor-to-ceiling drapes hung by the windows looking out on the landscaped backyard, but it wasn't a normal window treatment. The curtains didn't end at the corner, but followed the rod around and down the adjoining wall about two or three feet. I'd noticed it when I walked in the room and thought it gave the room a warm, embracing feeling. It seemed that it served another purpose.

The Chief was in charge and things happened fast.

"Jeff, take the cleaning lady outside and…"

"Can't do that, Chief. She took off when we started the search."

"Then wait outside and if the suspect arrives, detain him until we're finished here." The officer rushed out and the Chief eyed the door and the wall it was on. "What's on the other side here?"

"The garage, I think," said another officer.

"Go out there and see what you see. No sense breaking down a door that only leads to the garage. If you don't see the door, knock on the wall when you get to the corner." He crossed his arms while we waited for the telltale knock.

When it came, it was only halfway down the wall, nowhere close to the door.

He used his radio to have the officer see if the door led to the outside. The answer came back quickly.

"Chief, the wall is flush with the back of the house. No windows. There's no way the garage comes all the way back here."

"Okay," He turned to the last officer. "Get me through this door."

"You want me to…"

The chief nodded and the big man took a couple of running steps and slammed his shoulder into the door that caved in without protest.

I tried to see over the Chief's shoulder as he peered through the shattered door, but his height blocked my view.

"Stay where you are," he ordered.

"What is it? What do you see?" Then a terrible thought flew through my brain. "It's not Edward, is it?"

I couldn't handle another sad ending.

"No, no. But it's bad enough." He stepped aside so I had a clear view. "We found what we came for."

I could see a table and a messy pile of cut-up pages. Considering the tall stack of newspapers and magazines on the floor, it must have taken a lot of patience for Edward to search for the right words to glue to the puzzles. A large drawing table tilted flat so it worked as a desk was against one wall. Calligraphy pens, ink bottles, scissors and glue bottles lined the top of the work area. That's where he must have prepared the letters left at the church and the museum. A strong lamp was angled up so it would shine in his face. He must have used it to check the pinholes on the House Divided letter.

My stomach rolled and I wanted to sink to the floor.

A strong hand closed on my arm. "Abby, come with me." The Chief led me outside to my car. "You sit out here until you feel better; then drive back to Fair Winds. I can't spare any of my men right now to take you. You understand."

"Yes, of course." Another thought made me feel sick again. "He's methodical, we could see that. If the chalice isn't there, where is it?"

"I don't know. Look at the Bible verses. When you get back to Fair Winds, figure it out."

He walked back into the house with his cell phone glued to his ear.

I got in my car and turned on the heater. It was smart to wait until my head cleared. So, I sat alone with my thoughts. *It was Edward all along. Such a distinguished looking gentleman. So kind, so concerned, so supportive...*

and all the time, he had the chalice. Why, why? That word kept crashing around my head. *If both he and his wife Laura loved this church, why would he do something to harm it and its special possession?*

The shadows on the courthouse wall from the night Kat died danced in front of eyes. *Kat must have overheard the argument I had with the Pastor.* In my mind, I heard the echo of a door closing. I'd thought it was a staff person. It must have been Kat leaving for the courthouse. *She thought she'd found her ticket out.* My hands started to shake and not from the cold.

Is Edward a killer? The Chief said the details surrounding Kat's death did not fit the legal definition of murder. However, the unknown man—the man I now knew to be Edward—could be charged with a lesser crime.

I made myself visualize that horrible night in the courthouse square. I felt the chill breeze stroke my cheek as it caused the tree branches to creak above my head again. Dark shadows moved in rhythm with the wind. Beads of sweat slid down my arm. My body trembled, knowing that something sinister was about to happen and the realization that I was here and truly alone.

I shivered and tried to toss off the emotions created by those frightening memories and the feeling of being so alone. I needed to remember exactly what I saw. I closed my eyes and dredged up the memory so it would play like a movie in my mind's eye.

It was dark except for the spotlight on the statue of the Confederate soldier. Only the statue was lit by the spotlight. The pedestal base was in shadow. *Good, I was viewing the scene without all the emotions I felt that cloud my memory.* The base was in shadow so it was obvious when someone struck a match and lit a candle. Then another flame appeared and a second candle was lit. At the main entrance to the square where the wrought iron fence framed the sidewalk, a figure appeared. Wearing high heels and carrying a large purse suggested the figure was a woman: Kat. *My emotions reared up: Anger at her greed and reckless behavior, sadness at the unfairness, regret and a little guilt that I might have done something... STOP! The only thing I can do for Kat is to find out what happened, why and who.* I took a deep breath and tried to settle myself again.

She walked up the sidewalk and turned toward the statue. I lost her in the shadows, but heard muffled voices during a lull in the wind. Though I concentrated, I couldn't make out the words, but I remembered now, it was a heated exchange... between Kat and a man. Their shadows moved on the brick wall as if they were dancing. They came together in a move of the tango then her shadow moved away... No, it fell away from his. There was a wail that rose above the wind and his shadow disappeared. When her shadow fell away... that was when she fell, her head striking the corner of the granite pedestal.

I wanted to stop the movie in my head. I wanted to mourn the loss of this artistic woman, a mother, who only wanted one thing – to go home. If I pushed through the pain building in my mind, something might rise to the surface, something important.

I closed my eyes one more time and watched the

dance of shadows on the wall again. They came together and rocked a little back and forth… as if grappling over an object. The chalice? Were they grabbing and tugging on the chalice? Then, I realized with a start, the larger shadow, the man's shadow pulled away. His arms were not outstretched as if pushing her. Only then did her shadow fall away and disappear.

Maybe he didn't push her. Maybe she just lost her balance and hit her head on the corner of the granite pedestal. Could the Chief be right? Maybe it wasn't murder? Maybe it was only an unfortunate accident?

It didn't matter. Based on the little part that Edward revealed to me, the justice system couldn't hurt Edward any more than his own feeling of guilt at breaking one of the Ten Commandments: Thou shalt not kill. It would change the man forever.

It didn't have to happen, none of it. But the fact remained that it did. *But why? And where is the silver Communion chalice?*

I grabbed the papers from the seat next to me and thumbed through them until I found a copy of the last letter stuck in the stack of sheet music. The Chief identified the list of symbols and numbers as Bible passages. The couple that we identified together seemed to explain why the thief had done what he had. Once he made us understand the reasons for his actions, maybe he used the last passage to identify the location of the chalice. It was a little unnerving to me that I was starting to think like the thief, but I shrugged off the creepy feeling and scanned down to the last clue.

6 19

I tried to remember my studies from Hebrew school before my Bat Mitzvah when I turned 13. Yes, there was something about Kings in the Old Testament. Could this be a reference to Chapter 6, Verse 9 of First Kings? Quickly, I searched online using my phone and found the passage:

So he built the house and finished it, and he made the ceiling of the house of beams and planks of cedar.

Everything, all of it, has revolved around the church. The chalice, the messages, the… I froze. *Everything revolved around the church, the building itself.*

On the night of the choir concert, I told him I hoped the chalice was all right. He reminded me what he always told Laura when she asked him if everything would be all right. He said, "I'm sure it will be all right. The Lord is watching out for it, I'm sure." I was focused on what he always told Laura. He was telling me that the chalice was someplace where the Lord was expected to be present. He was telling me the chalice was in the church. It never left. Edward must have known about another secret hiding place and stashed the chalice so it would be safe from accidents and prying eyes.

How could I be so blind? The chalice is at the church. Edward wants us to come to the church!

But there was something else nudging me, something at the back of mind or just beyond my sight out of the corner of my eye. I threw my head back against the headrest – once, twice. Maybe I could shake it loose. *Stop! I'm only giving myself a headache.*

I closed my eyes, took a deep breath and zeroed in on the question.

I know what: the chalice. Now I know where: the church. When I get there, I'll find out who because he said he'd be there. My eyes popped open. In the last message, he said he'd be there. He said,

You must come by the time the clock strikes the day you were created.

The day you were created, I thought. *If we're talking the Bible, he must be referring to Genesis. Man was created on the sixth day. Six o'clock!*

I looked at my watch. Twenty minutes until six! So little time. It had to be enough. Somebody had to get there by six... the time he said he was going to destroy the silver chalice.

I opened my window as I started the car and yelled out to the officer standing guard. "Tell the Chief that Edward and the chalice are at the church and we have to get there before six. Tell him to meet me there and to hurry!" I sped out of the driveway and called Lorraine with the same information. Maybe she could talk Edward into giving her the chalice and surrendering quietly to the police. Nobody else had to get hurt.

Fumbling with the phone while I was driving, I finally found the number for the Pastor's office from the many times he'd called me for updates. When he heard who was calling, his voice turned hard from either exasperation or exhaustion… or both.

"Did you find it?" He demanded.

"No," I said and heard a deep groan from the other end of the call. "But I know where it is. It's there, at the church. It never left except… except that one night."

"Don't be ridiculous," he countered. "If it was in my church, I'd know it." I heard his words as he handed away the phone. He said, "Here, you talk to her. I can't take her crazy ideas anymore."

"Hello?" The voice was tentative. "This is Pastor Paul."

"Oh, thank goodness. I'm on the way to the church right now. Tell me one thing. Is Edward there? Have you seen him today?"

He stammered. "Why, yes, I saw Edward a little while ago going into the sanctuary. He was carrying some supplies. Abby, did something happen? Is the chalice…?"

"The chalice is at the church. Edward has it. Take a phone and meet me by the side entrance to the cemetery." I promised myself I'd watch the clock and call back if the timing was too close. "Don't go in by yourself."

"But we can just—"

"Don't do it, Paul. Remember how things went terribly wrong at the courthouse. Get the Pastor and meet us by the entrance."

"How long?" He sounded stronger, probably relieved that it was almost over.

"I'll be there before six." *I hope.*

"We'll be there, both of us. I hope you're right."

"Unfortunately, I am."

I hung up, put both hands on the wheel and drove like I was running moonshine.

CHAPTER TWENTY-NINE

The beauty of every silver piece depends in great measure upon the care given to it. That care is the responsibility of the Butler of the household. If the silver is not lustrous and in perfect condition, the fault is on his shoulders and tarnishes his reputation.
—"The Butler's Guide to Fine Silver" Mr. Hollister, 1898

Heavy gray clouds hung low in the sky as if the heavens were grieving too as the truth became clear. I approached the church as a big SUV turned in ahead of me: Lorraine. I parked behind her and as she opened her door, I heard her questions.

"Abby, what in the world? Do you really think it's here?" Her eyes jumped from me to the church building and back again. How? Who?" She gave up on completing her questions.

I wanted to appear calm, though my stomach was churning. "The chalice is inside, I'm sure of it." I laid a hand on her arm to forestall her questions. "It was Edward, it was Edward all along." I could hear the hitch in my voice caused by tears of betrayal. I was taken in completely by this man. To think that I wanted Lorraine to… I shook off that thought and all the others crowding my brain. I needed to think clearly and find the chalice.

A shiver ran through me. *When I find the chalice, I'll find Edward.*

The pastors came running from the parish hall, the older man bursting with demands, not questions. Funny how people respond so differently to stress and emergency, but this time he wasn't taking charge. I was.

I held up my hands for them to stop on the sidewalk with us. "No questions. Unlock the church. We go in and—"

The Pastor sputtered. "Young lady, this is—"

"It's my turn to make it right. You had your chance and a woman died." The words in my heart finally crossed my lips but I didn't care. Truth hurts sometimes, and from the stunned look on his face, it cracked his pompous exterior, leaving a man who was scared and ashamed. "We go inside slowly. The chalice is there and that's what we find first."

"First?" asked Paul, sounding pained.

"Yes, once we have it, leave. Don't stop for any reason." I looked around the group. They didn't understand, but quietly accepted my direction. "Let's go."

Paul unlocked the side door and glanced at me. I nodded. He depressed the handle and opened the door. I went in first, followed by the Pastor and then everyone else.

We moved into the sanctuary. Shadows lurked along the walls and in the corners. The brilliant lights of the choir concert night, even those on the Christmas tree, were dark. The silence was palpable, so thick it stroked my face. The holiday aromas of cinnamon and pine were overwhelmed by some kind of rancid odor that made my nose twitch. My eyes did a quick sweep of the area, but couldn't find the source. It smelled familiar, but I couldn't place it.

The clouds must have parted to let the sun's rays pour through the stately stained glass windows above the altar. My eye wasn't drawn to the rich colors of crimson and sapphire and jade. I looked to the altar instead. Glistening in the wintery light stood the stately silver chalice. All the talk since its disappearance didn't describe the effect this one piece of silver could have on someone. I wasn't a believer. It didn't have a special significance for me, but its beauty took my breath away. It wasn't the jewels. It wasn't the quality of the metal. The hand of the craftsman of centuries past had created its perfect line and balance. Beauty, love and life can transcend time, even when it's expressed in a chalice of sterling silver.

I heard someone gasp next to me. "You were right. It's here where it belongs," the Pastor said, his face wreathed in a light that could only come from within. "Thanks be to the Lord." He walked solemnly toward the altar and slowly mounted the steps. He took his place where he'd stood for so many years, leading his supplicants in prayers for forgiveness and blessing.

"Now, it is time to give thanks." Slowly, he placed his hands, wrinkled with age, on each side of the chalice and raised it in the filtered sunlight toward heaven in supplication and praise.

"Thank you Lord for delivering this back to us, the

symbol of the path to everlasting life."

I added my own silent prayer of thanks only to be shocked back to reality by a deep male voice from on high, issuing a command.

"Put. That. Down." The deep resonant voice filled the sanctuary.

It wasn't the voice of the Almighty. It was a mortal man standing in the balcony at the back of the church. A man, prone to err, to make mistakes, to sin.

It was Edward.

"You don't deserve to touch the sacred cup." His words reverberated throughout the sanctuary and spread chills over my skin. This was no longer the man I'd met only a few days earlier. Now, he was the commander issuing orders that demanded immediate attention and obedience.

"Step away from the chalice and the altar." The Pastor didn't move. "NOW!"

The Pastor jumped away from the altar where the chalice stood and rushed down the aisle where Lorraine and Paul were standing. We stood silently while the bells high above our heads rang out the hour.

As the last peal faded away, the man standing above us spoke again, but this time in a friendly tone, the commander being benevolent. "It was good of you to show up, all of you. Glad that mess with the Framptons didn't keep you away. And now you're here, just in time. I wouldn't want you to miss what's going to happen."

Pastor Paul stepped forward. "Edward, we can talk about this."

"I have nothing to say to you. You have the gall to

call me a thief? Ha! Isn't that the pot calling the kettle black?"

"Wh-what?" Paul stammered. "I don't understand."

"I know what you're doing. Stewart told me all about it. Did you really think you could steal church funds with a fully accredited Certified Public Accountant watching? If so, you're dumber than I thought."

"You know about the special account?" Paul's words were strained.

"Of course I do."

"What account? What is he talking about, Paul?" asked the Pastor. "I'm supposed to know about..."

Paul's shoulders sagged and a groan escaped his lips. He didn't have to admit his guilt. His body language said it all.

I really know how to pick 'em. First, Edward is a thief turned killer. Now, Paul is an embezzler. My assessment of men is couldn't be more wrong.

Paul started to explain. "I set up the special account to collect any money we'd save on a project. A few dollars here and there really add up."

The Pastor stepped forward, his chest puffed up and his mouth stretched tight. "Paul, how could you?"

Paul straightened up and turned around slowly to face his boss. His face was empty of emotion and his voice was soft. "Just this once, don't..."

"You are in no position—" His voice pointed an invisible finger of condemnation at the young man, but the assistant pastor raised his voice and cut him off.

"It's for you. The money is for you." Paul's shoulders sagged again, not from guilt but frustration. I wanted you to have a really special gift when you retire and with the economy the way it is, I was afraid we wouldn't have the dollars we'd need. All the money is there... so we'll have it when we need it."

The sound of one man clapping in the church was eerie. We all looked back to the balcony. "How touching, but it's all too little, too late. It's time to cleanse this place."

"Edward," the Pastor's voice was thin with fear. "What are you going to do? Don't hurt the church."

"Ah, always the one to jump to conclusions, aren't you? You always have an opinion and it's usually on the negative side." He paused. "Why don't you go stand at the pulpit, Pastor?"

"Edward, I don't think—"

"That's your problem. You don't think." Edward's voice was getting louder. "Do it!" His anger ricocheted off the wood paneled walls, leaving invisible gashes in the sanctuary he worked so hard to nurture and protect.

The Pastor sprinted to the pulpit and paused. His face was pale and he looked like he'd faint away on the spot. Slowly, he put his right hand on the railing that led up the few steps to the podium where he stood to deliver his sermons on the many Sundays of his career. He drew in a shallow breath, tightened his grasp and pulled himself up to the lectern that normally held his notes. As he moved to the exalted position set higher than those seated in the congregation so all could see him, he raised his head, pulled his shoulders back and stood tall in the rightful place of the pastor.

"That's better," said Edward. "When you speak to

us from there, you speak of forgiveness and redemption. Your kind words light the path we all should follow. But, I swear, when you step down from there, you become an idiot."

The Pastor's head jerked back in shock, then he murmured, "Too often, I feel like one." Then he lowered his head to his chest as if in shame.

I walked out of the shadows into the light showing in the center aisle of the sanctuary so Edward could see me. "Edward, I—"

"Quiet! I'll get to you. Did you think I didn't know you're here? Of course you are, right here in the middle of what's happening since all this started. I wish from the depths of my soul that you were never called in to help with the first puzzle. It was so easy, but he didn't try. He called for help and expected everyone else to do his bidding, as usual. No, don't move," Edward called out.

I looked over my shoulder to see the Pastor resume his place at the pulpit.

"If you stay there, maybe you'll hear me at last," Edward continued to address the Pastor. Standing in the church, the rest of us were nothing more than observers. I wasn't sure how this situation would resolve itself, but felt a small wave of confidence that it could all work out if only the Chief would hurry.

"Edward, I'm listening. What do you want?" pleaded the Pastor.

"I want you to hear me, really hear me at last. Do you know why I took the chalice? Do any of you?" We all kept silent. "Ha! Just as I thought. No clue. Pastor?"

The leader of the church barely shook his head. He looked like he was aging right before our eyes. "Let me enlighten you as you enlightened me from that spot with your sermons over the years.

"It was a wakeup call. You weren't listening over the past two or three years. I tried to make you see when we talked in your office, when we debated in meetings – endless meetings – with the elders and committees. I was concerned for all the members of the congregation, but when..." His voice cracked. "When the cancer took my Laura, I listened to the words you spoke at the funeral. That's when I knew you were endangering my immortal soul. If I didn't repair what you had done, change the direction you were leading us, I would never be allowed to take my place next to Laura for all eternity."

Paul raised his hands and his fingers covered his mouth as he uttered a muffled *No*. Lorraine sank down to the hard seat of a nearby pew, her back stiff.

"Edward," The Pastor's voice, filled with remorse, was barely loud enough to be heard. "I-I didn't—"

Edward leaned over the balcony railing, his finger stabbing the air with each word. "No, you didn't!" the unseen man high above us snapped. "It started with the little things... like a guitar player to accompany the choir instead of the organ, then you didn't speak out in your sermons about the changes forced upon members of other denominations: same-sex marriage, women priests and now gay members of the clergy." He spat out the words. "It started other places and will be here in our little town soon because *you* didn't speak out. *You* haven't drawn the line. *You* haven't set boundaries,

boundaries to protect us. You're even setting the stage to welcome these sinful changes into our church."

The Pastor was shaking his head slowly back and forth in disbelief. "Edward, Edward, you are—"

"I am the champion who had the courage to step into the void where you should have been. I spoke out against all the changes you would allow, including the simple decision to change the color of the carpeting here in the sanctuary. This is no place for blue carpeting. It's always been red... to remind us of the wine we take in His name."

The Pastor put his head in his hands. "No, no..."

"That's right. *No* should have been your answer. But you'd rather give in to the voices of the new people moving into our town and into our church. People who want to force change before they know what we are about."

Paul stepped forward and cried out, "Edward, you were new once and we listened to you. Look at all the good work you've done."

"Ah, another man who finally found his voice again. Better late than never, Mr. Assistant Pastor. You should have spoken up when it became clear that our church leader..." He said those last words with contempt. "Had grown tired of the battles. You should have been a source of strength, but you weren't. You caved in to the pressure and had the gall to ask me, pressure me to step down from my position as a leader of this church."

Sounds of shuffling came from the balcony as though Edward was moving things around. The acrid smell I'd noticed earlier suddenly became stronger.

What is he doing up there? Is he going to hurt himself? Is he planning to damage the church? I wanted to do something, but I was afraid. Since I couldn't see what he was doing, I might make things worse.

"You encourage women to step out of their traditional roles. You push and push until they're more macho than most men. No wonder they have to marry each other. No self-respecting man would have them."

The Pastor started to sputter a response, but Edward cut him off.

"Don't bother trying to defend yourself. The proof is clear for everyone to see. You allowed that stupid woman to step into my place with all her grandiose ideas… modern ideas, you called them. You and all the weak, spineless leaders in all the churches are shoving change down the throats of your true believers and I, for one, am fighting back. When you put her in the highest position of authority, I knew I had to get your attention. I had to make you hear my message. That's when I began my preparations to take the chalice." He laughed, but there was no happiness in the sound. "Imagine my delight when I found the hallmark *Ladyman*. The poor guy went through life with that horrible name. No wonder he didn't make a lot of pieces. Remember when you found that nugget of information, Abby? It was perfect for my warning. You almost caught on but dropped it."

It felt like it was my turn to step forward. "You were meticulous in your preparations."

"And how would you know that?" There was a suspicious note in his voice.

"I know because I saw your work area. You organized your supplies – your scissors, glue and pens – so neatly. You lined up your reference books on sterling silver and hallmarks. You stacked the ravaged pages of the newspapers and magazines where you clipped out the words for the puzzles so no one could find them in the trash. You kept them in your secret room."

"You broke into my house?" He was incredulous.

"Edward, you knew the Chief was going to follow every clue... and they led to your house. He did it by the book – search warrant and everything – and once we were inside, we found the evidence. The Chief is on his way right now, so why don't you—"

"You went into *our* home, into *our* bedroom? You touched *her* things?" Strain pulled his words thin like taffy.

In the quiet, Lorraine looked at me, her face filled with disbelief. Then her expression changed and her eyes flicked from the door to me and back again.

Before we could act, Edward spoke again, but something had changed. His voice was calm, resonant and filled with resolve. "It doesn't matter. I won't be going back there."

Fear tickled the back of my neck. "Edward, where are you going?"

"I am going to HELL!" His answer thundered throughout the sanctuary, each word rolling over me like a boulder. "The flames of hellfire shall lick and sear my skin, but they will not burn away my sin, a sin you made me commit."

There was the shuffling sound again and a new

burst of the acrid smell. Like a shock of electricity, I realized that the smell was some kind of fire starter fluid like the kind used with charcoal-burning grills. There was a scraping. A small flame appeared.

With a great whooshing sound, a ball of fire flared. High above our heads, Edward appeared in the snapping flames of a torch he held high over his head.

"I killed a woman. I will burn in the fires of hell in eternal damnation. My final punishment will start here. You say you've done nothing wrong... but you have sinned. After I'm gone, you'll continue in your misguided ways, Pastor, leading the good people of this congregation astray. The least I can do is destroy this sacred place so you cannot inflict your wickedness on another soul that only aspires to good."

As the fire found the starter fluid and the carpeting and wood of the church balcony, it reached up toward the ceiling paneled in planks of wood hewn in the 1800's when the church was built. They looked good, but I wondered how dried out they were. I scanned the church quickly. A hint of the firelight danced in the gleaming silver surface of the chalice. Dragging my eyes away from the mesmerizing image, I kept scanning. As the flames grew, I knew the church interior would be no match for the torch of retribution.

"Edward!" I had to raise my voice to be heard over the sound of the blaze. "What sin, what sin did you commit?"

Paul's head whipped around and he stared at me in surprise. His tortured expression said, *Are you crazy? Murder, MURDER!* I ignored him and turned my face up to look at Edward again.

"Abby, you know as well as I do. You saw it, you saw me break one of the Ten Commandments." His voice rose. "And it's your fault."

"Me? What did I do?" Every minute he stood there talking and doing nothing gave the Chief more time to get here. Though it had felt like hours since we discovered Edward in the church, I had to believe the Chief was on his way. He just had to be coming.

"You sent that woman to me. You knew the answer to the puzzle, but you sent *her* to me and all she wanted was to take the chalice from me and sell it." His voice cracked. "She was nothing more than another Judas willing to do anything for money," Edward shouted.

The confirmation hit me in the stomach like a fist. Lorraine was right. Kat put her nose in places she didn't belong. She couldn't fight the temptation of making her dream of moving back to the mountains come true. If I'd only... *No, this is not the time, not the time. Now, I have to do something to protect the people here and this beautiful building. I need to keep him talking, but if he thinks I'm attacking him, he might go ahead and do whatever he came here to do. He has to think I understand and I'm on his side. I hope whoever is watching over us forgives me for what I say. Here goes...*

With a chuckle, I said nonchalantly, "Edward, Edward, Edward." I sauntered up the aisle toward the back of the church. "You're right about that woman. She was only after the money she could make, but why would you think I sent her to you? I wasn't the one." I swung around, stretched out my arm and pointed at the pulpit. "It was him!"

Behind me, I heard Lorraine gasp and whisper my name. I shot her a glance and hoped she'd keep silent. At the front of the sanctuary, blood drained from the Pastor's face so it was as ghostly white as Kat's had been that night at the base of the soldier's statue in the courthouse square.

I heard Lorraine clear her throat and I glanced at her over my shoulder. With a little tip of her head, her eyes flicked back and forth between me and a shadowed area underneath the balcony. She must have caught on to what I was doing and wanted me to know there was a staircase to the balcony in that direction., that's what Lorraine was telling me with her eyes.

I hurried to pick up the conversation with Edward. "Your pastor never understood your message. He didn't hear you when you tried to tell him in the meetings. I know how you must feel. He didn't hear me either when I told him the House Divided was his very own church!" I kept taking slow steps up the aisle. "Edward, look what happened because this one man refused to hear us and understand."

Then Edward said something unexpected. He agreed with me. "You're right, Abby. It's all his fault. He denied me entry to heaven, to be with my Laura. So I shall deny him that which is the center of his life, his church."

"No! No," the Pastor wailed. "No, it's not my fault." He jumped down from the pulpit and, with tears running down his face, he grabbed up the chalice and fled.

"STOP!" The word thundered throughout the church. "Sit down." Edward ordered as he clipped each syllable. "You're not going anywhere." The Pastor staggered to a nearby corner, pressed his back against the wall and slid to the floor. A flood of his tears splashed on the chalice cradled in his hands.

Edward stood by the balcony railing, tall and erect and made a proclamation. "You will burn in a hell of your own making. You cannot escape..." He started swinging the lighted torch up and around in a wide arc. The flames left a path that seared its form in my eyes and made me blink.

"You cannot escape for you have sinned!" The torch left his hand and flew high in the rafters towards the altar.

It struck a hanging brass chandelier and fell to the floor between two pews. Lorraine raced to the spot and lifted the torch away from anything that could burn while Paul stomped out the burning embers.

"You cannot stop me so easily!" Edward laughed.

I can try.

I took off for the shadowy area, found the staircase and half ran, half hauled myself up to the balcony. I had to reach Edward before he used the lighter again.

When I emerged onto the balcony, I could see the shadowy lines of the pews set in descending rows toward the railing. There, Edward stood in silhouette against the stained glass window at the other end of the church above the altar. Silently, I stepped down past each row toward him.

Without warning, he swung around and challenged

me. "Don't, don't take another step."

The face I'd once thought so handsome was contorted by agony. *He doesn't want to do this,* I thought. *There's still a chance.*

"Abigail, step away from me," he roared, as he thrust the torch at me.

In the most soothing voice I could muster, I said, "Edward, I want to help. I—"

"No one can help me now."

"That isn't true. The Chief thinks it was an accident and about the theft—"

"It doesn't matter what the Chief thinks or anyone else in this world. I have to try to make amends and then accept my punishment." Tears were in his voice.

"Burning down the church is not making amends." He started to speak but I kept on. "Yes, I heard what you said, but you're wrong. Doesn't it say in the Bible that two wrongs do not make a right? What happened to you was wrong, but taking a torch to this church is wrong." I moved down two more steps. "It's over, Edward."

"It will never be over," he pronounced. "If you don't go away, I will have to condemn you to hell."

His words didn't stop me. "I don't care, Edward. I'm Jewish, remember? We don't believe in hell. We're supposed to take care of today and the Creator will take care of tomorrow." As I spoke, he raised the lighter. "And I'm going to take care of *right now.*"

I lunged at him and knocked the lighter out of his hand. It flew high in the air, then fell with a clatter to the floor below.

"No!" Edward screamed. He surged against me as I

grabbed hold of his arm holding the torch. He wrenched it, but I didn't let go. The bottle of stinking fluid tipped over and leaked over the edge of the balcony to the carpeting below.

He stopped struggling, but I didn't release my grip on him. "You leave me no choice. I will end this now. And you are coming with me." He jerked me over the edge. The railing cut into my back. I felt my hair fall free. I looked over my shoulder to see nothing but air beneath me. The scent of the white roses that made up the Star of Bethlehem filled my nostrils. Was I smelling the flowers marking my own death?

I sucked in a breath and squeezed out my last plea. "Edward, you don't have to do this. It can be all right."

In the fading light, I saw the look in his eyes change from desperation to regret. He made the connection, the connection to his wife and what he'd tell her when things were going wrong. He told her because he believed it. I hoped he'd believe me now.

"It will be all right," I whispered.

He searched my face with eyes glistening with tears. He must have found something there, because he eased his grip on my wrist and gently lifted me back to safety and didn't let go until he sat me down safely on the bench of the front pew. The strained expression on his face spoke the apology that couldn't cross his lips.

He looked over the rail and up to the altar. A muffled cry escaped his mouth and his body lurched.

Not over the edge, but away from the railing. Slowly, he sank to the floor.

Had he chosen not to tumble over the railing for

fear of committing the sin of suicide... or had the words he often spoke to Laura made a difference? Whatever the reason, he'd made his choice and he sat sobbing silent tears.

A last ray of sunlight shone through the stained glass window painting colors everywhere.

The voice I'd been waiting to hear roared behind me and the Chief pounded up the steps toward us.

"It's over," I said and tasted a salty tear of my own.

CHAPTER THIRTY

There is an ancient saying that it would benefit a Butler to keep in mind: It is best to cure an evil before it happens. The family depends on the Butler to keep the sterling silver in fine condition. If a piece is damaged, the Butler must find another to rectify the situation and repair the piece, if it is even possible.

—"The Butler's Guide to Fine Silver" Mr. Hollister, 1898

The first night after the confrontation at the church was hard. Fortunately, Lorraine didn't feel like going to sleep either, so we stayed up talking about nothing and everything until dawn. Somehow it was easier going to bed after the sun came up. Though more than a week had passed, flames still popped up in my dreams and I'd wake up frightened and sweaty.

Simon and I had just come back from breakfast at the big house. He curled up exhausted from his run and I settled down to go through a stack of mail. One envelope caught my eye. The return address read *First Presbyterian Church of Saint Michaels*. I opened it and found a letter from Assistant Pastor Paul.

Dear Abby,

Hope this letter finds you well or at least better after your ordeal. Things are back to the normal craziness here as we are in the final preparations for our Christmas celebration. The Pastor has taken some much needed time off to rest before the services begin. I find myself in the thick of things now, making decisions, resolving little disputes and offering encouragement and appreciation to everyone who is working so hard to make this Christmas special.

I must say that I still get a horrible feeling in my stomach when I think about what happened... and what almost happened. I look at our parishioners and I'm torn. Part of me is grateful that they have no idea what happened and how you stepped us back from the brink of destruction. But part of me wishes that they knew so they could thank you. I have to accept that things are as they should be and hope that my own heartfelt expression of gratitude will suffice.

Wishing you all the best always, Abby,

Paul Thomas

I refolded his letter, tucked it into a desk drawer, then paused. *I wonder.* It took a little digging, but I found a copy of Edward's final puzzle that we never completely solved. *I wonder what he was trying to tell us?* I sat down at the computer to find out.

When I first started working on the puzzle, the Chief figured out that the set of clues were based on different Bible chapters and verses. The first clue translated into a well-known quote:

313

The Chief had explained the rationale: The patron saint (HALO) of lawyers (SCALES) and law enforcement officers (HANDCUFFS) as well as those dealing with insect bites and is the saint known as the "Lion-hearted" = Mark 12:31- "You shall love your neighbor as yourself."

From this, I suspected that all Edward wanted was to have his concerns about changes in the church be taken into consideration and treated with respect, as anyone would.

 14 15 =

The next clue asked us to identify the patron saint (HALO) of writers (PEN and WRITING) and artists (PALETTE and PAINTING) = John 14:15 - "If you love Me, you will keep My commandments."

That awful afternoon in the church, Edward said he believed people in his church were leading the congregation astray. He thought it started with little things like changing the color of the carpeting in the sanctuary. He sincerely believed that soon the church leadership would rationalize more serious actions that would not be in keeping with the commandments.

 26 5 =

In the next clue, the line of music suggested the Song of David which led me to Psalms 26:5 - "I hate the assembly of evildoers, and I will not sit with the wicked."

During our conversations, I got a sense of how important the church was to Edward. He volunteered hours and hours over the years to its well-being. From the way he talked, he also believed the teachings. After his wife died, his priorities must have changed. All he wanted was to earn his place with her in eternity. Because of the changes – both in the church building and the attitudes of the clergy and parishioners – Edward must have believed his immortal soul was in danger. In good conscience, he could not sit with people whose actions and beliefs put him in peril of losing his place in heaven with his wife. He had to stand up and separate himself from those who were taking him down the wrong path.

5 25-28 =

This clue took me a long time to crack. It was the statue of the maiden with the stag that finally reminded me of the European tour with Gran right after my high school graduation. We saw that statue of a Greek goddess in the Louvre in Paris. The hunting bow identified her as Diana, goddess of the hunt. I searched through the internet and found that one of the seven wonders of the ancient world was a temple dedicated to Diana located in Ephesus where the people adored her.

Edward had worked hard to make up this clue and I was anxious to see what verse was so important to him. A quick look at the listing of the books in the Bible led me to Ephesians 5:25-28. I read the verses about the love a man should have for his wife and his church. A storm of emotions made me sit back in my chair to catch my breath. The whole sequence of events – the theft of the communion chalice, puzzles, treasure hunt and the death of Kat – everything was driven by Edward's love for his wife and his grief at losing her. For him, their love transcended death.

I spent the next few minutes thinking about the power of love and what we do for it. I was having a hard time understanding how a man, so in tune with his church and its teaching, could do like the horrible things that Edward had done. I went back to work, hoping the remaining clues would tell me.

 10 12 =

Thank goodness, the next clue was easier. The owl is the universal symbol for wisdom. In the Bible, the book of wise sayings is Proverbs which led me to 10:12: "Hatred stirs up strife, but love covers all sins."

When Edward lost his power and influence within the church, he took action, thinking that anything he did to save the church would be excused because he did it out of love. I noticed my hand had curled into a ball of frustration. *Where were his friends, his —*

Stop it! Just finish working out the clues, I told myself.

 **25 41, 46 =**

Again, the puzzle referred to a patron saint who, in this case, watched over those associated with money, such as banks = Matthew 25:41 - "Then he will say to those on his left, 'Depart from me, you cursed, into the eternal fire prepared for the devil and his angels. And, Verse 46: "And these will go away to eternal punishment, but the righteous into eternal life."

This whole puzzle of Bible quotations explained why he did what he did. If we had worked it sooner, that whole scene at the church... No, I can't blame myself or change anything. All I can do now is try to understand why Edward did what he did.

I took a deep breath and went back in my mind to that night at the courthouse square. When Kat confronted Edward and tried to take the chalice, he fought her off, thinking he was doing the right thing to keep the chalice away from someone who wanted it only for its monetary value. When Kat fell and died, he believed he'd broken the commandment *Thou shalt not kill.* For that act, he would burn in the fires of hell. But, in his mind, it was the actions of the church leadership and congregation that drove him to do what he did and they should be punished. If he was going to suffer the fires of hell for his sin, so should they. With the church building destroyed, the congregation could begin again with a clearer vision. It all made sense in a weird way. It was so sad that his logic was colored by his grief.

The memories of this sad experience were crowding me out of the small cottage.

"Come on, Simon." I grabbed my coat. "Let's go for a walk."

Outside, the sun had broken through the bank of clouds. The Miles River still flowed toward the Bay. Eight white swans bobbed on the calm waters. In the distance, a lone goose called out to his flock... or his mate. His plaintive cry made me think of Edward. The authorities were handling his case with gentle care. He was in a hospital for observation. His fate wasn't clear, but his son was with him, watching over him. Evidently, he hadn't realized the depth of his father's grief. Now, he was giving him the support and love that he needed.

He wasn't the only one getting a lot of attention from family. Mrs. Bolinsky, the lady with the dogs, had agreed it was time to move closer to her children and was spoiling her grand and great-grandchildren terribly. According to reports, they were all loving every minute of it.

I felt a little sorry for Sonny. He was picked up in Chestertown for some minor offense. The Chief suspected Sonny agreed to a one-month stay in jail instead of paying the fine to get away from Carly. Sonny's mom had arranged to take the baby, much to Carly's relief. She'd realized that she wasn't ready to raise a child and Sonny's mom was happy to open her home, especially since her son would be moving in to help.

As the Chief said, all's well that ends well. Working with him on the puzzles and the forensics of Bobby Gee's murder, gave me a keen insight into the man. He acted like a regular police officer, but there was a depth of understanding he kept well hidden. He confided to me that we owed Edward a debt of gratitude. If the chalice hadn't disappeared triggering the treasure hunt, he would never have uncovered the antique scam perpetrated by Rennie and her pal, Jeff. This is how it worked: He'd tell Rennie where the good antiques were and she would swoop in, make the deals that were not to the advantage of the sellers, and deliver the goods to her friends, clients and contacts in New York at a tidy profit.

It seemed that Mrs. Bolinsky would be reunited with her Staffordshire dogs. The Chief had them under lock and key after a state trooper who'd heard the bulletin about Jeff's van, pulled it over for a burned-out taillight. I still didn't understand all the legalities but he was able to search the van and take Jeff into custody along with the dogs. Now, the court would sort it out. I suspected that Belle Antiques would never reopen. I had to laugh. It was the kind of thing that would happen to good ole Conrad Jeffries.

As for Rennie, her hotshot lawyer managed to keep her out of jail and was negotiating some kind of restitution for her targets. Her grandiose home with the four-car garage was on the market and I figured she'd only return to the area for court appearances.

And then there was poor, clueless Grant. He was in a daze and claimed he had no clue. The Chief believed him, but would keep an eye out, just in case. Miss Cunningham felt sorry for him and invited him along to the many holiday parties now on her schedule. Her proximity to the theft and treasure hunt had made her a popular guest at luncheons and dinner parties where she regaled people with inside information and impressions that she embellished with each telling. The attention had bolstered her confidence. She'd even gone to a hairstylist and I almost didn't recognize her when I saw her out shopping the other day.

Yes, this was a beautiful place, an island of peace, but life could still jump up and surprise me, in both good and not-so-good ways. I was getting cold so I called Simon and we went back inside.

CHAPTER THIRTY-ONE

*There are many large pieces, such as the epergne, that are made
in sterling silver. Each is dramatic in its own right but, when
embellishments such as flowers or sweets are added, the true
beauty and design of the piece become apparent.*
— "The Butler's Guide to Fine Silver" Mr. Hollister, 1898

At the end of the afternoon, I opened the door to
my clothes closet and started a hunt for something nice
to wear. Lorraine had invited me to the big house for
dinner – a festive dinner, she'd said. The least I could
do was bypass my jeans and wear something festive. I
put on a pair of black cashmere slacks and a cashmere
sweater in a deep shade of turquoise. It brought out
the auburn shades of my hair and I was thrilled that my
curls were starting to behave. My consultation with the
spa ladies was paying off. Simon romped on our way up
the path, as usual, but when he got to the door, he shook
his body from his nose to the tip of his tail as if he was
primping for our dinner engagement, too.

The house seemed quiet and I headed toward the
kitchen, as usual, but found the door closed. Then I
remembered that Lorraine had asked me to come straight

to the dining room. So, I bypassed the kitchen and went down the hall with Simon at my heels.

All the lights were on making the decorated rooms of Fair Winds very festive. Holidays were holidays and there was no reason why I couldn't appreciate the decorations for Christmas.

I took a moment to look at the tree in the living room and remember the painstaking care Kat had put into the ornament selection and decorating. There was no way I could bring her back or ease the sadness for her son, but, in my heart, I felt some satisfaction and closure. The mystery was solved and there was justice for Kat. If only... *If only* would change a lot of things in life.

"Abby?" Lorraine glowed in the light from the crystal chandelier. It was easy to see that she too had benefited from the peace of the last several days. "I'm glad you're here. Come into the dining room."

I followed her into the large room and almost had a heart attack.

"Happy Hanukkah!"

A crowd of people I was coming to know and love stood together by the largest silver menorah I'd ever seen outside of a synagogue.

"You've been celebrating with us. Now, we want to celebrate with you!"

Everyone surged around me, sharing hugs and laughter. The Chief was all smiles. His tasks had settled down to watching over St. Michaels, now a very quiet town since many residents had fled the cold weather for Florida or the homes of their family in other parts of the country. He had already lectured me about putting myself in danger. He stopped just short of ordering me to stand in the corner for punishment. Seeing him now, I was glad all was forgiven.

Paul was there. He was acting pastor of the church now. The situation with the chalice had frayed Pastor Francis's nerves so the bishop had given him a leave of absence until his retirement date. By then, he would be well rested to enjoy the gift Paul and the members of the church were arranging for him. It was the fulfillment of a lifelong wish: a trip to the Holy Land. The young pastor was right that little cost savings added up to big rewards. In addition, the congregation rallied behind Paul and planned a series of meetings to discuss changes, rather than instituting them as directives.

Dawkins, standing by the door to the butler's pantry, caught my eye and nodded ever so slightly. Then, he gave me a huge smile, his eyes twinkling. What a surprise! Maybe it was true that there was a real human being under that oh so proper façade.

As people made their way around the table looking for their names on the white cards held by the silver placeholders, Ryan stepped up to me and took my breath away again, looking good enough to eat in his hunter-green sweater that brought out the green flecks in his eyes. He grabbed my hand and hustled me around the corner and down the hall.

"What are you doing?" I asked with a laugh.

"I have to ask you a question. Since we're all here to help you celebrate Hanukkah, I have to know if there's an equivalent to mistletoe?"

Confused, I shook my head, then I realized that he

wanted to accept me for who I am. I too had thought about what had happened between us in the boat and decided we could learn a lot about each other.

I stepped closer and said, "Why do we need mistletoe?"

He wrapped his arms around me and I felt the warmth of his kiss down to my toes.

It wasn't long before a discreet *ahem* from Mr. Dawkins reminded us about the party waiting for us in the next room. Holding hands, we joined the others.

Lorraine stood at the other end of the table, gave me a wink as we sat down and then introduced a man with short silver-white hair wearing a yarmulke. "Abby, this is the rabbi from Easton. He helped us arrange everything so it'd be just right." She gestured to the large piece of Judaica on the table. "He even brought this antique menorah."

The silver piece stood on the table about four feet tall and gleamed. One of the eight cups had a wick floating on oil, ready for the ritual.

"Shall we light the menorah? Then, we can eat!" The rabbi winked and everybody laughed as he guided me to stand next to him at the menorah.

"Hanukkah is a time for praise and thanksgiving," he said.

Lorraine and I exchanged looks across the table. The rabbi had no idea how grateful we were.

He continued. "First, we light the shamus or helper that is used to light the Hanukkah candles or oil. Tonight is the first night so we'll light one cup of oil and sing three prayers." He intoned the prayers in Hebrew as he lit the oil with the shamus and repeated each in English then he sang a couple of songs that I remembered from my childhood.

As he sat down, I rose from my chair. I raised my glass. "I want to propose a toast to all the wonderful people... friends in my life. L'chaim! To Life!"

Everyone clinked glasses and drank as waves of delicious foods flowed out of the kitchen. We called for Mrs. Clark to come and join us.

"How did you do it, Mrs. Clark?" I said in delight. "Everything is terrific!"

Her face was turning pink with all the attention. "I couldn't have done it without the rabbi's wife. She brought her recipes and even fried the potato pancakes – the latkes herself." She looked to the rabbi to be sure she had pronounced the word correctly.

He nodded and said with laughter and love, "She's still in the kitchen as usual!" He raised his voice. "Sadie, enough already. Come and join us!"

A small woman wrapped in a huge white apron with strands of gray in her dark hair came to the door and we broke out in wild applause.

When Ryan offered me another jelly doughnut – a Sufganiyah, the name I never could pronounce, I squealed, *No!* But I couldn't resist.

When I finished devouring it, I dropped my hands and let them hang at my sides full to bursting. It was the moment Simon was waiting for. He zoomed over and sat merrily licking the powdered sugar off my fingers! His holiday was complete, too.

ACKNOWLEDGEMENTS

Every story requires an inspiration, and the inspiration for this one is on display at Christ Church, St. Michaels, Maryland: a communion chalice given to the St. Michaels Parish by Queen Anne in 1710. Thank you to the parishioners for sharing your special sterling silver treasure.

Getting the details right is so important. Chief Anthony Smith of the St. Michaels Police Department and his officers work hard to protect this special place for visitors and residents. Thank you for your time and attention to detail in helping me keep the law straight and siting the "new church" within your jurisdiction, Chief. Forensics played a key role in this investigation. Terry Alston, a former state trooper and Chesapeake College professor of criminal justice and forensics, guided me through procedural questions and approaches. Though Abby's part in the investigation might sound unusual, it is one way the authorities might proceed. Terry was precise ... and any mistakes are mine.

Thank you to the wonderful people at The Inn at Perry Cabin, St. Michaels, Maryland – owned by Orient-Express – who came up with the fabulous menu for

Lorraine's buffet dinner served to the Christmas in St. Michaels volunteers. A deep bow of appreciation goes to Daniel Pochron, Executive Chef, who created the mouthwatering menu, Michael Pfister, Banquet Manager, who helped select the appropriate serving pieces, and Brian M. Plaska, Director of Sales & Marketing, who facilitated its creation. My only regret is that its appearance was only fiction. See the complete menu following these acknowledgements.

Captain Bob Luff, sailor and amateur radio operator extraordinaire, clued me into the family home of the osprey and helped Abby and Ryan safely navigate the St. Michaels Harbor and Miles River.

People on the Eastern Shore have shared their memories of The Cove in the old St. Michaels drugstore. Unfortunately, the company chain that bought the independent store thought it was a good business decision to close the Cove. The local residents were not pleased and now the store is gone as well. It was great to stroll through the old memories with John Swann who started his career as a knowledgeable and caring pharmacist with Dr. Young at the original drugstore.

Lulu Mae's work with the banana was inspired by the servers at the Denny's on Airport Road, along Route 70 in Zanesville, Ohio. They practice the fine art of waitressing in this day of crank-it-out fast food joints. These ladies can carry on a conversation while they slice a banana, make coffee and pour out maple syrup. Watching them work brought back vivid memories of the Cove and now I stop there for lunch whenever I'm in the area. Keep up the good work, Ladies!

Puzzles are curious things. The staff at the National Cryptologic Museum, part of NSA, described many actual alternatives for this story. It's worth visiting this fascinating museum outside Annapolis. Also, many thanks to www.silvermarkersmarks.co.uk for the makers' marks images.

There are special people who stay close for encouragement: To Tim and Mike, thank you for your warm and unwavering support in so many ways. And to Sarah, it's a glorious, challenging and lonely experience to write a story so our afternoon strolls for a little sanity were always a welcome break.

As always, many thanks to the wonderful, knowledgeable, and supportive librarians at the St. Michaels branch of the Talbot County Free Library especially Shauna, Shirley, Ted and of course, Betty who works so hard on my ILL requests.

Thanks to Bruce who sat through hours of story discussions and read my drafts with incredible patience and encouragement. Thanks for helping navigate all those pesky rules about commas! And Jen who understands the creative writing process and always has a rousing word that sends me back to the keyboard.

To my family –Matt, Barry, Erin and little Zoe – your love and support mean the world to me. You, along with the whole family in Chicago, pour love into the void we all feel as life goes on and our family grows.

PERRY
CABIN

Christmas Buffet
Fair Winds - St. Michaels

Chilled Seafood Display
Poached Colassal Gulf Shrimp
Fresh Shucked Choptank Oysters
Perry Cabin Smoked Scottish Salmon Display

Mixed Salad Selections
Traditional Caesar Salad
Brioche Crouton, Confit Tomatoes, Shaved Parmesan,
Anchovy Mixed Artisan Greens
Corn Bread Croutons, Candied Sweet Potato,
Shallot Tarragon Dressing
Waldorf Salad

International & Domestic Cheese and Charcuterie
Selection of Artisan Cheeses
Assorted House Made Jams and Chutneys
Venison Salami, Country Pate, Duck Rillette
Mascerated Apricots and Figs, Wine Mustard, IPC Honey Comb
Toasted Baguette and Lavash
Assorted Pickled Vegetables

Chef to Carve
Roasted Prime Rib, Natural Jus
IPC Honey Glazed Ham

Sides
Garlic Mashed Potatoes
Harvest Blend Rice
French Beans, Caramelized Shallots
Roasted Brussels Sprouts, Grain Mustard
Scalloped Oysters

Desserts
Dutch Apple Pie
Candy Cane Cheesecake
White Chocolate and Brandied Cherry Bread Pudding
Lime Tarts with Chambord Mousse

ABOUT THE AUTHOR

Author Photo by Bob Bader

Susan Reiss trained as a concert pianist then moved into television as a writer/producer for many years. Her work has received a Silver Medal, New York International Film Festival, the Cine Golden Eagle, three Tellys and numerous Emmy nominations. She started collecting sterling silver pieces decades ago and blogs on the topic of sterling silver, sailing, Eastern Shore life at www. SilverMystery.com. A native of Washington, D.C., she spent wonderful years with her husband Joey in the Midwest and now makes her home in St. Michaels, Maryland.

COMING SOON!

Abby and Lorraine's next adventure
in the Silver Mystery/St. Michaels Series!

HAMMERED SILVER

Sailboat racing in Chesapeake Bay country brings together sleek Lasers, stately Hinckleys. historic log canoes and more. Many silver trophies are coveted, but the Governor's Cup – hammered into existence by a skilled silversmith – is the biggest prize of all.
Shadows of almost a century of fierce competition hang over the Cup. For this year's winner, will it runneth over with champagne... or blood?